BACKLASH

Recent Titles by Sally Spencer from Severn House

THE BUTCHER BEYOND
DANGEROUS GAMES
THE DARK LADY
DEAD ON CUE
DEATH OF A CAVE DWELLER
DEATH OF AN INNOCENT
A DEATH LEFT HANGING
DEATH WATCH
DYING IN THE DARK
A DYING FALL
THE ENEMY WITHIN
FATAL QUEST
GOLDEN MILE TO MURDER
A LONG TIME DEAD
MURDER AT SWANN'S LAKE
THE PARADISE JOB
THE RED HERRING
THE SALTON KILLINGS
SINS OF THE FATHERS
STONE KILLER
THE WITCH MAKER

The Monika Paniatowski Mysteries

THE DEAD HAND OF HISTORY
THE RING OF DEATH
ECHOES OF THE DEAD
BACKLASH

BACKLASH

A Monika Paniatowski Mystery

Sally Spencer

This first world edition published 2011
in Great Britain and in the USA by
SEVERN HOUSE PUBLISHERS LTD of
9–15 High Street, Sutton, Surrey, England, SM1 1DF.
Trade paperback edition first published
in Great Britain and the USA 2011 by
SEVERN HOUSE PUBLISHERS LTD

British Library Cataloguing in Publication Data

Spencer, Sally.
  Backlash.
  1. Paniatowski, Monika (Fictitious character) – Fiction.
  2. Police – England – Fiction. 3. Missing persons –
  Investigation – Fiction. 4. Detective and mystery stories.
  I. Title
  823.9'2-dc22

ISBN-13: 978-0-7278-8055-0 (cased)
ISBN-13: 978-1-84751-357-1 (trade paper)

Except where actual historical events and characters are being
described for the storyline of this novel, all situations in this
publication are fictitious and any resemblance to living persons
is purely coincidental.

All Severn House titles are printed on acid-free paper.

Severn House Publishers support The Forest Stewardship Council [FSC],
the leading international forest certification organisation. All our titles that
are printed on Greenpeace-approved FSC-certified paper carry the FSC logo.

Typeset by Palimpsest Book Production Ltd.,
Falkirk, Stirlingshire, Scotland.
Printed and bound in Great Britain by
MPG Books Ltd., Bodmin, Cornwall.

For Ray and Brenda Griffin

*Very good and very kind friends, excellent people
to have on a quiz team, and the best babysitters our dog
Sadie could ever wish for.*

ONE

With even the walking wounded working a double shift, it was inevitable that tempers would become frayed as the day wore on, so it was only to be expected that when Constable Bates sneezed – loudly and wetly – into his own right hand, Constable Moore's response was somewhat less than measured.

'For Christ's sake, Phil, why can't you use your bloody handkerchief?' Moore demanded, in a voice much too loud for an enclosed space like the inside of a parked police patrol car.

Bates sniffed. 'Sorry, Trev,' he said. 'I think I must be coming down with the flu.'

'Of course you're coming down with the flu,' Trevor Moore agreed. 'We're *all* coming down with the bastard flu. But you're not helping matters by spreading your germs everywhere, are you?'

'Fair point,' Bates agreed reluctantly – because it undoubtedly was.

At this time of year – November – flu was *always* a problem in Whitebridge, because that same dank, damp air which had made the town the perfect location for cotton mills had also made it the perfect incubator for the influenza virus. And, according to the copy of the *Whitebridge Evening Telegraph* which was currently residing on Moore's knees, this *particular* year – 1973 – it was even more virulent than usual.

Moore carefully folded the newspaper, then glanced, almost apathetically, through the windscreen.

Dozens of cars – their headlights cutting a swathe through the thick darkness of the night – were approaching along the two left-hand lanes of the dual carriageway. Dozens more – their tail lights bobbing around like demented fireflies – were travelling in the opposite direction.

'Mind you, looking at all this traffic, you wouldn't know there *was* an epidemic,' he said to his partner, in a placatory tone.

'You're right there – folk'll drive when they're not fit to walk,' Bates replied sourly.

The sound of the motor horn seemed to come out of nowhere.

Had it been a single beep – or even a series of beeps, in which one driver showed his annoyance with another – the two officers would have ignored it.

But it wasn't.

Instead, it filled the night air like the wailings of a demented banshee.

'That kind of behaviour's simply not on,' Moore said, his foot already feeling the clutch and his hand reaching for the gear stick.

The blaring grew louder, and a green Ford Cortina suddenly appeared. The headlights were on full, and the driver was weaving in out of the traffic as if he had a death wish.

'Jesus, he must be doing at least a hundred!' Bates gasped, as the Cortina shot past the lay-by where they were parked.

'Bloody maniac!' Moore said grimly, switching on the siren, throwing the vehicle into gear, and pulling out.

The patrol car's flashing lights and siren were already having the desired effect on the cars ahead of them. Some of the drivers had slowed almost to a standstill. Others had pulled over on to the hard shoulder. But the green Cortina was impervious to it all, and continued to accelerate into the darkness.

'At the rate he's going, we'll never bloody catch him,' Bates said, reaching for the radio.

'We'll catch him,' Moore said firmly, as the speedometer needle rapidly climbed its way around the dial.

Bates clicked the switch on the radio, and was connected to HQ.

'Bloody mad driver on the loose,' he said, after giving his call sign. 'He's travelling north on the dual carriageway. He's between Mill Lane and Piper's Brook at the moment, but Christ alone knows *where* he'll be five minutes from now.'

'Very professional, Phil,' Moore said, as he pressed his foot down hard on the accelerator. 'Almost textbook. You're a credit to the force.'

'Piss off,' Bates said, though without any real rancour.

A bend was looming up just ahead of them.

'We're nearly at the Piper's Brook roundabout,' Moore said, coaxing the maximum speed out of the engine. 'If the sod takes one of the turn-offs before we're round that corner, we'll have no bloody idea where he's gone.'

It was as the patrol car was screeching round a bend – two of the wheels momentarily leaving the tarmac – that they saw all the traffic in front of them had stopped.

'Shit!' Moore shouted, stamping down on the brake pedal.

The patrol car skidded through forty-five degrees, and came to a halt frighteningly near the closest stationary car.

Bates opened his door and climbed out.

A man in a heavy overcoat, standing next to his own vehicle, shouted, 'Thank God you've arrived! There's been an accident!'

'Tell me something I don't know,' Bates said, as he weaved in and out of the parked vehicles, heading towards the large road island that the driver they were chasing had clearly failed to negotiate.

The Cortina had mounted the island and crashed into a massive oak tree which stood in the centre of it. Its bonnet had buckled, and there was steam rising from it.

'Bloody tree!' Bates muttered.

They should have cut it down when they were building the road, he thought. They *would* have cut it down if the anorak-and-green-Wellingtons brigade hadn't protested that it was four hundred years old, and so had historic importance.

Historic importance!

When all was said and done, it was still no more than a lump of wood, and if the nature nuts *really* felt the urge to look at trees, well, there were thousands of the buggers in the Whitebridge area.

Bates heard a puffing, wheezing sound at his side, and realized that Moore had caught up with him.

'We'll have to get the feller out of there,' Moore gasped. 'And quickly – before the bloody thing blows.'

'If we *can* get him out,' Bates said.

By the time they reached the car, small flames were already starting to lick what was left of the bonnet.

They could see the Cortina's driver now, slumped over the steering wheel. But he *was* wearing a seat belt – so there was a good chance that he would have survived the crash.

Please God, let the bloody door not be jammed shut, Moore prayed silently, as he reached for the handle.

For a moment it looked as if he had wasted his prayer, because when he pulled, nothing happened. Then, with a metallic groan, the door swung open.

As Moore reached inside, he felt a huge wave of relief sweep over him – and then a blinding rage quickly took its place.

'You stupid bastard!' he shouted at the slumped-over driver. 'You stupid, irresponsible, *dangerous* bastard!'

The driver groaned, and muttered a single word.

'What did he say?' Bates asked.

'Sounded like "lane",' Moore replied.

But then again, it could just as easily have been 'rain' or 'pain' – and whatever it was, it didn't matter now.

Moore unfastened the seat belt and placed a hand under each of the driver's armpits.

Don't move him! warned a voice in his head. Wait for the ambulance men to arrive. *They're* the professionals. They'll be able to get him out without doing further damage. Wait for them!

'Can't bloody wait,' Moore told the voice, as he watched the flames growing bigger and bolder by the second. 'Leave the feller where he is, and he could be burned to a crisp by the time the ambulance arrives.'

He hauled the driver from the car, and the moment he was clear, Bates grabbed his legs, so that at least now he was horizontal.

'Where shall we take him?' Bates asked.

'As far away from here as possible,' Moore told him.

A small crowd had gathered on the edges of the traffic island, and a few people were even advancing towards the wrecked car.

'Get back, you bloody idiots!' Moore screamed. 'It's about to blow!'

But it didn't.

Not then.

In fact, the two policemen and the victim had almost reached the patrol car when there was a huge explosion behind them and the sky turned red.

'Lay him on the ground,' Moore said urgently. 'Now!'

'Why should we—?' Bates began.

'Just do it!' Moore barked.

They lowered the injured man on to the road, and Moore immediately huddled over him.

Around them, small pieces of shattered glass fell through the air like sharp-edged raindrops. Chunks of metal, some of them the size of a man's leg, hit the asphalt and bounced several times before settling. And still the boom of the explosion lingered – if only in the eardrums of those who had been too close to it.

There were new sounds now – the demanding scream of several police sirens, the wail of at least one ambulance.

Moore straightened up.

'Let's take a look at him,' he suggested. 'Got your torch?'

Bates nodded, and shone the beam on the injured man's face.

'Bloody hell, it's . . . it's . . .' he stuttered.

'It's Chief Superintendent Kershaw – that's who it bloody is,' Moore said.

He knelt down again, and put his mouth close to the injured man's ear. 'Can you hear me, sir?' he asked softly.

The chief superintendent opened his eyes.

'Where's Elaine?' he groaned.

'What was that, sir?' Moore asked.

'Elaine,' Kershaw repeated, making an effort to sit up, and then falling back again.

'Who's Elaine?' Moore asked.

'My wife,' Kershaw groaned. 'I don't know where she is. I can't find her anywhere.'

TWO

Detective Inspector Colin Beresford – early thirties, good-looking, muscular, and a guiltily secret virgin – gazed up at the house from his vantage point at the end of the front garden.

It was a three-storey Victorian dwelling, which had probably once – long ago now – belonged to the manager of a small cotton mill. There were still a good number of such houses to be found in Whitebridge – though most of them, admittedly, were living in the shadow of the demolition ball – but Beresford couldn't think of a single example of another which was still a one-family residence.

The fact was, he reflected, the moderately prosperous had long since moved out of the centre of Whitebridge, and re-established themselves on executive estates, where it was almost possible for them to forget that they had any connection with a grimy, declining mill town. But Chief Superintendent Kershaw had stuck it out, and still lived in the house he had bought probably twenty years earlier, even though it was now in an area which catered for the transient bedsitter.

Beresford turned his attention to the garden. Unlike most of those in this street, it had not been paved over to accommodate off-the-road parking. It was, he decided, studying it more closely, a garden which had not so much been planned as just allowed to happen.

There was a wishing well, squarely in the centre of it – and what a lot of stick Mr Kershaw must have got for that when he had his 'hard-man' colleagues round for dinner! There was a fish pond, with a delicate waterfall which was topped with a painstakingly constructed watermill. There was even a palm tree in one sheltered corner, and though it was well known that you simply couldn't grow palms in Whitebridge, it seemed, through infinite care and attention, to at least be surviving.

The whole garden, Beresford thought, was as individual, original and idiosyncratic as the man who had created it.

The roar of a sports car engine alerted him to the fact that his boss was about to arrive, and turning round he saw that DCI Paniatowski's red MGA was just pulling up behind the row of police vehicles already parked in front of the house.

And Monika was not alone, he noted. There was another woman in the passenger seat.

He watched the two women emerge from the car, and told himself that they could not have looked much less alike, even if they'd really worked at it.

Paniatowski was in her late thirties. She had soft, wavy blonde hair, and a largish central European nose that could have made her less attractive – but didn't. She also had a sensational figure which, most of the time, Beresford did his best to ignore.

The other woman was a complete stranger to him. She was probably in her late twenties, he guessed. She had a slim – almost pixie-like – figure, short cropped brown hair and big oval eyes. Very, very different to Monika, Beresford thought – but equally as fanciable.

Paniatowski stopped in the gateway to light a cigarette, then said, 'Why are we here, Colin?'

What, no cheery greeting? Beresford thought. No, 'How are you, Colin?'

'Mrs Kershaw's gone missing, boss,' he said aloud.

'I know that,' Paniatowski replied, with a hint of exasperation in her voice. 'What I asked was, why *we* are here.'

Beresford smiled. 'Ah, you mean why is a crack team like ours – the finest investigative force in the whole of Central Lancashire – being handed such a mundane job?' he said.

'That's right,' Paniatowski replied, either completely missing his humorous intent or choosing to ignore it.

'Everybody's short-handed,' Beresford said. 'With the flu epidemic, we're all expected to fill in wherever we're needed.'

Paniatowski sighed. 'Yes, I suppose we are,' she said reluctantly. 'And how long has Mrs Kershaw been missing?'

'Hard to say,' Beresford admitted. 'It could be as little as two hours, or it might be as much as eight.'

'What!' Paniatowski exploded. 'Eight hours at the most – and there's a full-scale manhunt!'

'Mr Kershaw *is* one of our own,' Beresford pointed out.

Monika Paniatowski scowled. 'Well, that's certainly one way of looking at it,' she said.

The younger woman – the pixie – had been standing perfectly still at Paniatowski's heel, and somehow managing to give the clear impression that she was the sort of person who knew enough to hear just what she was intended to hear, and no more.

Now, however, she coughed discreetly, and said, 'What would you like me to do, ma'am?'

Paniatowski turned to face her. At first, she seemed almost surprised to find the woman there. Then she smiled and said, 'Well, you can start by not calling me "ma'am", Kate.'

'Sorry, I . . .' the pixie began.

'Don't worry about it,' Paniatowski told her airily. 'And excuse my lack of manners for not introducing you to this handsome devil straight away. This is Detective Inspector Beresford, the rock I cling to when the storm breaks. Colin, this is DS Katherine Meadows, my new bagman.'

Meadows held out her hand. 'Pleased to meet you, sir,' she said. Then she added, slightly uncertainly, 'It is all right to call you "sir", isn't it, sir?'

'It's more than all right,' Paniatowski told her, before

Beresford had time to answer for himself. 'Not only will it make him *feel* important, but it might even remind him that he *is* important.'

That was better, Beresford thought, with some relief. The bad-tempered shrew who'd been standing there only moments earlier was quite gone, and the Monika he knew was back.

'I think I'd better talk to Mr Kershaw first,' Paniatowski said. 'So while I'm down at HQ, I'd like you, Colin, to supervise the team in the house.'

'HQ?' Beresford repeated.

'HQ,' Paniatowski confirmed.

'But Mr Kershaw isn't down at HQ.'

Paniatowski looked puzzled. 'Have they taken him to hospital, then? From what I heard, he only got a few cuts and bruises in the crash.'

'He isn't in hospital, either,' Beresford said, with a sudden sinking feeling.

'Then where the hell *is* he?'

Beresford gestured towards the house. 'In there.'

The shrew was back with a vengeance. 'Let me see if I've got this straight,' Paniatowski said. 'Kershaw was driving down the dual carriageway at such a speed that it's a wonder he didn't kill anybody. Right?'

'Right,' Beresford agreed.

'And the only thing that stopped him doing more damage was that he crashed into the oak tree on the roundabout?'

'Yes.'

'If anybody else had done that, they'd have been in the cells by now, wouldn't they?'

'I suppose so.'

'But he's in his own house! Now why is that?'

'Like I said, boss . . .' Beresford began.

'I know,' Paniatowski interrupted. 'He's one of our own.'

Kershaw was in his study, sitting at the desk with his large head held in his powerful hands. When Paniatowski and Beresford entered, he looked up, and it was obvious to both of them that he'd been crying.

Poor bastard! Beresford thought.

Because even if everything turned out all right in the end

– even if it eventually emerged that there'd *never* been anything to worry about – it was clear that Kershaw was suffering now.

'We'd like to ask you a few questions, if you don't mind, sir,' Paniatowski said.

Her voice was cold, Beresford thought – so unlike the one she normally used when she was talking to victims.

Kershaw nodded. 'Of course I don't mind, Chief Inspector,' he said miserably. 'I want to do anything I can to help.'

'The first thing I'd like to know is why you're so *worried* about your wife, when she's only been missing for a few hours.'

'Her name's Elaine,' Kershaw said. 'I'd like it if you could call her that when you refer to her.'

'Why are you so worried when *Elaine's* only been missing for a few hours?' Paniatowski said, her tone still unyielding.

'She was in no fit state to leave the house,' Kershaw explained. 'She's had a very bad attack of flu. She's been in bed for the last four days. She was getting a little better, but she certainly was not well enough to . . .' He waved his hands helplessly in the air. '. . . to even contemplate . . .'

'So what's *your* theory?'

Kershaw glared at her. 'Isn't it obvious? She's been kidnapped!'

'Who by?'

'I don't bloody know! If I *did* know, I would not be sitting here now – I'd already have my hands round the bastard's throat!'

'Why would anyone kidnap her? For ransom?'

Kershaw shook his head. 'I'm not well off. I earn a decent screw – you know that yourself – but I've never been one for saving. I live from pay packet to pay packet, like most bobbies, and anybody who'd done even a bit of research on me would know that.'

'Let's take a couple of steps backwards,' Paniatowski suggested. 'When did you discover she was missing?'

'When I got home from work.'

'Did you inform headquarters that you thought she'd been kidnapped?'

'No.'

'Why not?'

'Because, at that point, I didn't think that she *had* been kidnapped. It's not the sort of thing you *do* think, is it? Kidnapping's something that only happens to *other* people.'

'That's right,' Beresford murmured softly. 'That's exactly what it is.'

'So if you didn't call headquarters, what did you do?' Paniatowski asked Kershaw.

'I rang up all her friends, to see if she might be with them.'

'I thought you said she was too ill to leave the house.'

'She was, but I could see she wasn't here, so she had to be *somewhere*, didn't she?' Kershaw took a deep breath. 'Look, Chief Inspector, I wasn't thinking straight. If the truth be told, I think I'm coming down with the flu myself.'

'None of her friends had heard from her?' Paniatowski asked.

'That's right.'

'So what did you do next?'

'I went to see Elaine's mother.'

'Why didn't you just ring her?'

'I couldn't, because she isn't on the phone. And when I got there, and Mum told me she hadn't seen Elaine since last week, that's when I really started getting frantic.'

'But you still didn't think to call it in?'

'No, I . . .'

'So what *did* you do?'

'I decided to see if she was at her sister Mary's house. She lives at the other side of Whitebridge – almost the opposite end of the dual carriageway from their mother. I was driving normally at first, and then I thought, "What if Elaine isn't at Mary's either?" That's when I think I must have lost my head. I had to know for certain whether she was there or not, you see, and I started driving like a madman.'

'And crashed,' Paniatowski said.

'And crashed,' Kershaw agreed.

'Have you and your wife – you and Elaine – been having any marital difficulties recently?' Paniatowski asked.

'What kind of question is that?' Kershaw demanded.

'I should have thought it was obvious what kind of question it was – and why I was asking it,' Paniatowski told him. 'We've got at least twenty officers on this case, and before I use up any more of their valuable time, I want to be certain that your wife's not simply done a bunk.'

Kershaw nodded slowly. 'You're right,' he said. 'You do have to ask that question. I would have done the same, in your place.

But I like to think I would have phrased it differently – with a little more compassion.'

Yes, for God's sake, why *don't* you show a little compassion, Monika? Beresford thought.

'You still haven't answered the question, sir,' Paniatowski pointed out, in a flat voice.

'Elaine and I are not having any marital difficulties,' Kershaw said. 'We have the occasional tiff – what married couple doesn't? – but we're as much in love now as we were when we first tied the knot.'

Paniatowski nodded, as if finally satisfied.

'Do you know of anyone who might have some sort of grudge against Elaine?' she asked.

'At last!' Kershaw said, with evident relief. 'Finally, you're taking this seriously.'

'*Does* anyone have a grudge?' Paniatowski persisted.

Kershaw shook his head. 'Everyone loves Elaine. There's not a malicious bone in her whole body. She'll help anybody who asks for her help. Half the charities in this town would *collapse* without her support.'

'So your theory is that *if* she was snatched, she was snatched by a stranger,' Paniatowski said.

Kershaw's face collapsed. 'I don't . . . I can't think . . . I don't *want* to think . . .' He took a deep breath. 'If I was the officer in charge of this case, that's probably the conclusion I would draw,' he said, as crisply as he seemed able.

'I won't insist that you come down to the station, sir . . .' Paniatowski began.

'I should bloody well hope not,' Kershaw said, with a hint of anger in his voice now.

'Instead, I'll ask the police doctor if she wouldn't mind coming here.'

'The police doctor? I don't need a doctor. I've already been checked over by the ambulance men and given the all-clear.'

'The doctor will need to take a sample of your blood,' Paniatowski said.

'I haven't been drinking,' Kershaw said firmly. 'I haven't touched a drop since I first got the sniffles. You have my word on that.'

'Nevertheless, I'm afraid that I must insist you give a sample of your blood,' Paniatowski said. 'It's standard procedure in a case like this one – and you should know that better than most.'

Kershaw's eyes blazed with genuine anger. 'You really are a vengeful bitch, aren't you?' he demanded.

Well, I don't know anything about the vengeful part, but she's certainly being a *bitch* tonight, Beresford thought.

THREE

DS Meadows was standing in the corridor outside Kershaw's study, looking as if she didn't mind at all that she had not been included in the interview.

And maybe she didn't, Beresford decided. Maybe she'd already learned the most vital lesson in climbing the promotions' ladder – that you advance at the speed your boss wants you to advance at.

'Would you make the arrangements with Dr Shastri, please, Colin?' Paniatowski asked him.

'The arrangements?'

'For one of her staff to come here and administer the blood test to Mr Kershaw.'

'Is it really necessary?' Beresford wondered aloud.

'It's not only necessary, it's mandatory,' Paniatowski snapped.

Yes it is, but she'd bend the rules if she actually wanted to, Beresford told himself. God knows, she's done it often enough before.

But aloud, all he said was, 'Yes, I'll see to that.'

Paniatowski nodded. 'Good. And while you're making the call, Kate and I will go and see how the rest of the lads are getting on.'

It was a big house, which appeared to have been inspired not by the dwellings which had preceded it, but by a rabbit warren. Countless rooms opened up off any number of corridors, and, in normal circumstances, it would have taken a normal team of officers a long time to search it from top to bottom.

But these were not normal circumstances, and this was not the normal team. There were policemen everywhere – so many of them, in fact, that they were almost tripping over one another.

Paniatowski wondered briefly who had authorised this extravagant use of manpower, but quickly recognised that such speculation was pointless. As far as *all* the top brass were concerned, she accepted, nothing was too good for Chief Superintendent Tom-bloody-Kershaw.

She and Meadows started their tour of inspection at the top of the house – the attic, where the servants would have spent their short nights – and worked their way down to the basement at the bottom – in which those same servants would have spent their long days.

There was no evidence of its former use about the basement. The Victorian fireplace and kitchen range were long gone, and in their place was a card table, a snooker table, a dartboard and a bar.

'Proper little boys' club,' Paniatowski said.

'Yes, it must be every man's dream,' Meadows replied.

'So what's your impression of the house as a whole?' Paniatowski asked.

Meadows frowned. 'Why did you ask that, boss? Has it anything to do with the crime?'

'We don't know if there has *been* a crime yet,' Paniatowski pointed out. 'But no, it doesn't. I just want to find out how observant you are.'

Meadows grinned. 'So it's sort of like a test?'

'It's *exactly* like a test,' Paniatowski told her. 'And as long as you're working for me, Kate, you can expect to be tested every day. That's how you'll get better at the job.'

'I see,' Meadows said. 'Well, it's very tidy and very organized. The kind of house in which everything has its place, and there's a place for everything.'

Paniatowski nodded. 'Go on.'

'But it's not clinical, if you know what I mean. It feels like a real home – somewhere the people who live here could feel comfortable.'

Yes, it did, Paniatowski agreed silently. And that had come as something of a surprise to her, because whenever she thought about Kershaw – and she tried not to think about him *at all* – she never pictured him in a house in which he would 'feel comfortable'.

*   *   *

DC Jack Crane had heard all about the recent arrival of DS Kate Meadows, and as he walked down the stairs to the Kershaws' basement, he was already more than willing to dislike her.

This dislike wouldn't stem from anything about Meadows as an individual, he admitted. She could be the nicest person you could ever hope to meet, and it wouldn't make any difference – because the fact was that she'd taken his job.

You're not being fair, he told himself. It was never your job to lose.

And nor had it been. In the time he'd been working for Paniatowski, she'd had two sergeants who, each in their own way, had been a disaster, and though he'd filled in after both their departures, that was *all* he'd been doing – filling in.

Besides, having a first-class honours degree – which he was still careful to keep quiet about – was all very well if you wanted to be a university lecturer, but if you aspired to be a successful bagman, you needed to get some heavy policing experience in first.

'Jack?' said a familiar voice.

Crane snapped out of his musings, and realized he'd already reached the foot of the stairs, and was now in the basement.

'Did you want something?' asked the same voice.

Crane looked across at Paniatowski and her new sergeant.

Bloody hell, he thought, that DS Meadows is a stunning woman!

'The lads have found something, boss,' he said aloud.

'What kind of something?'

'It just might be evidence of a forced entry.'

The window was at the back of the house. It couldn't have let much light in, even on a bright day, because it was surrounded by shrubbery.

And it was that same shrubbery, Paniatowski thought, which would have shielded any intruder from the curious gaze of neighbours who might be looking out on to the garden.

The window frame was splintered, close to the inside catch, and there was no doubt that it had been forced.

'It's hardly what you'd call very secure,' Crane said.

No, it wasn't, Paniatowski agreed, and you'd really have thought that a policeman would be more security conscious.

And then she pictured her own home – the one she shared

with her beloved adopted daughter – and realized that it was almost as bad.

I'll see a builder first thing in the morning, she promised herself.

'What's in the room on the other side of this window, Jack?' she asked Crane.

'Not much. An ironing board, an old television and two or three clothes hampers.'

'And how far is this room from the main lounge and the kitchen?'

'Just about as far as it could be.'

Which made it the perfect entry point, Paniatowski thought, because even if Elaine Kershaw hadn't been in bed with the flu, she probably wouldn't have known someone was breaking in until it was far too late.

'Get some searchlights out here, and have a few of the lads go over the garden with a fine-toothed comb,' she told DS Meadows. 'I also want all the houses that overlook this one canvassed right away. I need to know if anybody saw any strangers – or strange vehicles. And if any of the neighbours noted anything unusual today – even if it's something that doesn't seem as if it could possibly be connected with Mrs Kershaw's disappearance – I need to know about that, too.'

'Got it,' Meadows said.

'Then, once the lads have finished with those houses, they can start widening the search. Tell them it doesn't matter if they have to drag people out of their beds to question them – and that if there are any complaints about their lack of consideration, I'll take the heat personally.'

'Right.'

'I also want all motor patrols and foot patrols put on full alert. Give them the same brief as the canvassers – if they can find Elaine Kershaw, I'll be over the moon, but if they can't, I want to know about anything that isn't quite as it was yesterday. Have I missed anything out?'

'I don't think so, boss.'

'Actually, I have,' Paniatowski said. 'When the police doctor's finished drawing the blood sample, tell him to try and persuade Mr Kershaw to take a few sleeping pills. If he refuses the pills, move on to Plan B.'

'Plan B?'

'Find a bottle of booze, and sit down and have a drink with him – but make sure he drinks more than you do.'

'Wouldn't it be better if *you* did that, boss?' Meadows asked.

'He won't want to drink with me, and the feeling's mutual,' Paniatowski told her. She paused to light a cigarette. 'And when you've finished all that, you'll find me in the public bar of the Drum and Monkey. Do you know where that is?'

Meadows smiled. 'Yes, boss. When I learned I'd be working with you, it was one of the first things I made it my business to find out,' she said.

This was always one of the worst times of year for her business, Marie thought, as she stood shivering in the toy shop doorway.

Part of the reason was the weather, of course. Once you were inside your own home, sitting snugly in an armchair in front of a toasty warm fire, it must take a real effort to haul yourself up again, and face the frosty night air.

But if that was the *main* reason, business would be just as bad in January – and it never was.

The punters were all saving up for Christmas, she thought bitterly – putting money away so that, on Christmas morning, they could stand around the tree and hand out presents to their dowdy wives and demanding children.

If only those wives and kids knew what those perfect fathers and perfect husbands got up to when they *did* have a bit of spare cash in their pockets. If only they could see them when they looked shiftily up and down the street before asking some poor bloody girl how much she charged.

They'd be disgusted – these happy families – if they heard the things that some of these men asked some of those girls to do.

She was often disgusted herself – but in her situation, there wasn't much bloody choice but to agree anyway, was there?

She lit up a cigarette, and noticed, in the flickering light of the match, that her hands were shaking. And *that* wasn't just the cold air, either, she told herself – it was fear.

She heard the distant sound of the clock on the Boulevard striking the hour and, almost simultaneously, the click-clacking sound of high-heeled shoes coming up the street.

Every hour on the hour – that had been the agreement they reached. And if you happened to pick up a punter when it was your night 'on duty', the first thing you had to do was make sure one of the other girls knew about it.

It wasn't a perfect system, of course – but then it wasn't exactly a perfect life, either, and even *some sort* of security was better than *no* security at all.

The clicking heels came to a halt in front of the doorway.

'Doing much?' asked the wearer of the heels.

Marie shrugged. 'I've had one lad, still wet behind the ears, an' as nervous as a frightened rabbit. Sad little thing, really.'

'It's often sad,' the other woman – Lucy – said wistfully.

'He must have been savin' up his pocket money for months,' Marie continued, 'an' I felt so sorry for him when he shot his load before we'd even got properly down to the business, that I was tempted to give him a discount.'

Lucy laughed. 'You were tempted, but you didn't give in to temptation, did you?'

'No chance,' Marie confirmed. 'Times are hard, an' if he can't hold himself back, then that's his problem.'

Lucy looked up and down the street. 'You haven't seen Grace, have you?' she asked casually.

Marie felt her stomach turn over. 'No, but that's hardly surprisin',' she said, trying to keep her voice steady. 'Grace's pitch is outside Woolworths.' Then she forced herself to add, 'What made you ask that?'

'Just wondered,' Lucy said evasively.

'Why?'

'Well, because I haven't seen her either, and I've been past Woolworths every hour, just like we agreed.' She paused. 'Do you think we should tell the police?'

And that was where all the planning broke down, Marie thought – because even if something had gone seriously wrong, what were the bobbies likely to do about it in the middle of the night?

'She's probably just struck lucky,' she heard herself say aloud. 'Found a punter with a lot of money, an' a lot of stayin' power.'

'Yes, that will be it,' Lucy agreed, far too readily. 'She'll just have struck lucky.'

Marie lit up a fresh cigarette from the butt of her old one.

We've got to keep reassurin' each other that everything's all right, she thought. And maybe, if we say it often enough, it really will be.

FOUR

For Monika Paniatowski, the corner table in the public bar of the Drum and Monkey – at which she was now sitting with Crane and Beresford – was nothing less than a time machine. It was at this table that she had first decided that she hated DI Bob Rutter, and then realized that she had fallen in love with him. It was on this very chair that she sat – heartbroken – when Rutter's sense of duty forced him to end the affair, and it was where she had come to grieve when she learned he had taken his own life.

But the table held happy memories, too. It reminded her of working with DCI Charlie Woodend, the man who had made her the policewoman – and perhaps even the person – she was now. It recalled for her the joy – even amid the despair – when she finally accepted that Bob's last wish had been that she should raise his daughter, Louisa, as her own.

There were times, it had to be admitted, when she'd considered breaking with the past and using another pub – or, at least, another table – but she knew, deep inside herself, that was never going to happen.

Paniatowski took a sip of her vodka and banished the time machine to the back of her mind.

'All we've got so far is a forced window – and a woman who went missing sometime in the last ten hours,' she said to her team. 'Now maybe, even as we speak, DS Meadows is on her way here with a vital piece of information which will help crack this case – a car number plate, or a description of a strange man, for example – but I don't think that's at all likely.'

'Any particular reason for believing that, boss?' Crane asked.

'Yes. The intruder was very careful. He didn't choose just *any* window to break in through – he chose one that was hidden from the neighbours and in the emptiest part of the house, which suggests to me that he's been planning this for some time. And given that he's been so careful about that, he's not likely to have been sloppy over other things. So we won't find his prints in the house, the car he used was probably stolen, and if he thought there was any chance of him being spotted, he was probably wearing a disguise.'

'How would he have got her out of the house?' Crane asked.

'I don't know,' Paniatowski admitted.

'She's not a big woman,' Beresford said. 'In fact, she's quite tiny. He could have fitted her into a sack or a largish box.'

Paniatowski's eyes narrowed. 'Oh, you know her, do you, Colin?' she asked sharply,

'I've . . . err . . . met her,' Beresford said.

'And what's she like?'

'As I said, she's petite.'

'I mean, as a person.'

'I only met her the once,' Beresford said, evasively.

'But you must surely have formed some impression of her.'

'Lively,' Beresford said. 'Charming. Very outgoing.'

'Did she also strike you as the kind of woman who might consider doing a bunk?'

'I thought you'd already dismissed that as a possibility, boss,' Beresford protested.

'*Did* she strike you that way?'

'The window was forced, boss.'

'If she's done a bunk, she could have forced it herself in order to throw everybody off the scent – and you still haven't answered the question,' Paniatowski said.

'No, she didn't look like that kind of woman,' Beresford said. 'In fact, she seemed quite devoted to Mr Kershaw.'

'Well, isn't that nice,' Paniatowski said sourly. 'All right, we'll go back to the assumption she's been abducted, even if we don't know how he got her out of the house. Now who'd have been likely to snatch her?'

'Could be a kidnapper – for ransom,' Crane suggested.

'We'd already dismissed that possibility before you arrived – and there are two good reasons for that,' Paniatowski told him. 'The first – as Kershaw pointed out himself – is that he's not a rich man.' She paused and turned to her inspector. 'He *isn't* a rich man, is he, Colin?'

'How would I know?' Beresford wondered out loud.

'And the second thing is that if she's been kidnapped for ransom, then the kidnapper must be a hardened professional criminal,' Paniatowski continued, ignoring the question. 'And no professional criminal is going to snatch such a high-risk target as a Chief Superintendent's wife.'

'Do *you* have a theory, boss?' Beresford asked.

'I think it was personal,' Paniatowski said, '*so* personal that the kidnapper was prepared to take on the whole of the Mid Lancs police force if he had to.'

'What sort of motive are we talking about here?' Crane asked.

'I don't know,' Paniatowski confessed. 'He may have wanted to get back at her, or he may have wanted to get back at Kershaw. But whichever is the case, he will have known her, and that's why, first thing in the morning, we'll be talking to all – and I do mean *all* – of the Kershaws' friends and relatives.'

'That's a bit of a tall order, especially with the friends,' Beresford said. 'They're a very popular couple.'

'Yes, well, you'd know more about that than I would, wouldn't you, Inspector?' Paniatowski said.

The clock struck the hour, and once again Marie heard the click-clack of Lucy's impossibly high heels approaching.

'I've got some good news for you,' Lucy said, the moment she drew level with the doorway. 'Grace hasn't disappeared at all. Ruby saw her going off with a punter.'

Marie gasped with relief, but then, almost immediately, fresh worries and doubts began to set in.

'And we know him, do we?' she asked hopefully. 'Is he a regular?'

'Ruby didn't *interview* him, to see if he was suitable, you know,' Lucy said with a smile. 'She only saw them from a distance. But he was definitely driving a big car, and it was definitely Grace getting into it.'

'And when was this?' Marie asked.

'Ruby said it was just after it went dark. So what would that make it? Five hours ago?'

Five hours! Five whole bloody hours!

'That's a long time for her to be away,' Marie said, as the fear bubbled up inside her.

'Driving off in cars, with men, is what we do,' Lucy countered. 'And it's not as if it's unheard of to take that long – a bit uncommon, I'll grant you, but not unheard of.'

Yet two words kept pounding away mercilessly at Marie's brain like a steam hammer.

Five hours . . . five hours . . . five hours . . .

'What if it was *him*?' she asked tremulously.

'What if it was *who*?' Lucy asked – though she knew well enough who Marie meant.

'What if it was the *Ripper!*' Marie replied, almost choking on the name.

Lucy clamped her hands on her hips in a show of exasperation.

'I should have put my foot down the moment the rest of you girls started calling him that,' she told her friend. 'I should never have allowed it.'

And despite the situation – despite her own, still-present fear – Marie could not help herself from smiling at what Lucy had just said.

I should have put my foot down!

I should never have allowed it!

As if Lucy thought of herself as their leader!

And then it struck Marie that, in a lot of ways, Lucy *was* just that.

When one of the girls had a problem, it was Lucy she talked it out with. When a helping hand was required, it would more likely than not be Lucy who provided it. And it was Lucy who had come up with the idea of these safety patrols.

'I should have insisted we called him the Dribbler or the Panter,' Lucy continued. 'Calling him the Ripper was just stupid – it makes him sound much more frightening than he actually is.'

'But he *is* frightening,' Marie insisted. 'Just thinking about him is enough to scare the crap out of me.'

Lucy laughed again. 'Then look on the bright side – you must be saving yourself a fortune in laxatives,' she said. 'Seriously,' she continued, 'I know he's not a nice man, but then *most* of the men we have to deal with aren't *nice* – in fact, you can count on the fingers of one hand the ones who are. And he's never done any real damage, now has he?'

'Try telling that to Denise,' Marie countered. 'She had to have ten stitches in her arm.'

'Yes, she did,' Lucy agreed. 'But that's almost as much down to her as it is down to him.'

'What do you mean?'

'She won't learn how to handle the punters. She always says the wrong thing, or does something to annoy them. And there's really no need for that, because this is a business like any other business – and the customer is always right.'

'In most businesses, the customers don't carry a razor around,' Marie pointed out.

'And neither do most of our customers,' Lucy said soothingly. 'Listen, if it had been you or me in that situation, we probably wouldn't have got cut at all. And anyway, cutting her must have frightened him as much as it frightened her. He's nothing to worry about.'

'If he's nothing to worry about, why do we take it in turns to patrol the streets?' Marie asked.

'We're just being careful, that's all,' Lucy said unconvincingly. 'Anyway, why would you think it was the Ripp— why would you think it was *that* man, who Grace went off with?'

'Because she's been gone for five hours!' Marie screamed. 'Five bloody hours.'

'She's a smart girl,' Lucy said. 'She wouldn't take any unnecessary risks.'

But *was she* so smart? Marie wondered.

Grace *said* she was nineteen, and that she'd been on the game for three years. But sometimes, when you caught her without any make-up on, she didn't look more than fifteen. And even *with* make-up, there was still a hint of the fresh-faced innocent about her which reminded Marie of herself, when she'd first started out walking the streets.

And how long did *you* keep that look, girl? she asked herself. Six months at the most!

'I'd better be moving on,' Lucy said. 'You want to learn to relax a bit, Marie. Carry on worrying the way you are, and you could end up a basket case.'

I could end up a lot of things, Marie thought. I could end up *dead*.

FIVE

DS Kate Meadows appeared in the doorway of the Drum and Monkey's public bar, looked around, and spotted her new boss and the rest of the team at the table on the other side of the room.

Studying the deliberately purposeful way she strode across the room, Paniatowski felt a momentary glimmer of hope that perhaps – against the odds – Meadows was the bearer of some important piece of information which would help them to wrap up this bloody case in no time at all. Then, taking a closer look at Meadows' elfin face – and reading the very adult frustration that was residing there – she felt that hope flicker and die.

Paniatowski gestured towards the empty chair next to Crane, and said, 'Anything to report, Kate?'

'Kershaw's neighbours are either deaf or dumb – or both,' Meadows said, sliding gracefully into her seat. 'None of them – not a single one – appears to have seen a bloody thing.'

Paniatowski felt her recent grumpiness start to evaporate, and did her best to hide a half-smile which had forced itself on to her lips.

She had been like Meadows once, she thought – young, enthusiastic, expecting every investigation to open up as neatly and easily as a tin of sardines.

'You look like you could use a drink, Kate,' she said. 'What's it to be? A pint of best? Or would you prefer a short?'

'A tomato juice, thank you,' Meadows told her.

Around the table, three sets of very surprised eyebrows involuntarily rose, and then, when the wearers realized how rude that might appear, were quickly lowered again.

'So you just don't fancy a drink tonight, then, Sarge?' Crane said, to cover his own embarrassment – and possibly that of the others. 'Well, I can sympathize with that – I sometimes don't feel like one myself.'

'Not that that happens *very* often, young Jack,' Colin Beresford said, with a chuckle.

'It's not that I'm not drinking tonight – it's that I don't drink at all,' Meadows said, and though she appeared to be addressing the remark solely to Crane, it was plain that it was intended for the whole table. 'And, in case the thought's crossing your mind that I might be a recovering alcoholic, Jack, let me assure you, here and now, that I'm not.'

Crane blushed. 'I didn't mean to . . .' he began.

'I know you didn't,' Meadows said, with a softening smile. 'But it's better to get these things straight right from the start, don't you think?'

She was clearly a woman who knew her mind, Paniatowski thought approvingly.

'As a matter of fact, I'll skip even a tomato juice,' Meadows said. 'I think I'd rather get back to Mr Kershaw's house, and see if there have been any new developments.'

'There won't have been,' Beresford said. 'Take it from me, Sergeant, the earliest we're likely to get a break is tomorrow morning, and if you go back now, you'll just be wasting your time.'

'That's probably true, sir,' Meadows agreed. 'But, when all's said and done, it will be *my* time I'm wasting.'

'Fair enough,' Beresford said, as discomfited as Crane had been earlier. Then he added, 'Why don't you walk the sergeant back to her car, DC Crane?'

'I don't need anyone to walk to me to my car, thank you, sir,' Meadows protested.

'I never said you did,' Beresford replied, now fully back in control of himself. 'But young Jack could use the exercise – couldn't you, Jack?'

'Err . . . that's right, sir,' Crane said unconvincingly.

'And once you've seen the sergeant safely to her vehicle, why don't you take a few minutes to stroll around the car park,' Beresford suggested.

'Uh . . . right,' Crane agreed.

Paniatowski watched Meadows and Crane leave the bar, then turned to Beresford and said, mischievously, 'You slipped up there.'

'Sorry, boss?' Beresford replied, in a flat voice.

'Well, you obviously fancy her something rotten, so what are you doing letting Crane have the first crack at her?'

'Crane's just a baby,' Beresford said, dismissively. 'Besides, we need some time alone, so we can talk.'

'What's all this leading up to, Colin?' Paniatowski asked.

'What do *you* think it's leading up to, Monika?' Beresford countered.

'I've no idea,' Paniatowski said, in a voice which didn't sound convincing, even to her. 'But whatever it is, I don't imagine I'm going to like it, so let's get it over with as quickly as possible.'

'Don't you think that you were being a bit hard on Mr Kershaw earlier?' Beresford asked.

'Hard? I'm not sure I know what you mean.'

But she did know – he could tell from the expression on her face that she did.

'I'm talking about the way you questioned him,' Beresford pressed on.

'He had information about a serious crime, and . . .'

'So you do think it *is* a serious crime now?'

'Of course.'

'Because not half an hour ago, you seemed to be suggesting she'd done a bunk.'

'I considered it as a possibility, and now I've rejected it. A woman with a bad case of flu doesn't suddenly decide to leave home on a chill winter night, however unhappy she is – and according to you, she isn't unhappy at all.'

'Which makes not only Mrs Kershaw – but also her husband – a victim of a crime,' Beresford said.

'It makes *him* a witness,' Paniatowski said firmly.

Beresford tried again. 'Kershaw's a good bobby.'

'Is he?'

'I think so. He's got an excellent track record for solving crime, he's generally acknowledged to be honest and straightfor-ward, and – most importantly for anybody who's ever worked for him – he looks after his lads.'

Paniatowski's eyes narrowed.

'Tell me about the time that you met Mrs Kershaw,' she said.

'It was . . . it was at a summer barbecue.'

'Where?'

Beresford sighed. 'At his house.'

'So he's a mate of yours?'

'Of course not. He was a chief superintendent, and I was only a sergeant. Our paths hardly ever crossed.'

'But he still invited you to this barbecue of his.'

'That's true, but it was rather a big do – there were a lot of other bobbies there as well.'

'When was this?'

'I'm not sure I can pin it down exactly.'

'Try!'

'It must have been two or three years ago now.'

'And what did you – out of all the sergeants on the force – do to earn your invitation to this barbecue?'

'Nothing much. He was my boss at one time.'

'Ah!'

'It wasn't for long. He was my chief inspector when I was first starting out on the beat.'

'But even though he was as high above you as the sun is over the earth, he still noticed you.'

'He noticed everybody. He was that kind of boss.'

'That kind of boss,' Paniatowski repeated, rolling the words carefully round her mouth, as if they were poison. 'And I expect he encouraged you in your career, did he? I expect he was almost like a father to you.'

She stopped, suddenly, remembering that Beresford's father had died when he was young – and that he had spent a great deal of his teenage years looking after a mother who was slipping ever deeper into the pit that her Alzheimer's disease was digging in her brain.

'I'm so sorry, Colin,' she said.

'Forget it,' Beresford said, brusquely.

'I really didn't mean . . .'

'The point is, boss, that you – and I do mean *you* in particular – can't afford to make enemies,' Beresford said.

It was true enough, Paniatowski admitted to herself. Since she had been a DCI, she had solved three major cases – and, though she'd had help from her team, she *was* the one who'd solved them. But that didn't play well with some of the people who mattered at headquarters. As far as they were concerned, the first case had actually been solved by a rogue sergeant who'd since been promoted, the second by a 'spook' from London, and the third by her old mentor, Charlie Woodend.

And why did they think that?

Because she was a woman – and a woman couldn't possibly have produced those results!

'All I'm saying, boss, is that you need all the support you can get – and going out of your way to turn fair-minded fellers like Mr Kershaw against you is just bloody insane.'

'I was just doing my job,' Paniatowski said stubbornly.

'Have you got something personal against the man?' Beresford asked, exasperatedly.

'Something personal?' Paniatowski repeated. 'Yes, I suppose you could say that I have.'

It has been a long hard climb from police cadet to detective sergeant – and Monika has had to take a lot of abuse along the way – but she has finally made it. Now, she believes, her troubles will be over, because she has proved herself – has shown that she is equal to any man.

The euphoria lasts for perhaps one day, and then the pictures start to appear. She ignores them at first, telling herself that they are no more than the last dying gasp of the prejudice which has stalked her throughout her career.

But it doesn't stop.

In fact, it grows worse than it ever has been – and it doesn't take her too long to work out why.

It is because her promotion has not taken her out of the danger zone at all – rather it has simply made her a bigger target. And her hunters have become more desperate, too, because while it is easy to dismiss a woman handing out parking tickets as a nothing – an aberration – it is much more difficult when she becomes a successful part of a serious investigating team.

She holds off for three weeks, but finally she sets up an interview with her immediate boss.

She likes Detective Inspector Kershaw for a number of reasons, but the main one is the way he looks at her – or perhaps it would be accurate to say the way he doesn't look at her.

Some of the men she works with might despise her as a bobby, but they have not failed to notice her as a body, so that while their eyes may look at her with contempt, those same eyes are, at the same time, undressing her. But Kershaw is not like that at all. She senses that he feels no attraction to her – or at least, if he does, he is professional enough to mask it.

And strange as it may seem, this lack of interest in her increases her own interest in him, for though she cannot normally bear to have a man touch her – even lightly, even in a friendly way – she is starting to feel that, with DI Kershaw, it might be different.

But it will never happen, she has promised herself. She will never get any closer to him than she is now, because that might damage their working relationship, and, at that moment, her job is the most important thing in the world to her.

Kershaw is sitting at his desk when she enters his office, and he looks up and smiles at her.

'What can I do for you, Monika?' he asks.

She does not want to show him the pictures she has in the folder she is holding – she feels almost ashamed to, though she knows she has absolutely nothing to be ashamed of. No, she doesn't want to, but she forces herself anyway.

She places them on the desk.

'I've come about these,' she says.

There are five pictures in all, and she has found each and every one of them taped to her locker. They have all been cut out of what surely must be the most hardcore – and probably illegal – magazine in circulation. The models in them have adopted poses which degrade not just them, but all women.

And perhaps they realize this. Perhaps, on their faces, there are expressions which show both disgust for themselves and disgust for the men in whose sweaty hands the pictures will eventually end up.

Perhaps!

But there is no way of being certain now, because where their faces once were, someone – some evil, filthy swine – has pasted a photograph of DS Paniatowski's head.

Kershaw glances at the pictures, but only long enough to get the general idea. Then he sweeps them off his desk and on to the floor.

'You were right to bring these to me,' he says.

And Monika feels a wave a relief sweep over her, because she has been worrying – somewhere at the back of her mind – that Kershaw will dismiss them as a harmless prank, and her as an over-sensitive fool.

'*How do you feel about them?*' *he asks.*
'*I'm sickened, sir,*' *she says.*
'*And upset?*'
'*That, too.*'
'*You don't* look *upset,*' *Kershaw says.*
'*I'm holding it in,*' *Paniatowski tells him.*
'*I went on a psychology course recently,*' *Kershaw says.*
'*Did you?*' *Paniatowski asks.*
But she is not really interested – because she doesn't want to hear about his courses, she wants him to solve her problem.
'*And one of the things we learned on that course is that it can be very destructive to hold your feelings back – very destructive indeed.*'
'*I don't see . . .*'
'*What you really want to do, Monika, is have a good cry. But you don't want to do it in front of your boss, because you think I'll think less of you. Well, let me assure you, I won't. We'd all be better people – better police officers – if we gave in to our emotions now and again.*'
A silence follows, eventually broken when Paniatowski says, '*I'm not going to cry, sir.*'
Kershaw smiles. It is a wise, benevolent, understanding smile.
'*Of course you're not,*' *he agrees.* '*Because you don't quite trust me yet. Because you don't know me well enough to accept that I mean exactly what I say. It doesn't matter. I said you were right to bring these disgusting objects to me, and so you were. This will stop. I'll see to that personally.*'
'*Thank you, sir,*' *Paniatowski says.*
And now she almost does *cry, but not through pain but because she feels so grateful.*
But she doesn't *cry.*
Not then – and not later.

The lights were flashing behind the bar, signalling last orders. Paniatowski looked down at her empty vodka glass and decided she'd had enough for one night.

'Let's get a few things straight, shall we, Colin?' she said. 'I don't like Kershaw . . .'

'You've made that fairly obvious.'

'. . . but I'll bust my gut trying to get his wife back to him, just as much as I would if I thought the sun shone out of his arse. Because that's my job, Colin.' Paniatowski paused for a moment. 'No, it's *not* because it's my job – it's because it's who I am. It's *me*.'

'I know that, boss,' Beresford said.

'Do you?' Paniatowski asked sceptically. 'Somehow, I'm not so sure about that.'

SIX

I t was a cold, crisp morning. The pavements glinted with frost, and there had been a warning about black ice on the roads, so Beresford drove with extra care.

He sniffled involuntarily, and wondered if he was catching flu. He half-hoped he was, because that would give him an excuse to withdraw from this case which his boss – for reasons of her own – was handling all wrong.

A sudden sense of shame engulfed him. Even if Monika was handling it badly, that was no reason to wish he could abandon her. In fact, it was when she was rushing headlong into what might turn out to be a disaster that she really needed him by her side.

As he approached Chief Superintendent Kershaw's house, he was expecting to see a considerable amount of activity, but rather than the half a dozen official vehicles he'd assumed would be parked outside it, there were only two – and the only *person* in evidence was DS Meadows, who was standing by the gate.

He parked his car behind Meadows', and walked over to the gate.

'Is Mr Kershaw awake yet?' he asked the sergeant.

'Wouldn't know, sir,' Meadows said. 'He's not here.'

'Then where is he?'

'He's staying with his bagman. He left the house soon after the police doctor had taken a blood sample.'

'I'm surprised he was willing to go,' Beresford said.

'He wasn't willing,' Meadows replied. 'I told him he had to.'

'You told him *what*?' Beresford exclaimed.

'I told him he had to leave,' Meadows repeated calmly. 'I said if he stayed here, he'd only get in the way of the investigation.'

So a young sergeant, only recently posted to the area, had told a chief superintendent that he had to move out, Beresford thought. Kate Meadows had really got some nerve.

'How did Mr Kershaw take it?' he asked.

'He seems like a good bobby, and *as* a good bobby, he could see the sense in what I was saying.'

'Yes, he is a good bobby,' Beresford agreed. 'Did the search of the house throw up any clues?'

Meadows smiled. 'If it had, don't you think I'd have been waiting for you out in the road, with my tongue hanging out like an eager dog's at supper time?' she asked. Her face grew more serious. 'No, we found nothing at all of any use.'

'Fingerprints?'

'Hundreds of them – from what I've heard, the Kershaws are very sociable – but I'll bet a year's pay that none of them belonged to the intruder. And there's no sign of a struggle inside, sir. My guess is that he took her completely by surprise, and then either drugged her or knocked her out.'

'What about the garden?' Beresford asked.

'I called the search of the garden off. Even with the spotlights on, there were too many shadows, and I was worried that if there *was* any evidence, some clumsy Plod would end up planting his size-nine boot on it.'

'So *you* called it off?' Beresford said. '*You* made the decision?'

'Yes, sir, I believe it's called showing initiative.'

And maybe it was called having just a little *too much* nerve, Beresford thought.

'It's light, now,' he said, with growing irritation. 'Why hasn't the search resumed?'

'I thought you might want to have a look at the scene before the uniforms got a crack at it, sir,' Meadows said.

'You mean you thought *you* might want to have a look at it before the uniforms did!' Beresford said accusingly.

'That as well,' Meadows agreed.

Joan Williams, Elaine Kershaw's mother, lived in an area of Whitebridge which, even in living memory, had been a village

in its own right. And there was still a distinct village feel about
the place, Paniatowski thought, as she drove past the local butcher's and post office.

Mrs Williams lived at the end of the former village, in a sturdy
stone-built cottage that was almost on the edge of the moors. In
the summer, it must have been a glorious place; the garden full
of fragrant old-fashioned roses, celebrating the sheer joy of living.
But on that chill November morning, the cracked and frozen
earth spoke more of death and decay.

As she was walking up the garden path, it suddenly occurred
to her that Mrs Williams would already know her daughter had
gone missing – her son-in-law's frantic visit the night before
would have ensured that – but was likely to have heard nothing
since.

Poor bloody woman, she thought, as she lifted the old-fashioned door knocker. She must have been up all night worrying.

The woman who answered her knock was in her seventies.
She had white, tightly permed hair and was wearing a pink
cardigan – and she didn't look half as concerned as she should
have done.

'Yes?' she said.

'Mrs Williams?' Paniatowski asked.

'That's right.'

'I'm from the police, and—'

'She hasn't turned up yet, has she?' the old woman interrupted.
'If she had, Tom would be here himself.'

'No, she hasn't turned up yet,' Paniatowski agreed. 'But you
mustn't go getting unnecessarily worried,' she added quickly.

'Oh, I'm not worried at all – at least, not about our Elaine,'
Mrs Williams said firmly. 'It was very silly of her to disappear
like that, but wherever she is, Tom will find her.'

'If you're not worried about her, then who *are* you worried
about?' Paniatowski wondered aloud.

'About Tom, of course. He's so protective – so responsible
– and he must be going through agony.'

'I'd like to ask you a few questions, if you don't mind,'
Paniatowski said.

'Of course I don't mind,' Mrs Williams replied. 'But if you
want my advice, dear, you'll take careful notes so you'll know
exactly what I said – because Tom's a stickler for details.'

'I won't be reporting back to Chief Superintendent Kershaw
– I'm in charge of this investigation,' Paniatowski said.

Mrs Williams shook her head slowly from side to side. 'I think
you must be a little confused, dear,' she said. 'But never mind,
why don't you come inside and have a nice cup of tea.'

The last time that Beresford had been in this garden, it had been
a happy place, full of people who'd had just a little too much to
drink and were talking just a little too loudly.

That had been in August, he remembered, when the garden
was in its full glory. Now, in November, bereft of its visitors and
vegetation, it seemed to him to have assumed an almost funereal
aspect.

But maybe that had more to do with the way he was seeing it
than the way it actually was. And maybe the fact that he was seeing
it that way was due to a feeling in his gut which told him that
something truly horrible had already happened to Elaine Kershaw.

'The chances are, this is the route he chose to get his victim
away from the house,' Meadows said.

'What makes you think that?' Beresford wondered.

'There'd be much less risk in that than in taking her out of
the front door, especially given what lies beyond the fence at the
bottom of the garden.'

'And what does lie beyond it?' Beresford asked.

'I'll show you,' Meadows replied.

She led him down the crazy-paving path, past the rhododendron
bushes, to the perimeter fence. It was a lattice fence, supported
by concrete posts every few feet, and it would certainly not have
been difficult for the kidnapper to have thrown Elaine over the
fence, and then climbed after her.

But what was more interesting, as Meadows had said, was
what lay beyond the fence.

The houses which backed on to the garden were probably
about the same age as the Kershaws' home, but considerably
cheaper and nastier. And more importantly still, there was a patch
of wasteland – which had probably once contained the toilets
and washhouses for the whole street – between the house on the
left and the house on the right.

'He could have driven his car right up to the fence,' Meadows
said.

Yes, he could, Beresford agreed, and using both the bushes and darkness for cover, he could have been reasonably certain that no one would spot him. And there would have been no danger of leaving any telltale footprints either, because the night before, the ground had been frozen.

It was when they turned to walk back to the house that Beresford noticed the flash of colour under one of the rhododendron bushes. He bent down, and retrieved the object. It was bright red, about five inches long and narrower at one end than it was at the other.

'Either she did finally start to struggle, or he got careless when he was carrying her,' Beresford said, holding the stiletto heel up for Kate Meadows' inspection.

Mrs Williams led Paniatowski into a living room which was almost swamped with bric-a-brac. There were the pottery ducks flying on the wall, horse brasses hanging on each side of the chimney breast, and the china dogs guarding the hearth.

It was, Paniatowski thought, almost a cliché of what an old lady's living room *should* be like.

'I'm *really* not worried about Elaine, you know,' Mrs Williams said – a cup of tea held carefully in her hand – as she eased herself into an armchair with a floral motif, opposite the one she'd invited Paniatowski to sit in. 'And *you* shouldn't be worried about her either. Wherever she is, Tom will find her. He's always looked after her.'

'He's not—' Paniatowski began.

Then she stopped herself – because what would be the point?

She took a sip of her tea, which was just the sort of mild, not-very-stimulating tea that old ladies always seemed to prefer.

'I'd like to ask you about Elaine's friends, Mrs Williams,' she said, 'and I'd be especially interested in hearing about any *boyfriend* who there might have been some unpleasantness with.'

'Why don't you just ask Tom?' Mrs Williams asked, maddeningly.

Paniatowski sighed. 'Because you'll know more about her before she was married than Tom will.'

'There's not much *to* know.'

Paniatowski sighed again. 'All right, just give me the names and addresses of all her old friends and, like I said, her old boyfriends. If you don't know their addresses, then just their names will do.'

'She doesn't have any old friends,' Mrs Williams said. 'And she certainly doesn't have any old *boyfriends*.'

'Everybody has friends,' Paniatowski protested.

Oh really? asked a mocking voice in the back of her head. And what friends did *you* have before you joined Charlie Woodend's team?

'You didn't know our Elaine before her marriage, did you?' Mrs Williams asked.

I don't know her now, Paniatowski agreed. But I'm *trying* to get to know her.

'Why don't you tell me about her?' she suggested aloud.

'Elaine and her big sister were as different as chalk and cheese,' Mrs Williams began. 'Mary was always outgoing and confident. But Elaine was such a frightened, mousy little thing. Maybe that was because her dad died when she was very young – or maybe it was just because she was such a late baby. I don't really know the reason – but I do know I always felt guilty about it.'

This was getting her nowhere, Paniatowski thought.

'Tell me a little about her life,' she suggested.

Mrs Williams shrugged helplessly. 'There's so little to tell,' she said. 'Elaine worked as a bookkeeper for her Uncle Michael, and when she wasn't working, she was here at home, with me.'

'She lived with you?'

'Yes, right up until the day she got married. I tried to persuade her to go out more – to have a life of her own – but she just wouldn't. I thought she might have been one of those women who . . . who . . . you know.'

'No, I don't,' Paniatowski said.

'One of those women who don't like men, but only like women. A Wesleyan, is it?'

'A lesbian.'

'That's right. I even asked her about it once. I told her I didn't really approve, but I supposed that if that was the only way she could find happiness, then it was all right with me. And she said she wasn't one of those women – she said even the thought of it made her sick.'

'So, if she lived as quietly as you say she did, how did she ever manage to meet her husband?' Paniatowski asked sceptically.

'Destiny,' Mrs Williams said, with a dreamy look coming to her eyes. 'We were burgled, and one of the policemen who came to look around was very rude to Elaine.'

The robbery has reduced Elaine to a nervous wreck. Her sanctuary – the one place she felt safe from the world – has been violated, and will never be the same again.

Two police constables are sent to investigate the robbery. One is middle-aged and steady, but the other is young, arrogant and seems to feel that the task he has been given is beneath him.

The older constable pulls rank on his partner, and nips off to the local café for a cup of tea and a cake, while leaving the younger one in charge. This only adds to the younger man's sense of grievance, and he stamps around the cottage like a Nazi storm trooper, looking for an excuse to get even angrier.

His attitude makes Elaine's nerves even worse, but there are things she feels have to be said, and she finally plucks up the courage to speak to him.

'Do you think you'll catch them?' she asks.

'Catch who?' the constable demands, rudely.

'The . . . the men who broke in.'

The constable looks around the room. 'What did you say they'd stolen?'

Though she has already told him once – and observed that he wrote nothing down – Elaine lists them again.

'There was a portable television, my mother's jewellery box, five pounds forty-nine pence from the drawer in the kitchen, my piggy bank . . .'

'Your piggy bank!' the constable interrupts. 'Your bloody piggy bank?'

Elaine wants to rebuke him for swearing, but she just can't muster the courage.

'It's where I put all my loose change,' she says meekly. 'It soon adds up, you know.'

'Anything else?' the constable asks.

'My photograph album. I don't know why they took that – but they did.'

'All in all, a very valuable haul,' the constable said. 'Well, madam, I don't think we should have much trouble catching your criminals for you.'

'You don't?'

'Not at all. The thieves are bound to want to fence your piggy bank for a king's ransom, and when they do, we'll arrest them.'

'It's not funny,' Elaine says. 'Those things might not seem much, but they mean a lot to me. All my pictures of my dad were in that album.'

Listening to the exchange from the doorway, Mrs Williams is amazed. Elaine has raised her voice – she is actually shouting – and it's the first time her mother can ever remember her doing that.

'I'd advise you not to raise your voice to a police officer, madam,' says the young constable, suddenly sounding very grave and official.

But, just this once, Elaine is not to be intimidated.

'You're a disgrace to your uniform, and I'm going to report you,' she says – and now she has progressed from shouting to actually screaming.

The constable's official veneer, never very thick, now cracks and shatters.

'Oh, you'll report me, will you?' he hectors. 'Well, go ahead – you pathetic dyke.'

'I never thought she'd do it, but she did,' Mrs Williams told Paniatowski. 'She phoned police headquarters and Tom came round himself – personally – to investigate. He was very angry when he learned what the constable had said to Elaine, and not three hours had gone by before that constable was back here, apologizing for his behaviour.' The old woman chuckled. 'I don't think I've ever seen a man look so dropped on as he did at that moment, but he sounded sincere enough when he said he was very sorry, and – do you know – I think he might actually have become a better policeman because of what Tom said to him.'

Because Tom's a bloody marvel, Paniatowski thought sourly. Because Tom can work miracles!

'And then, I think it must have been two or three days later, Tom came round to see us again,' Mrs Williams continued. 'And you'll never guess what he brought with him.'

'Your stolen property,' Paniatowski said, guessing anyway.

'That's right,' Mrs Williams agreed. She paused again. 'Tell

me, how often do the police manage to recover things that have
been stolen in a burglary?'

'Not often enough,' Paniatowski admitted.

'That's what I thought,' the old woman said, almost complacently. 'But Tom brought everything back, even the piggy bank!
And on top of all that, he invited us out for afternoon tea.'

'That was nice of him,' Paniatowski said, in a flat voice.

'Of course, I could tell – even though he was being so polite
about it – that he wasn't really inviting both of us, he was inviting
Elaine.'

'And she agreed.'

Mrs Williams smiled. 'She didn't want to, but I pushed her
into it. And then one thing led to another, and within a year they
were married.'

'I see,' Paniatowski said.

'You don't believe me, do you?' Mrs Williams asked, and now
there was a hard edge to her voice.

'I'm sorry?'

'You don't believe anything I've told you about Elaine. You
think I'm nothing but a mad old bat, who just sees what she
wants to see, but really has no idea of what's really going on.'

'I assure you—' Paniatowski began.

'I'd like to show you something,' Mrs Williams interrupted
her.

She stood up and hobbled over to the sideboard. Paniatowski
heard the sound of a drawer being opened, and when the old
woman turned round again, she had a photograph album in her
hands.

Mrs Williams sat down again, and opened the album.

'Elaine would be furious if she knew about some of the old
pictures I've still got,' she said. 'That's why I keep them well
out of sight.' She selected a page, and handed the album over to
Paniatowski. 'Look at that!' she commanded.

Paniatowski studied the photograph. For a moment, she thought
the woman she was looking at might be a much younger Mrs
Williams, but then she began to see the differences. Certainly,
the two women looked alike, and certainly the girl in the photograph was wearing the same kind of frumpy clothes that Mrs
Williams was wearing now, but there was a look in her eyes – a
downcast, defeated look, the sort of look which said that taking

her photograph was simply a waste of film – that clearly distinguished her from her mother.

'That was taken a few months before she met Tom,' Mrs Williams said. 'Now turn over to the next page.'

It couldn't be the same woman, Paniatowski thought, as she did as instructed – though it clearly was.

This woman was smartly dressed and exuded an air of confidence. And the dull downcast eyes were now vivacious and intelligent.

'That photograph was taken a year after the other one,' Mrs Williams said, with just a hint of triumph in her voice. 'Do you see what I'm getting at, now?'

'Yes,' Paniatowski admitted. 'I do see.'

'Tom made a new woman out of her,' Mrs Williams said. 'There's nothing Tom *can't* do, when he puts his mind to it. And that's why I'm not worried that she's gone missing, because *he'll* find her.'

Have I got it all wrong? Paniatowski asked herself. Have I got *him* all wrong?

Because maybe he was no longer the man she had known. Maybe love of Elaine had changed him, just as her love for him had so obviously changed Elaine herself. Maybe he was a better police officer than she was. And maybe Mrs Williams was right and he really *could* work miracles.

There were no shoes in Elaine Kershaw's wardrobe to match the heel found under the rhododendron bush.

'It's not hers,' Meadows said.

'What isn't?' Beresford asked.

'The heel.'

'Are you saying somebody else left it there?'

'No. I think she was wearing them when the heel became detached, but they're not her shoes.'

'I don't see how you can possibly have decided that,' Beresford said.

'Look at the rest of the shoes in the wardrobe, sir. There's plenty of them – she likes her shoes – but there's nothing that's anything like as extreme.'

'So?'

'So if she liked this style of shoe, she'd have had at least one other pair. That's why I guarantee that when you show this particular heel to Mr Kershaw, he won't recognize it.'

'Then if the shoes weren't Elaine's . . .'

'Her killer brought them with him—' Meadows came to an abrupt halt. 'I mean, her abductor brought them with him,' she continued, slightly shakily.

'Why did you say "killer" just now?' Beresford asked.

'I don't know,' Meadows replied.

And Beresford was almost certain she was lying.

'Go on with what you were saying,' he told the sergeant.

'The kidnapper brought the shoes with him, and then either made her put them on, or put them on her himself,' Meadows said.

'Why would he have done that?'

'I don't know,' Meadows repeated.

And once again, Beresford was not sure he believed her.

'Perhaps I'm wrong,' Meadows said. 'Perhaps Mr Kershaw will recognize them. He may even have bought them for her himself.'

'Maybe he did,' Beresford agreed. 'But that still doesn't explain why a woman with flu was wearing them around the house.'

'Would you like to go for a drink tonight, sir?' Meadows asked, out of nowhere.

'We always go for a drink when we're in the middle of an investigation,' Beresford said. 'We've done some of our best thinking at the Drum.'

'I didn't mean that, sir,' Meadows said. She paused, as if considering exactly how to phrase what she wanted to say next. 'You do know I've only just been posted to the Mid Lancs Division, don't you?'

'Of course.'

'Well, I've got my flat set up – it's small but it's nice and cosy – and I've worked out where to go to do my shopping and where to take my dry cleaning.'

'Yes?'

'So I'm pretty much settled in. But I still don't know anybody – socially, I mean. And so I thought it might be quite nice if you and I went out for a drink. Unless you think that might be inappropriate – what with you being my superior officer and everything.'

'No, it's not inappropriate,' Beresford said. 'I often go out for a drink with the boss, even when we're not working on a case.'

'Yes, but the boss is older than you, isn't she?'

'And what do you mean by that?'

'Just that, since she is an older woman, there are not likely to be any complications, are there?'

'And do you see any complications in us going out together?' Beresford asked, as his heart began to beat a little bit faster.

'I don't know,' Meadows said – and this time, when she used the phrase, she really was being honest. 'Neither of us can know. We'll just have to try it and see how it turns out, won't we. If you're willing, that is.'

'Oh, I'm willing,' Beresford said – though he knew that he shouldn't.

SEVEN

The tailback began about half a mile from the Piper's Brook roundabout. Had Paniatowski wished to, she could have turned on her siren and shot along the hard shoulder. Instead, she chose to edge slowly forward with the rest of the frustrated motorists, because it gave her time to think, to examine what she'd learned – and to ask herself if she was seeing it as she *should* see it, or whether she was viewing it through a lens darkened by something that had happened long ago.

At about a hundred yards from the roundabout, the two lanes shrank down to one, and she could almost hear the groans from the other drivers trapped in their own metal boxes on wheels.

Several uniformed officers were on duty, waving the vehicles through to a twisting lane marked by bollards. Paniatowski swung to the right and parked on the hard shoulder.

She was just climbing out of the MGA when one of the uniformed bobbies strode furiously towards her.

'What's your problem?' he called from the distance. 'Are you blind? Or are you just stupid?'

He was probably twenty-two or twenty-three, Paniatowski thought, as she watched him draw closer, and though that made

him too young to possibly be the officer who had called Elaine
Kershaw a pathetic dyke, he was cast from the same mould.

'You're new to the force, aren't you?' she asked.

'That's none of your bloody business, luv,' the constable said.

'You should call me "madam",' Paniatowski told him. 'I am,
after all, a member of the public who you've sworn to serve.'

'You've got a nerve,' the constable told her. 'You're too
thick to obey simple instructions, and yet you expect me to
call you . . .'

He stopped, abruptly, when he saw the warrant card Paniatowski
was holding out in front of her.

'All right,' she conceded, 'don't call me "madam" – call me
"ma'am".'

The constable looked down at the ground. 'I'm sorry, ma'am,
I didn't realize that . . .' he mumbled.

'Name!' Paniatowski barked.

'Perkins, ma'am. Roger Perkins.'

'Right, Perkins, I'll be watching you,' Paniatowski promised.
'And maybe you could return the favour by watching my car
while I go and look at the scene of the accident.'

'Yes, ma'am,' the downcast Perkins replied. 'Certainly, ma'am.'

The main wreckage of Kershaw's car had already been towed
away, but there was still ample evidence of the crash and explosion – broken glass, pieces of metal, chunks of rubber – on the
closed-off lanes which had not yet been fully cleared.

Paniatowski mounted the roundabout.

Kershaw's tyres had gouged a deep track through the grass as
he had struggled to keep control of his vehicle, but, despite what
must have been a desperate effort on his part, he had still hit the
oak tree with some force, as was evidenced by the scarring on
its mighty trunk.

Paniatowski wondered briefly if anything would ever make
her desperate enough to drive so recklessly – to risk not only
her life, but the lives of others. Then she realized that she
already had the answer – understood that if Louisa's safety was
at stake, she would take any risk at all, without even thinking
about it.

'Mr Kershaw was lucky to come out of that alive,' said a voice
to her left, and turning, she saw a sergeant she knew.

'Yes, he was,' she agreed.

But would Kershaw think the same, if things turned out as badly as they very well might?

Marie was used to going to bed late. It was, as Lucy said, 'an occupational requirement'. And what Lucy really meant was that it was much easier to get a punter to part with his money if he was drunk, and the later it got, the more likely that possibility became. Which was why, while a lot of the trade came when the pubs closed their doors, the more 'lucrative contracts' – Lucy's words again – were negotiated at around two o'clock in the morning, as the private drinking clubs finally shut up shop for the night.

Going to bed late usually meant getting up late, too, and normally Marie slept straight through until noon.

But not on that particular morning.

That morning, after a restless night in which she'd tossed and turned and tried to persuade herself she was asleep, she finally admitted, at a quarter past seven, that she was in fact wide awake.

She felt lost with this totally unexpected free time suddenly on her hands. She simply didn't know what to do with it.

She knew what she *wanted* to do, of course. She wanted to go down the hallway, open Grace's bedroom door, and see if her friend was safely tucked up in her bed, just as she was supposed to be.

But that would be tempting fate, she told herself.

She couldn't exactly explain what she meant by that, but it ran along the lines of, 'If I think things have gone wrong, then they probably will have. If I go and look in Grace's room now, she won't be there, because something terrible will have happened to her. But if I leave it till later – if I go into her room at the same time as I normally do – she *will* be there. She will have been there *all night*.'

None of it made sense – she accepted that – but it brought her a little comfort – and comfort could be very thin on the ground.

She lay perfectly still, convinced she wouldn't fall asleep, but trying to empty her mind, so time would have passed before she knew it. Then, at a quarter past eight, when her landlady, Mrs Dawkins, began vacuuming noisily downstairs, even keeping her mind empty became an impossibility.

Marie didn't like the landlady, and tried to avoid her whenever possible, even going so far as to get one of the other girls to hand over her rent for her.

It wasn't that Mrs Dawkins was unfriendly. Far from it, she treated all her guests like young ladies. And not only treated them like it, but pretended that was what they actually were.

What skill that took – ignoring the whispers in the hall at two o'clock in the morning, as one of the girls led a punter upstairs; being seemingly oblivious to the fact that when 'respectable' girls were already at work, her guests had not even got up.

Yes, it was her hypocrisy that Marie really hated, because when rent day came around, her guests handed her a rent for their shabby bedsits which was five or six times as much as the shorthand typists and shop assistants would be paying for theirs.

The vacuuming stopped, and Marie looked at her bedside clock.

'I'll give it two hours – a full two hours – before I go and see Grace,' she promised herself. 'If I leave it that long, I'll have made sure that nothing could possibly have gone wrong.'

Mary Philips was a brisk, energetic woman in her early fifties, who did indeed live at the opposite end of the dual carriageway to her mother.

Her lounge, into which she invited her visitor without hesitation, contained no mementoes or even personal touches. It was, in fact, as stripped down and functional a living space as Paniatowski had ever seen.

'Would you like a cup of coffee, or should we cut to the chase and start hitting the gin?' Mrs Philips asked her guest.

'Vodka's my drink . . .' Paniatowski said.

'Got some of that, as well – bottles of the stuff.'

'. . . but, at this time of day, I think I'll stick to coffee.'

Mary Philips sighed regretfully. 'And so another beloved stereotype – the hard-drinking copper – bites the dust. Very well, I'll make you a cup of coffee – and you might just have shamed me into joining you.'

She swept into the kitchen, and returned with two mugs of coffee.

She gave Paniatowski the one which had an image of Whitebridge town hall on it.

'They give them out free to employees, in lieu of paying us a decent wage,' she said.

Her own mug said, 'Bitch On Wheels'.

'I bought that for myself,' she told the chief inspector.

Paniatowski grinned. 'You must let me know where you got it,' she said. 'I could use one, too.'

'Poor Tom,' Mary Philips said, sitting down in the minimalist armchair opposite Paniatowski's. 'I suppose, in a way, it's my fault the crash happened, because if I'd had a phone there'd have been no need for him to drive like a bloody maniac.'

'You're a social worker, aren't you?' Paniatowski asked.

'That's right,' Mary Philips agreed. 'Though I wouldn't want you to get the wrong idea about that,' she cautioned.

'The wrong idea?'

'I'm not one of those namby-pamby bleeding-heart types who can see the good in everybody and know it's only their upbringing that makes them act as they do. Once I get my hooks into some man who's been beating up his wife and kids, I don't rest until I've got the bastard firmly behind bars.'

Paniatowski smiled. 'I was wondering why, given your job, you don't have a phone?'

'It's precisely *because* of my job that I don't have a phone,' Mary Philips replied. 'I once heard that you can measure your success in any job by the number of people who dislike you – and if that's true, I must be *very* successful indeed.'

'You kept getting anonymous calls,' Paniatowski guessed.

'Dozens of them – and while it was very gratifying, in a way, to engender such hatred, most of the callers would insist on ringing after the pubs closed, which meant that I was losing a great deal of my beauty sleep.'

'Why didn't you go ex-directory?'

'I tried that, but it didn't work. Because though the foul-mouthed scum who rang me are so lazy that they've never done a decent day's work in their lives, they somehow summoned up the energy to track down my new number, and, in the end, I simply had the phone taken out.' She paused for a moment. 'But you're not here to listen to me recount amusing anecdotes of my life in the sewer – you want to ask me about Elaine.'

'You don't seem very concerned about the fact she's gone missing,' Paniatowski said. 'Is that because you don't think there's anything to worry *about*?'

Mary Philips shook her head vigorously. 'No, it's not that at all. In my line of business, you learn to discipline yourself not to worry about something bad happening until you know – for a fact – that it has. It's the only way to survive. So in answer to your implied question – which may actually have been a veiled criticism – yes, despite myself, I am concerned. But I'm not going to show it – even to a thoroughly nice young woman like you.' She paused again. 'Would you like something stronger to drink now?'

'No, thank you.'

Mary Philips shrugged her shoulders. 'Always worth a try,' she said, philosophically. 'I expect you've already been to see my mother.'

'I have.'

'And did she tell you that there was really no problem at all, because *Tom* would find Elaine?'

'Yes, she did.'

Mary Philips laughed. 'And so he would – if he were allowed to. But I'm a little bit more worldly than Mother – and I know he'd never be let within a mile of the case.'

'You sound like a big fan of his,' Paniatowski said.

'Let me tell you about my sister,' Mary Philips suggested. 'Elaine's twenty-odd years younger than me – which, if you think about it, makes her almost twenty years younger than Tom. She was only eight when our father died, and it hit her very hard. She was like most kids – she thought the world centred on her – so if anything went wrong, it had to be *her* fault.'

Paniatowski knew what she meant. As a child herself, constantly on the run with her mother in war-torn Europe, she'd often had the feeling that if she'd been just a little bit better, none of this would have happened.

'So Elaine clung to the one certainty she had left,' Mary continued. 'She tried to be exactly like Mother, but that didn't work, of course, because she was still a kid and Mother was already in her forties.'

'Did she get picked on in school?'

'She most certainly did. And there was nothing that even a bossy busybody like me could do about it. When she left school, she went to work for our uncle, and she'd probably have been working for him still, if she hadn't met Tom.'

And now we come to the point that still puzzles me, Paniatowski thought. Just *what* did Kershaw see in her – and just *what* did she see in him?

'You're speculating about how the relationship ever got off the ground,' Mary Philips said.

'I am,' Paniatowski admitted.

'We'll probably never have a completely accurate answer to that, because if we don't really know our own partners – or even ourselves – how can we ever really know *anybody*?' Mary Philips said. 'But I'll make a stab at answering, if you want me to.'

'I want you to.'

'Tom, to do him credit, must have caught a glimpse of something none of the rest of us saw – the real Elaine, the one that froze when Father died.'

'And Elaine?'

'I think it was that she sensed he really wanted her. I'm not talking here about just *loving* her, you understand – she got plenty of love from Mother and me – but actually *wanted* her. And with a tall, handsome, confident man like Tom Kershaw virtually falling at her feet, she was finally forced to admit that she couldn't be quite as worthless as she'd always imagined herself to be.' Mary Philips waved her hands helplessly in the air. 'That's not a good answer. It's probably not even the *right* answer. But it's the best I can do.'

'Are they happily married, would you say?'

'Very happy indeed. I'd go so far as to say they complement each other perfectly.'

'So there's no chance Elaine might have been having an affair?'

'You think she might have run off with a lover?'

'It's a possibility we can't dismiss.'

'Maybe you can't – but I certainly can. If she'd been having a bit on the side, she'd have told me. She wouldn't have been able to help herself.'

'And if she found out Tom was having an affair? What would she have done then?'

'Tom hasn't been having an affair. Elaine's all the woman he's ever wanted.'

'Has he told you that himself?'

'No. And even if he had told me, it wouldn't necessarily make it true. But I've *seen* them together. I've seen the secret way he looks at her in company – as if he just can't wait to

get her to bed. It's a look most women go through their entire
life without experiencing. I know I've never had it. My Harry
loves me to pieces, but I've never felt that he was fighting the
urge to rip all my clothes off in a crowded room – and damn
the consequences.'

Paniatowski stood up. 'You've been very helpful,' she said.

'I haven't really, have I?' Mary Philips asked.

No, she hadn't, Paniatowski admitted silently.

'You've helped towards eliminating certain lines of inquiry,
and that's a valuable thing in any investigation,' she said aloud.

And then she noticed the tears that Mary Philips had been
working so hard to fight back.

'She will be all right, won't she, Chief Inspector?' Mary asked.

'Let's hope so,' Paniatowski replied.

Chief Superintendent Kershaw looked a wreck, but then it would
have been a marvel if he hadn't.

'We're sorry to drag you round to the . . . to the . . .' Beresford
began.

'To the scene of the crime?' Kershaw suggested.

'Yes, sir,' Beresford admitted uncomfortably. 'The scene of
the crime. We know this must be very hard for you.'

'If your sergeant hadn't thrown me out last night, you wouldn't
have needed to drag me round, because I'd already have been
here,' Kershaw pointed out. Then he looked Meadows straight
in the eye and said sincerely, 'I want to thank you for that,
Sergeant.'

'There's no need, sir,' Meadows said, looking embarrassed.

'But there is,' Kershaw insisted. 'I want to thank you for
reminding me that, despite my personal grief, a crime had been
committed and it was my duty to act like a police officer.' He
took a deep breath, then continued, 'Now what can I do for you,
Colin?'

'Like most men, you probably don't know half the stuff your
wife has got in her wardrobe,' Beresford said, 'but we'd appreciate you looking through it anyway, because there's always a
chance you'll notice that something is missing.'

A smile, too poignant to be called anything like amusement,
came to Kershaw's face.

'Is that what you think, Sergeant Meadows?' he asked. 'Do

you believe, as Inspector Beresford seems to, that I'll have only a vague idea of what's in Elaine's wardrobe?'

'No, sir,' Meadows replied. 'I think you'll know exactly what should be there.'

'And so I do,' Kershaw said. He turned his attention back to Beresford. 'Elaine has never bought a dress without asking me if I liked it, and I wouldn't even purchase so much as a handkerchief without getting her approval first.'

'I see, sir,' Beresford said.

'I don't think you do,' Kershaw contradicted him, 'but then I know for a fact that you're not married, and I *suspect* you're not in love.' He sighed. 'Even if I hadn't played a part in buying the clothes, I would still remember every dress that Elaine has ever worn, simply because she was the one who wore them.' He paused. 'You still don't understand, do you? Never mind. Let's go and look at Elaine's wardrobe.'

Kershaw gave the wardrobe a thorough inspection. 'There's nothing missing,' he said finally. He looked around the room. 'May I examine the laundry hamper?'

Meadows and Beresford exchanged glances, then Beresford said, 'As long as you're wearing gloves.'

Kershaw took a sterilized package out of his pocket, slipped on the gloves, and opened the hamper.

He rummaged through it for about a minute, before saying, 'The nightdress she was wearing when I left for work yesterday morning isn't here.'

'Could you describe it to us, sir?' Beresford asked.

'Certainly. It's in pale-blue chiffon, with a low neckline, dropped back, and slits up each side to the upper thigh level. Have you found it anywhere else in the house?'

'No, sir,' Meadows replied.

Kershaw gulped. 'Then we can only assume that she was still wearing it when the bastard took her away,' he said. He gulped again. 'And what further assumption can we make from that?'

'I don't think you personally *should* go making assumptions, sir,' Meadows said quietly.

'We can assume that he didn't expect anyone to catch sight of her between here and . . . and wherever he was planning to take her,' Kershaw said, ignoring the advice.

'We've one more thing to show you, sir,' Beresford said.

'And what's that?'

Beresford produced the red stiletto heel. 'Is this your wife's?'

'Good God, no,' Kershaw exclaimed. 'That heel must be nearly five inches high, and I don't mean to sound snobbish here, but Elaine has far too much style to ever contemplate wearing such a monstrosity. In fact, it's hard for me to imagine the kind of woman who *would* wear it. Would you think of wearing a pair of shoes like the ones this heel came from, Sergeant Meadows?'

Meadows' face suddenly lost all expression. 'With all due respect, sir, what I would or wouldn't wear is nothing to do with you.'

Kershaw nodded his head. 'Quite right, Sergeant, and I apologize for ever placing you in the position where you felt it was necessary to put me in my rightful place.'

'Apology accepted,' Meadows said.

'And now, Sergeant, if you wouldn't mind, I'd like you to leave the room while I have a private word with Inspector Beresford,' Kershaw said.

'Of course, sir,' Meadows agreed.

The interview with Mary Philips had shaken up Paniatowski, but that had more to do with Kershaw himself than with the investigation. It had seemed – as it had when interviewing her mother – that they had been talking about a different man to the one she knew.

No, she corrected herself – not *knew*, more a case of *had known*.

But as she drove into central Whitebridge, and despite all her efforts to fight it, she found her mind drifting back to those *had known* days.

It is a week since Paniatowski showed the obscene photographs to DI Kershaw, and two more have appeared since then.

She has taken them both to Kershaw, and he has been sympathetic, but unhelpful.

'There's a delicate balance that has to be maintained in any police force,' he said the first time. 'I want to find out who's been producing these disgusting pictures – I really do – but I

have to tread carefully, because I can't risk destroying the morale of the whole unit in the process.'

'You have to be patient,' he'd said on her second visit. 'And maybe you'd find that a little easier if you let yourself go and just had a good cry.'

She is not willing to do that – nowhere near ready to give her enemies the satisfaction of seeing her break down.

But she almost does break down when the third picture appears, because it is fouler – by far – than any that have preceded it.

The woman in the picture – the woman with her head pasted on to her – is lying on the ground, with her legs spread wide. And on top of her – mounting her – is a full-sized hog.

It is difficult to avoid vomiting, but she manages it, reducing what could have been a stream of spew to a few dry heaves.

Her first thought is to take the picture straight to Kershaw, but that will be even more humiliating than the last three times, and she can think of no reason why it might meet with any more success.

Out of desperation, a new idea comes to her mind. She cuts out a photograph of Kershaw, and pastes it on to the hog's head. Now, she argues to herself – surely now, that he is a partner in the humiliation – he will be forced to take some decisive action.

Kershaw has barely glanced at the other pictures she brought him, but he stares at this one for a full minute.

Then he says, 'Why, Monika?'

'Because they're sick bastards,' she tells him, though she is fully aware that she is not answering the question he's asked.

'It all comes down to a question of respect,' he tells her. 'You have to work hard to get it, and once it's yours, you have to make sure that you never do anything which might make it slip from your grasp.'

'I don't understand,' she says.

'I have the respect of my men,' Kershaw says gravely. 'Wouldn't you say that's true?'

'Yes,' she admits – because there is no point in denying it.

'And because I have the respect of my men, I know that none of them would have pasted my head on to this disgusting photograph. So the question is, who did put it there?'

'You can't be certain that one of them didn't . . .' Paniatowski begins.

'*I am* absolutely *certain,*' Kershaw says firmly. '*And now I am going to repeat my question, and I want it answered honestly. If they didn't do it, Monika, then who did?*'

'*If they didn't do it, then I have no idea,*' Paniatowski says.

But she knows he knows the truth, and that he knows that she knows.

'*I can't blame you, Monika, because I understand the pressures you're under,*' Kershaw says softly. '*Nor will I hold it against you in the future. But I will caution you again that if you continue to hold your emotions in, there is a serious risk that you will repeat this error of judgement.*'

'*Can I go now, sir?*' Paniatowski asks.

'*You may,*' Kershaw replies. '*Though I think you might be wiser to stay a little longer, and talk this thing through with me.*'

'*I want to go,*' Paniatowski says urgently, knowing she will fall into an emotional nosedive if she stays there a minute longer.

'*Then go,*' Kershaw says.

'I didn't cry,' Paniatowski said, as she pulled into the car park at police headquarters. 'I didn't cry. I didn't cry,' repeating it like a mantra. 'I had every excuse in the world, and I still didn't cry.'

But then she realized, as she put on her handbrake, that the tears she had held back for so many years were flowing freely enough now.

It was eleven thirty. Marie padded barefoot along the narrow corridor, stopped in front of Grace's room, and tapped lightly on the door.

'You awake yet?' she asked with a lightness of tone in her voice that she was far from feeling.

There was no answer.

'Come on, get yourself out of bed, lazybones, and we'll go for a drink,' Marie persisted.

There was still silence from the other side of the door.

It shouldn't be like this, Marie thought. I've been fair. I could have done this half an hour ago, but I waited. I've played by the rules. She *has to* be there.

She reached out for the door handle, and gave it a half turn. The door was not locked.

And still she hesitated, as if another ten seconds could make a difference – as if, though Grace had not been in the bed when she knocked, she would be by the time she opened the door.

She pushed, and the door swung open. She looked across at the bed, and it was obvious – even from the other side of the room – that it had not been slept in.

EIGHT

L ong ago, shortly after she and Bob Rutter broke up, Paniatowski had had a brief affair with George Baxter, a policeman she'd been working closely with on the other side of the Pennines. He had made all the running, and she – emotionally crippled by her unhappiness – had simply let it happen, because she liked and respected the man, and it seemed to be what he'd wanted. The affair had been doomed from the start, for though she tried her hardest to fall in love with him, she secretly knew that had never been a real possibility. It had been a relief to her when he ended it, even though that left her feeling lonelier than ever. And at least, she had consoled herself, she could finally put it all behind her.

And then, out of the blue, George Baxter – now married – had been appointed Mid Lancs' Chief Constable.

They had an uneasy relationship now, which, though much of it was based on mutual professional respect, also contained elements of regret, bitterness, and an abiding affection which terrified them both. So, understandably, it was not without some trepidation that Paniatowski answered his summons that morning.

Baxter was sitting behind his desk, rather than on one of the easy chairs in the corner which he reserved for more comfortable chats. She looked at him, and could not help, for a moment, seeing him as the big ginger teddy bear she had once known. But if he was *still* that teddy bear, he was an angry one – or perhaps only a troubled one.

He looked up from his paperwork, and said, 'Please take a seat, Chief Inspector.'

Paniatowski sat. 'What was it you wanted to see me about, sir?'

'Is there some bad blood between you and Chief Superintendent Kershaw?' the chief constable said.

'Why do you ask that, sir?' Paniatowski countered.

'I ask because, from the reports I've been receiving, you seem to be handling Mr Kershaw with a lack of tact which is extreme, even by your own somewhat volatile standards.'

'My somewhat *volatile* standards?' Paniatowski repeated.

'That's what I'd call them,' Baxter confirmed.

'I get the job done,' Paniatowski said stubbornly.

'Yes, you certainly have so far,' Baxter admitted. 'And that's been your saving grace. But a bobby who relies *only* on results to keep out of trouble is heading for a fall.'

An uneasy silence descended, only broken when Paniatowski said, 'Might I ask who has been giving you these reports?'

Baxter ran his hands through his shock of ginger hair.

'How would you reply to that question if it was put to you?' he asked.

'I'd reply that I wasn't at liberty to say,' Paniatowski confessed reluctantly.

'And can you expect any less from me?' Baxter wondered. 'Now, Chief Inspector, since I have answered your question as best I can, would you kindly answer mine?'

'Whatever history I might have with Mr Kershaw in no way influences the way I'm handling this investigation,' Paniatowski said stiffly.

'Doesn't it? I'm told you ordered him to have a blood test.'

'The man was involved in a car crash which could easily have resulted in the death of other drivers. I'd have been failing in my duty as a police officer if I hadn't ordered the test.'

'You know the result was negative, don't you – that he hadn't touched a drop of alcohol all day?'

'That still doesn't make it wrong to have ordered the test,' Paniatowski said, holding her ground.

'Tom Kershaw's not just a good bobby, he's a decent man,' Baxter told her. 'He's a deacon at my church.'

Paniatowski grinned involuntarily. 'I didn't know that you were a member of the God-bothering brigade, sir,' she said.

'There are a lot of things you don't know about me, Chief Inspector – there are a lot of things you never *took the trouble to find out*!'

So there it was, out in the open – a chunk of their own personal history, rearing up from the grave they had tried to bury it in, like the monster it was.

'Can I ask you what your own relationship with Mr Kershaw is, sir?' she asked.

'I'm his superior,' Baxter said.

'So it's no more than that?'

'You do realize you're bordering on insubordination with questions like that, don't you?' Baxter said.

'I must disagree with you there, sir,' Paniatowski said firmly. 'I'd be bordering on insubordination if I *demanded* to know what your relationship with Mr Kershaw was – but I'm only asking.'

'We're both very keen anglers, and sometimes we go fishing together,' Baxter said.

'So you'd say that once you've both taken off your uniforms, the chain of command is left behind and you're simply friends?' Paniatowski asked.

'Don't push it,' Baxter warned her.

'I'm just trying to get a clear picture, sir,' Paniatowski said flatly.

'You're just trying to insinuate that in any dispute between yourself and Chief Superintendent Kershaw, I'll come down on Tom's side,' Baxter said angrily. 'Tell me, Chief Inspector, do you intend to charge the chief superintendent with dangerous driving – because if you do, you'll have my support, if not my approval.'

'No, of course I don't intend to charge him,' Paniatowski said.

But she had considered it, she realized. There had been a small, malicious part of her which would have taken great pleasure from seeing Kershaw standing in the dock.

'Mr Kershaw and I got off to a rocky start yesterday,' she said, 'and I'll admit that was probably mostly my fault. But I want you to know I'll pursue this investigation with the same vigour I've pursued all the others.'

'I never doubted it,' Baxter said.

Bollocks! Paniatowski thought.

Lucy lived in a better class of boarding house than she did herself, Marie thought – but then Lucy *would*, because she knew how to handle money almost as well as she knew how to handle men.

But even so, the differences were only skin-deep. Lucy's landlady might be more smartly dressed than her own, but she had the same look of avarice and hypocrisy in her eyes when she opened the door. And though the wallpaper in the hallway was nicer, this was still no more than a dormitory, where girls who prostituted themselves returned nightly to lick their wounds.

When she knocked on Lucy's door, a voice from inside called, 'Come on in.'

But when Marie opened the door, it was plain from the expression on her friend's face that she was not the person who'd been expected.

Lucy was lying on her bed, reading a book – a slim, almost tiny book! – but when she saw Marie in the doorway, she quickly stuffed it under her pillow.

'What's that you're reading?' Marie asked.

'Nothing,' Lucy said awkwardly.

'Is it a *dirty* book?' Marie asked.

Lucy sighed. 'No, it's poetry,' she said. 'At least, it is to me.'

Marie didn't understand what she meant by that, but then she often didn't understand Lucy, because Lucy was so smart.

But anyway, understanding the way that Lucy thought wasn't why she was there.

'Grace wasn't in her room this morning,' Marie told her friend.

'She might be with a punter,' Lucy replied.

'Till eleven o'clock in the morning?' Marie asked. 'You don't really believe that, do you?'

'No,' Lucy agreed, with resignation. 'I don't really believe that.'

'We have to go to the police,' Marie said, desperately.

'What's this "we"?' Lucy countered. 'If you're so worried, why don't *you* go to the police?'

'Cos I'm not brave enough to go on my own – an' you know I'm not.'

Lucy reached under the pillow, and ran her fingers along the book she had been reading earlier.

'What would be the *point* of reporting it?' she asked. 'I reported what happened to Denise, and nothing happened.'

'That's cos you reported it to the wrong person.'

'And I suppose you know who the *right* person is,' Lucy said sceptically.

'Yeah, I do, as a matter of fact,' Marie said. 'There's this important bobby who keeps getting her picture in the papers. I think she'd help us.'

'I don't see *why* you should think that,' Lucy answered. 'She might be a woman, but she's still a *police officer*, isn't she?'

'She won't look at us like the men do,' Marie said stubbornly. 'She won't think we're nothing but dirt. She's a nice person. You can tell that from her photo.'

'You can tell it from a photograph in a *newspaper*!'

'That's right.'

Lucy sighed. 'Does she have a name – this important bobby of yours?'

'Course she does. Everybody has a name.'

'And what's hers?'

'I can't remember exactly, because it's a funny foreign name, but I've got it written down somewhere.'

'You're sure you're not making this up – or that you just imagined it?'

'I'm definitely not making it up,' Marie said hotly. She pursed her brow. 'It starts with a "pan". That's right – it's "pan-something"!'

Beresford and Meadows were standing by the garden gate of Kershaw's house when Paniatowski's red MBA pulled up at the kerb. Beresford was smoking, but Meadows had refused his offer of a cigarette – so maybe that was another vice that she had managed to steer clear of.

'Have the lab boys finished with the house?' Paniatowski asked Beresford.

The inspector nodded. 'Yes, boss, they're back at headquarters now, running a check on the fingerprints.'

That wouldn't lead anywhere, Paniatowski thought. The intruder had been far too careful to have left his prints.

'I suppose you might as well give Mr Kershaw his keys back, then,' she said.

'I've already done that, boss,' Beresford told her.

'Have you indeed?' Paniatowski asked, as a prickle of irritation ran through her. 'Well, I must be getting really absent-minded in my old age, because I've absolutely no memory of authorizing that.'

Beresford looked sheepish. 'You didn't authorize it,' he admitted, 'but, like I said, the lab boys had no more interest in the place, and Mr Kershaw seemed eager to get back into his home, so I didn't see the harm in letting him.'

'No harm at all,' Paniatowski said tartly, 'except that it weakens the chain of command, which is one of the most effective instruments we have at our disposal.'

Christ, I sound just like a bloody police manual, she thought.

But Beresford had taken the point anyway.

'You're right, boss, I was out of line and I'm sorry,' he said. Then he went and spoiled the apology by adding, 'It just seemed to me that Mr Kershaw might be a bit happier back in familiar surroundings.'

'You're not supposed to be his social worker, Inspector, you're supposed to be one of the police officers charged with investigating his wife's disappearance,' Paniatowski snapped. 'And if you really want to make him happy, you could do worse than turn your mind to thinking about how we might get his bloody wife back!'

'You're right, boss,' Beresford said, for a second time.

'Where is Kershaw now?' Paniatowski demanded.

'I think he's in the basement.'

'And do I have your permission to go and talk to him, Dr Beresford – or do you think that might upset him too much?'

'I made a mistake, boss, and I've apologized for it,' Beresford said. 'Can't you let it rest at that?'

A wave of shame swept over Paniatowski. She and Beresford had been through so much together – had covered each other's backs so often – that he didn't deserve this treatment, whatever he'd done.

'I'm sorry, Colin,' she said. 'I'm just in a bloody mood today. He's in the basement, you say?'

'That's right, boss.'

Paniatowski nodded, and walked towards the front door.

Beresford, feeling miserable, watched her progress. He had let Monika down, he thought, and – almost as bad, from his personal perspective – he had put himself into a position which had resulted in him being humiliated in front of the new – and increasingly appealing – sergeant.

*   *   *

Until that day, DC Jack Crane had never realized quite how many women's shoe shops there were in Whitebridge, but so far he had visited five, and he hadn't even really made a dent in his long list.

His heart sank when he saw that the one he was just entering was manned entirely by young women, because, however grave and official he tried to sound, young women always seemed compelled to flirt with him.

He showed his warrant card to a girl who said that her name was Cindy and she was assistant manageress.

'Doesn't it make me sound old – assistant manageress?' she asked coquettishly. 'But I'm only twenty-two.'

Crane, stuck for an appropriate reply, said nothing at all.

'It's the truth,' Cindy said. 'I won't be twenty-three until next April. Honestly!'

'I believe you,' Crane said gruffly. 'I'm looking for a shoe.'

Cindy giggled. 'Well, you've come to the right place, because this shop is full of them.'

'A specific shoe,' Crane said firmly. He took a photograph of the red heel out of his pocket. 'The shoe that this heel came from.'

Cindy examined the picture. 'Don't think we've ever stocked anything like that,' she said. 'June! Liz! Come and have a look at this.'

The girls crowded around the photograph – and around Crane.

'No, never had nothing like that,' June said. 'Most of the customers what we get in here would be frightened they'd fall off heels like them and break their bloody necks.'

'Language, June!' Cindy said, remembering, belatedly, that she was temporarily in charge.

'Well, they would,' June said defensively.

'The thing is, we'd have no call for shoes like that – not from our clientele,' Cindy said. 'The plain fact is that that heel looks a little bit . . . a little bit . . . well, you know what I mean.'

'No,' Crane admitted. 'I don't think I do.'

'It looks a bit *kinky*,' Cindy blurted out.

And her two companions almost split their sides laughing.

Paniatowski heard the click of snooker balls from the top of the stairs. But it was not the vigorous click that she would have heard if the player had been really absorbed in the game. Rather, the shots were spaced out, as if whoever was playing was merely forcing himself to go through the motions.

She had been in the basement the previous day, but then she had been looking for clues, and had divided it up – in her mind's eye – into a series of small squares which should be investigated individually. Now, as she walked down the stairs, she took in the whole room.

The dartboard was in one corner, the bar stood next to it and the snooker table, over which Kershaw was lethargically bent, was in the centre of the room. Several straight-backed chairs had been placed around a card table, and there were four easy chairs in front of a large television screen. On the far wall was a book-case, which – in the spirit of the room – was probably filled with books on sporting topics.

The whole place had been carefully thought out, and every component of it blended perfectly with the others, which meant that the large empty space near the foot of the stairs really jarred.

'That's where the cabinet for my sporting trophies is supposed to be going,' Kershaw said, following her gaze and reading her mind. 'I was looking forward to installing it. It would have given me real pleasure. Now, however things turn out, I don't think I'll bother.'

Paniatowski reached the bottom of the stairs. 'The chief constable has decided not to go public on your wife's disappearance,' she said. 'He thinks that all the media attention it would throw up would only serve to get in the way of the investigation.'

'He's probably right,' Kershaw agreed. 'But how do you propose to explain away all the police vehicles that were here last night?'

'Nobody saw them but the neighbours, and they probably thought that all those bobbies were just here for one of your celebrated parties,' Paniatowski said.

Jesus, I sound bitter! she thought.

'I never did invite you to one of those parties, did I, Monika?' Kershaw asked. 'But even if I had, you'd never have come.'

'No, I wouldn't,' Paniatowski agreed. She took a deep breath. 'We're going to have to put our differences behind us, you know – at least for the present.'

'Agreed,' Kershaw replied. 'But before we can do that, I need to apologize. It was wrong what I did when you were my sergeant, but I was a different man back then, Monika, I really was.'

Based on the evidence of his obviously happy marriage, she was inclined to believe him – but yet, remembering what a good actor he could be when the situation called for it, she was still not *entirely* convinced.

'I've talked to Elaine's mother and sister this morning,' she said.

'Oh yes?'

'And what they told me was enough to convince me that whoever abducted Elaine probably did it to get back at you.'

'Unless he wasn't trying to get back at *anybody*,' Kershaw said.

'What do you mean?'

'He could be just a psychopath, you know.' Kershaw swallowed hard. 'I don't want to think that's what he is,' a vein on his forehead began to throb alarmingly, 'because if he *is* a psychopath . . . if . . . he . . . is . . . a . . . psychopath . . .'

'Stop right there!' Paniatowski ordered. 'Take a few deep breaths.'

Kershaw did as he'd been instructed, and the purple sheen which had come to his face slowly drained away.

'Better now?' Paniatowski asked.

Kershaw nodded. 'It's still a possibility that has to be faced, you know,' he said, with great effort.

'Yes, it is,' Paniatowski agreed. 'And we won't be neglecting that as a line of inquiry. But I'll also be looking for anyone who has a grudge against you – and that's why I'm asking you now for access to the files on all the investigations you've conducted in the last five years.'

'And if I say no?'

'If you say no, I'll ask the chief constable to order you to give them to me. And if *he* refuses, I'll go over his head to the magistrate. But why *would* you want to say no?'

'You're quite right, why would I?' Kershaw agreed. 'But when your lads are working their way through the files, I want my lads sitting right next to them.'

'That's not possible,' Paniatowski said.

'Isn't it? Why not?'

'Because it would be highly irregular for them to become a part of the official investigation.'

'But they could be there unofficially,' Kershaw pointed out.

'And how would that work?'

'A couple of lads have taken some of the leave that's owed them. I didn't ask them to, but they insisted they'd do it whatever I said.'

'They've taken *leave*?' Paniatowski repeated incredulously. 'In the middle of a bloody flu epidemic, when we can barely scrape a skeleton staff together?'

'Yes.'

'And who rubber-stamped their request? You?'

'No, not me,' Kershaw told her. 'I'm too personally involved, so I passed the request up to the chief constable.'

'You knew I'd ask you for the files, and, with George Baxter's complete cooperation, you decided to stitch me up before I even made the request,' Paniatowski said, furious.

'I'm willing to do anything – and everything – I have to, if it will get my wife back safely,' Kershaw said.

'Then why won't you and your chief constable mate just let me get on with my job?'

'Maybe George doesn't completely trust you,' Kershaw suggested. 'Maybe he thinks your personal animosity to me will influence the way that you conduct the investigation.'

'And what about you?' Paniatowski demanded. 'Is that how you think?'

'No,' Kershaw said seriously. 'I think you're a good bobby – probably one of the best in the whole force.'

'Well, then?'

'But I'm better. I'm *the* best. And since it's my wife who's gone missing, I want the best bobby available looking for her, even if it's only unofficially.'

'And if I say no?' Paniatowski said, echoing his earlier comment.

'If you say no, I'll go above your head – and I'll win,' Kershaw replied, returning the compliment. 'Of course, it won't do either of our careers any good, but my career is the last thing I'm worrying about right now.'

'I need time to think about it,' Paniatowski said.

'There *is* no time,' Kershaw said. He looked around him. 'I hear you're a pretty good darts player,' he continued, his eyes resting on the board.

And so I am, Paniatowski thought.

She'd come to the game rather late, when Louisa had started to express a distinctly unfeminine interest in it, and had been surprised to find she was a natural. Perhaps, she sometimes thought, it was because she was capable of such single-minded concentration. Or maybe it was simply because she'd a stronger urge to win than almost all her opponents.

'I'll play you one game of three-oh-one, straight in and a double to finish,' Kershaw said. 'If I win, you'll let my lads work in tandem with yours. If I lose, I'll stay clear of the investigation.'

'Seems a bit of a desperate gamble,' Paniatowski said.

'That's because I'm a bit of a desperate man,' Kershaw told her.

She nodded. 'All right, you're on. How many practice darts do we have before we start?'

'None,' Kershaw replied. 'Life isn't about trying things out first – it's about meeting problems head-on, and dealing with them straight away.'

They bulled up, and she won the right to start.

Her first three darts landed firmly in the treble twenty. One hundred and eighty – the maximum score, and enough to make most of the opponents she'd ever played against all but give up the ghost.

But Kershaw was not about to give up, nor did he try to emulate her. Instead, he slammed three darts into the treble nineteen.

She had 121 left. Kershaw had 130.

She could finish it in the next three darts. Another treble twenty, a treble eleven and a double fourteen, and it was all over.

She found the treble twenty and followed up with the treble eleven. Kershaw was completely silent and perfectly still, but she could sense his tension.

She threw her third dart, and it landed just the wrong side of the double fourteen wire.

She stepped aside, and Kershaw walked up to the line.

For at least a minute, the chief superintendent stood staring at the board.

It wasn't that he was working out what he needed to win,

Paniatowski thought. Any real darts player would know that automatically. No, what he was doing was putting off the moment when he might have to admit that he'd lost.

Kershaw threw his first dart, and it landed inside the treble twenty by a hair's breadth. He should have followed through with his second dart immediately, while he still had the momentum – every darts player knew that, too – but he didn't.

He's scared, Paniatowski thought. He's really frightened.

Kershaw lifted his arm again – stiffly, and with effort, as if the dart in his hand weighed a ton. When it was finally at the right level, he threw carelessly – like a man already accepting defeat – but, despite that, the dart still found its treble ten target.

He needed double fifteen to win.

He turned to Paniatowski. 'You'll hold me to this agreement, will you?'

'I will.'

'Why, in God's name?'

'Because I think you'll be a liability to the investigation. Because I think I have more chance of finding your wife on my own.'

Kershaw turned back to the board, and this time his hand rose quickly – this time he released the dart as if he were depending on the righteousness of his cause, or divine intervention – or *something* – rather than his own skill.

The dart wobbled in mid-air, but landed in the double fifteen.

'You might not want me, but you've got me,' Kershaw said.

But there was no triumph in either his voice or his expression. There was only relief.

NINE

The two women seemed such an unlikely pair that it would have been difficult not to notice them under *any* circumstances, but the fact that they were standing squarely in the middle of the space in the police car park which said 'Reserved for DCI Paniatowski' made ignoring them a virtual impossibility.

As she put the MGA into reverse, and began slowly to back

towards her parking space, Paniatowski studied the women in her rear-view mirror.

One of them – the younger of the two, who was probably twenty-two or twenty-three – was dressed in cheap, flashy clothes, and heavily – if hastily – made-up, and if she wasn't already on the game, then she was at least teetering on the very edge of it.

The older one could have been twenty-five or twenty-six. She was slightly less attractive than her companion, but had a style – both in her dress and her manner – that the other woman could never hope to emulate.

As the back bumper of the MGA approached the yellow line which marked the edge of her space, she saw the two women step to one side. But they made no effort to move away. Instead, they stood in silence, and watched while she completed the manoeuvre.

Paniatowski shifted the gear stick into neutral, switched off the engine, and stepped out of the car.

'Is there something I can do for you, ladies?' she asked.

'It's our friend, Grace,' moaned the younger one. 'She's gone missing.'

'Gone missing?' Paniatowski repeated.

'I told you I'd handle this, Marie,' the older one said, firmly but kindly.

The younger one looked down at the ground. 'I'm so sorry, Lucy, I just forgot.'

'It's all right,' the older one – Lucy – cooed. 'We all forget things when we're upset.' She turned to Paniatowski. 'We've come about a friend of ours who's disappeared – and yes, before you ask, she's a prostitute.'

'We think the Ripper might have got her,' Marie said, on the verge of hysteria.

'What ripper?' Paniatowski said. 'I've no idea what you're talking about.'

'One of the other girls got slashed with a razor a couple of weeks ago,' Lucy explained. 'We think the same man might have taken Grace.'

I don't have time for this, Paniatowski thought. I really *don't* have time.

'If you're worried about your friend, you should report it,' she said aloud.

'That's what we're doing,' Grace told her.

'When reporting a suspected crime, there are channels to go through,' Paniatowski pointed out.

'You can drown in those channels,' Lucy said bitterly. 'It's happened often enough before. So we either report it to you – or we report it to nobody.'

Paniatowski hesitated for a second, then said, 'There's a café just around the corner. Why don't we go and have a cup of tea?'

It was a workman's café, which meant they got none of the disapproving stares which might have been aimed at them in a more genteel establishment.

'So, it's the fact that the one girl was slashed which makes you so worried about the other one, is it?' Paniatowski asked, when the waitress had deposited mugs of tea on the table and moved on.

'That's right,' Lucy agreed. 'It's because of that.'

'Grace is so young – and so tiny,' Marie sobbed.

A lorry driver had been eying them up for some time, and now he ambled over to the table.

'I wouldn't normally bother with a woman of your age,' he said to Paniatowski, 'but you look like you've got a bit of class about you.'

'Do you think so?' Paniatowski asked. 'I'm never sure myself. It's my nose I worry about. I think it's a bit too big.'

The lorry driver leered. 'It's not your nose I'll be most interested in,' he said. 'So how much will it cost me?'

Paniatowski's brow furrowed with concentration. 'Hard to say exactly,' she told him. 'But I'd guess that it would be somewhere around a hundred and fifty pounds.'

'A hundred and fifty quid?' the lorry driver said. 'For a quick jump in the cab of my lorry?'

'And then, of course, there's the fact that your name will be in the papers to be taken into consideration.'

'I don't know what you're on about.'

'Are you thick or something?' Paniatowski asked, reaching into her handbag. 'The fine for soliciting should be about a hundred and fifty pounds, and your name will be in the papers when it comes to court.' She held up the warrant card. 'I'm a police officer, so if I was you, I'd piss off.'

The lorry driver turned and rushed out of the café, leaving his bacon sandwich on the counter. Lucy was laughing throatily, and even Marie seemed to have cheered up a little.

'About this girl who was slashed,' Paniatowski said to Lucy, 'do you have any of the details?'

'I have *all* the details,' Lucy told her.

The man standing under the street light is a mess, Denise Slater quickly decides. With his thin nose and his blue eyes, he must once have been quite handsome. Not handsome like the young bricklayer who robbed her of her virginity, of course – no, not like that at all. More – she struggles for the right word – more posh-handsome. But now there is a slackness to his jaw and a lifelessness to his skin which makes even a girl like her – who has rented her body out to all kinds of creeps – think twice. And he is nervous – very nervous. He has a tic in one cheek, and those blue eyes of his – bloodshot now – dart nervously around like those of a frightened rabbit.

Still, a punter is a punter, she tells herself, and however bad it is, it will soon be over.

'If you want oral, it'll cost you more, and I don't do anal whatever you're willing to pay,' she says.

'Oral' and 'anal' are not the words she would have used a couple of weeks earlier. She didn't even know *them a couple of weeks earlier. But Lucy says they are good words, because they show you have a bit of class – and there are some punters who are willing to pay more for class.*

'Have you ever read any of the works of the Marquis de Sade?' the punter asks tentatively.

'Marquee?' Denise says. 'Isn't that some kind of big tent?'

The punter laughs – patronizingly, yet somehow still unsure of himself. 'De Sade was a French writer who believed that the greatest sexual pleasure comes through pushing back the barriers of pain,' he explains.

Denise shifts her weight uneasily from one foot to the other. 'Barriers?' she repeats. 'I don't know what you're on about.'

'I have all kinds of costumes at home,' the punter says. 'Tight corsets, masks, shoes which are so high they are almost stilts . . .'

'Look, I don't care what *you've got at home – do you want to do the business or don't you?'*

'I want to do the business,' the punter confirms, his confidence growing. 'I want to chain your hands above your head so tightly that you are forced to stand on tiptoe. I want to see your naked skin glistening in the candle light. And then I want to whip you!'

'You're sick!' Denise says.

'I am not sick,' the punter counters, in what sounds almost like the cry of a wounded animal. 'I merely have unusual tastes.'

She should take warning now – should remember that wounded animals can still be dangerous – but she doesn't.

'Sick!' she repeats. 'What's the matter with you? Can't you get it up, like normal men?'

'I am so much more than a normal man,' the punter tells her – loudly, as if this will somehow make what he is saying sound more credible. 'I am a superman.'

Denise giggles. 'Superman's got muscles of steel,' she says. 'You're not like him. You're a weed.'

The punter bellows with pain and rage, and Denise, alarmed, takes a step backwards. And it is as she retreats that she sees the naked blade of the razor shining under the streetlamp.

The man slashes out with the razor. He is aiming at her face, but she has already dodged to the side. Even so, she does not escape unscathed. The razor cuts into her coat. She feels no pain at first. That does not come for perhaps two or three seconds. And then it hurts – God, it hurts – and she is screaming at the top of her voice.

'It shouldn't have been like this,' the man mumbles to himself. 'This isn't how I planned it at all.'

He slips the razor in his pocket, and scurries away. And though Denise does not see it – being far too involved in her own anguish – he is crying.

'If I hadn't found her when I did, she'd probably have bled to death,' Lucy says, doing her best to speak matter-of-factly, but clearly shaken by even the memory of the experience. 'I took her straight to hospital.'

'And then?' Paniatowski asked.

'And then we reported it to the police.'

'I need a name,' Paniatowski told her.

'A name?'

'I need to know who you reported it to.'

Lucy nodded, to show she understood, 'We were moved from pillar to post for a couple of hours,' she said, 'but we finally got to see a sergeant called Bailey.'

'And what did he say?'

'He said he'd look into the matter.'

'And did he?'

'Not as far as we know.'

The first time that Beresford had stood on the podium in the police headquarters' major cases incident room (which, when there *were* no major cases, was more prosaically known simply as the basement), he had looked down on what seemed to him like a positive sea of fresh-faced detective constables, and had been sure it would not be too long before one of them unmasked him as the impostor he really was. But those days were behind him. Now, he had come to accept that he truly *was* a detective inspector, and that the words of wisdom he dispensed were – most of the time, anyway – actually quite wise.

'The motives behind the abduction might be very complex – we simply don't know, one way or the other,' he told the young policemen, who had been drafted in from all over central Lancashire, 'but the method used couldn't be simpler. The intruder entered here,' he indicated the window on the sketch map pinned to the blackboard. 'Mrs Kershaw was in the house. We can't say exactly where, but given that she had a bad case of the flu, the chances are that she was in bed. Now, there are no signs of a struggle, so he probably drugged her or knocked her unconscious before she had time to react.'

The detective constables, for many of whom this was their first serious case, were all furiously taking notes, and Beresford began to feel quite paternal. Then he reminded himself that they'd probably all had sex at least once or twice, while it was still unknown territory to him – and the feeling went away.

'We know the intruder took her through the garden, and that she was still wearing only her nightdress,' he continued. 'We suspect that he'd slipped a pair of very high-heeled shoes on her feet, though that is only speculation. It's speculation, too, that he had a vehicle parked in this alley, but it is *informed* speculation.' He paused briefly. 'Any questions so far?'

One of the youngest detective constables started to raise his hand – as if he were still a schoolboy – then lost his nerve and let it fall to his side again.

'The uniforms have done a door-to-door canvas of the area around Mr Kershaw's house, and have come up with sweet FA,' Beresford continued. 'That's why you'll be covering the same ground again. You'll also be setting up roadblocks on the roads leading away from the area. Have you any idea why you might be doing that?'

'So we can question motorists who regularly use that route, to find out if they noticed anything unusual on the night in question,' one of the older detective constables said.

'Correct,' Beresford agreed. 'Now, before you're given your assignments, I'd like to leave you with one last thought. Ninety-nine per cent of good police work is persistence and bloody-mindedness. If you ask a question and you're not happy with the answer, ask it again! And keep asking it until you get an answer you *are* happy with. Don't worry about annoying or offending the people that you're questioning – they'll get over it, and there's just a chance that they might finally let slip something we can use.' He paused again. 'Are there any questions now?'

The reluctant young constable raised his hand again, and this time he *kept* it in the air.

'Yes?' Beresford said.

'You keep saying the intruder did this, and the intruder did that, sir,' the constable said.

'So what's your point?' Beresford wondered.

'How do we know it was a *single* intruder, sir?' the constable replied. 'How can we be sure there weren't two or three of them?'

Bloody hell, we never thought of that, Beresford told himself.

Sergeant Bailey was in his late-thirties, and had the look of indolence about him which some policemen develop when they finally give up their dreams of becoming chief constable and accept that they have climbed as high up the ladder as they are ever going to.

'When you first asked me about it, ma'am, I drew a complete blank,' he said to Paniatowski, across the table in the police canteen. 'Fortunately, I've always been very good at keeping records.' He smiled complacently. 'So I only had to read my report to have all the details at my fingertips.'

'So let's hear those details,' Paniatowski said.

'It was around two o'clock in the morning, and I was just about to take a well-earned break when the duty officer asked me if I'd talk to this slag, and—'

'Her name's Denise Slater,' Paniatowski interrupted him. 'Call her Denise, if you must – though since she's a member of the public like any other, I'd prefer you to call her Miss Slater – but under no circumstances, Sergeant Bailey, are you to refer to her again as a slag.'

'Sorry, ma'am,' Bailey said, with more indifference than sincerity. 'Anyway, this Denise had her arm bandaged, and she told me she'd been slashed by a punter.'

'So what did you do?'

'I filed a report.'

'No more than that? Didn't you investigate the complaint?'

'Well, of course I did, ma'am. That's what we're here for.'

'So you showed her the book of mug shots?'

'I was going to, but she looked very tired, so I suggested we did it later.'

'And *did* you do it later?'

'Err . . . no, ma'am. According to the records, we don't actually seem to have done that.'

'But at least you went to the scene of the crime – or made sure that somebody else did?'

'Not exactly.'

'And what does that mean – *not exactly*?'

'I didn't, as it happens.'

'So you simply filed the whole thing away?'

'I was just about to go on leave, and there were a lot of loose ends to tidy up before I went,' Bailey said. 'If she'd come in again, I'd probably have given it a bit more of my time, but she didn't, so I thought, well, if she couldn't be bothered, I didn't see why I should be.'

'Do you realize how much nerve it must have taken a girl like her to come to the station even *once*?' Paniatowski demanded. 'And how hard it would have been – after the lukewarm reception she got the first time – to force herself to make a second visit?'

'Look, ma'am, you know what it's like,' Bailey said defensively. 'It probably wasn't a punter who slashed her at all. More than likely, it was her pimp, and she was using us to put pressure on him.'

'Oh, she has a pimp, does she?' Paniatowski asked.

'A lot of these girls have pimps,' Bailey said evasively.

'And is she one of them?'

'I'm not entirely sure.'

'Meaning you haven't a bloody clue – one way or the other!' Paniatowski said angrily. 'You're a disgrace to your uniform, Sergeant – and if I have my way, you'll spend the rest of your career directing the bloody traffic – preferably in the middle of the motorway!'

All Chief Superintendent Kershaw's case files had been moved from his domain to Paniatowski's, and now they stood on Monika's desk in three piles, each one so high that every time there was the slightest vibration, it wobbled dangerously.

'How many years' work did you say this was?' Meadows asked Sergeant Lee, who would be working through the piles with her.

'Let me see,' Lee said, counting backwards. 'Five years.'

'You handled this many cases in only *five* years?' Meadows said, incredulously.

Lee chuckled. 'Of course, that's only *calendar* years,' he said.

'What do you mean by that?'

'A year working with Mr Kershaw isn't like a year working with anybody else. There's no such thing as being "off duty" when you're on his team. If you want a life outside the job, you should think about getting yourself a new boss.'

'So he's a bit of a slave driver, is he?'

'More than just a bit of one. But the person he cracks the whip hardest over is Chief Superintendent Thomas Kershaw.'

Meadows picked up one of the files at random. 'This doesn't look like a job for the uniformed branch,' she said, flicking quickly through it. She handed the file to Lee. 'In fact, I'd say this *clearly* falls squarely within the CID's remit.'

Lee laughed again. 'Mr Kershaw's not one for what he calls "bureaucratic lines",' he said. 'If something that he's working on leads him into somebody else's territory, he jump the fence without thinking about it.'

'So he's a glory grabber,' Meadows said.

Lee sighed. 'I was planning to go to Spain for my holidays,' he said. 'It would have been the first time we'd been abroad, and the kids were really looking forward to it. Notice I said "would have been"?'

'I did.'

'Well, we can't go now, can we? I'm using up all my accumulated leave time in working with you. And why am I doing that?'

'Because Mr Kershaw asked you to?'

'Wrong! He didn't ask. He didn't even hint. It was all my idea.'

'All right, I'll accept that he's a good boss, and you're loyal to him,' Meadows said.

'And it's not just me. The reason I'm here is because it was my idea, but there's not a man on the team who wouldn't have willingly taken my place. Do you think that makes *us* "glory grabbers"?'

'Not you, no,' Meadows said, uncomfortably.

'And not him, either,' Lee said sharply. '*We* solved that case you've just handed me. Us! Mr Kershaw's team. But you're right when you say it was, strictly speaking, CID business, so when we'd cracked it, Mr Kershaw handed the file *over* to the CID, and they got the credit for making the collar.'

'I should think more before I speak, shouldn't I?' Meadows asked ruefully.

'It certainly wouldn't be a *bad* idea,' Lee agreed.

'So let's start again,' Meadows suggested. She held out her hand to him. 'I'm DS Kate Meadows.'

'And I'm Sergeant Bill Lee,' Lee replied, taking her hand and shaking it.

'Well, Bill, shall we get down to work?' Meadows asked.

'Might as well – now we're here,' Lee replied.

'I didn't expect to see you so soon after our last meeting, Monika,' the chief constable said.

Well, at least he was calling her Monika again, and that was a start, Paniatowski thought.

'You personally signed requests for leave for two of Mr Kershaw's men – in the middle of a flu epidemic – didn't you, sir?' she asked.

'I fail to see what that has to do with you,' Baxter said.

'Come on, George, please don't treat me like I'm an idiot,' Paniatowski said.

'Tom Kershaw is both a very worried husband and a very good bobby,' Baxter said. 'Having his people attached to your investigation can only enhance its effectiveness.'

'Enhance its effectiveness,' Paniatowski repeated. 'Where did you learn that, sir? Was it on one of your courses at the police college?'

'You can ridicule me all you like, Monika – though one day you will go *too* far – but if you want me to reverse my decision on this particular matter . . .'

'I don't,' Paniatowski said.

'I beg your pardon?'

'I don't want you to reverse your decision. I think the extra manpower will be useful, especially as I want to widen the investigation.'

'What do you mean – widen it?'

Paniatowski outlined what Lucy and Marie had told her about Denise and Grace.

'So a prostitute's gone missing,' Baxter said, when she'd finished. 'You don't know that any harm has come to her.'

'We don't know that any harm has come to Mrs Kershaw – but it still doesn't stop us from throwing resources that we can ill afford into searching for her.'

'You can't compare the two,' Baxter told her.

'*Why* can't I?' Paniatowski countered. 'Because one's a senior policeman's wife and the other's a common whore?'

'Essentially, yes.'

'You disappoint me,' Paniatowski said, knowing she might be pushing things more than was wise, but – by this stage – not giving a damn. 'They're both *people*, sir.'

'You're right,' Baxter admitted. 'They are.'

'And I think the two cases may be connected.'

'I'm listening,' Baxter said.

'The man who slashed Denise Slater was, at least potentially, a sadist. Agreed?'

'If she accurately reported what it was he said to her, then that does seem likely.'

'And before he ran away, he said, "It shouldn't have been like this." So maybe he rethought his entire game plan. Maybe he decided that since he obviously couldn't *persuade* women to go with him, he'd have to *force* them.'

'So perhaps he did kidnap this prostitute.'

'And perhaps he also kidnapped Mrs Kershaw.'

'On the same night? That's stretching the bounds of credibility a little, isn't it, Monika?'

'You've heard about the red shoe heel, haven't you?'

'Yes, but . . .'

'The shoes were not Mrs Kershaw's – her husband has confirmed that. So the kidnapper must have taken them with him. And despite the fact that it's difficult to dress anyone who's unconscious – which Mrs Kershaw probably was at the time – he slipped the shoes on her feet before he left the house. Doesn't that suggest that he was fulfilling some sort of fantasy?'

'It's possible,' Baxter conceded.

'And further support for the fantasy theory is that the two missing women are of the same physical type. You'd describe Elaine Kershaw as petite, wouldn't you?'

'Undoubtedly.'

'And when Marie was talking about Grace, she said, "She's so tiny". So what stretches the bounds of credibility the furthest? Believing that one man snatched two women? Or believing that there are two perverts in Whitebridge who decided to snatch women within hours of one another?'

'You may widen the scope of your investigation,' Baxter said reluctantly.

'Thank you, sir.'

'But I want you to keep clearly in mind that the main thrust of the investigation is to be aimed at returning Mrs Kershaw safely to her husband – and that if the investigation into the prostitute's disappearance looks like distracting you, in any way, from that central purpose, you will abandon it. Mrs Kershaw is – and must always be – your main consideration.'

'Naturally,' Paniatowski agreed.

Like hell! she thought.

Elaine Kershaw was the wife of an important man, and that made her important, too. She had the whole of the Mid Lancs constabulary on her side – from the lowly officers who admired Kershaw from a distance, to the chief constable who attended the same church as her husband and went fishing with him.

And who does Grace have on her side? she asked herself. Me – and *only* me!

TEN

D usk came early in November and, as it descended, half the life of Whitebridge shut down. The shops stayed open, but the shoppers were few. Offices continued to function, but the death of the day brought with it an accompanying demise of enthusiasm and initiative. Only in the few factories that were still left in the town did the relentless movement of the conveyor belt – which was affected by neither light nor darkness – manage to maintain a purposeful rhythm of activity.

The police force – especially those members involved in the Elaine Kershaw case – were exempt from this particular evening malaise, and long after the dark had firmly established itself, Sergeants Lee and Meadows were still ploughing their way through the files which chronicled the last five years of Chief Superintendent Kershaw's working life.

It was just after nine o'clock that Kate Meadows pushed the file she was studying aside and said, 'I have to go out for an hour or so, Bill.'

Lee looked up. 'Got a meeting with your boss, have you?' And without waiting for a reply, he added, 'Well, I expect you know your way to the Drum and Monkey by now.' He chuckled. 'Don't look so surprised, Kate. Your boss's fondness for the Drum is legendary around police headquarters.'

'Legendary – but disapproved of?' Meadows wondered.

'Far from it,' Lee assured her. 'You can sometimes get a lot of work done over a few pints – I often wish Mr Kershaw would take a leaf out of DCI Paniatowski's book.'

Meadows stood up. 'I'll get back as soon as I can.'

'If I was you, I wouldn't bother,' Lee told her. 'You've probably taken in as much of this stuff as you can for one day. When you've finished your meeting with DCI Paniatowski, your best plan would be to get yourself off to bed, so you can make a fresh start in the morning.'

'And what about you?'

'I won't be good for much more than another half-hour myself, so if you *do* come back, you'll probably find me gone.'

'In that case, I'll see you in the morning,' Meadows said.

'Sweet dreams – as if there was any chance of that,' Lee called after her, as she stepped out into the corridor.

'There's not a shoe shop in the whole town which will admit to ever stocking shoes with high red heels,' Crane told the rest of the team. 'Of course, we could try further afield – Bolton's a bit more cosmopolitan and sophisticated than Whitebridge – but I don't think we'll have any luck there, either.'

'And why's that?' Paniatowski asked.

'Because I'm rapidly coming to the conclusion that they won't have been made by what you might call an "ordinary" shoe manufacturer,' Crane explained. 'One of the assistants who I talked to said they were "kinky" – and the more I look at that heel, the more I'm sure she's right. I think they're the work of a specialist company which caters for customers with a particular requirement, if . . . er . . . you know what I mean.'

Paniatowski sighed. 'Yes, Jack, I think we *all* know what you mean.'

'So, suppose I wanted a pair of these shoes,' Beresford said. 'Where would I buy them?'

'There are a number of sleazy sex shops in Manchester which might possibly stock them – or so I'm told,' Crane said tentatively, 'but even if they do, I don't think the kidnapper will have bought them there.'

'Why not?'

'Because there'd always be a chance that the shop owner might remember his face – and he seems to have been far too careful to take that kind of risk unless he absolutely had to.'

'And you're saying that he *didn't* have to?'

'That's right.'

'So what would he have done instead?'

'Bought one of those magazines that the sleazier newsagents keep under the counter, flicked through the adverts until he found something he liked – in this case, the red shoes – then ordered the shoes, and had them sent to a post office box. There's some risk even in that, but it's much less.'

Paniatowski nodded. 'Good thinking, Jack. The first thing in the morning, I want you to go round all those newsagents and buy as many different magazines as you can.'

Crane grimaced. 'Does it have to be me who does that, boss? I don't even own a dirty raincoat.'

'I'll do it,' Kate Meadows said.

'You've got a mountain of Chief Superintendent Kershaw's files to work your way through,' Paniatowski reminded her.

'I'll need a break at some point in the morning,' Meadows said. 'I'll *have to have* a break, or I'll go stale – and that's when you start overlooking vital bits of information. So I'll do it.'

'When I pulled that face, it was only a joke, Sarge,' Crane said, sounding slightly guilty. 'I really don't mind making the rounds of the shops myself.'

'I'll do it,' Kate Meadows said, for a third time – and even more firmly.

'Fair enough,' Crane accepted. Then he turned to Paniatowski. 'That is, if it's all right with you, boss.'

'It's all right with me,' Paniatowski agreed, though she was puzzled why Meadows should have been quite so insistent.

She took a sip of her vodka, and mentally prepared herself to deliver the bombshell.

'The chief constable wants us to widen the investigation,' she said, as if it had all been Baxter's idea.

And then she told them all about little Grace Meade.

It took Paniatowski fifteen minutes to outline the details of Grace's disappearance, the attack on Denise Slater and her own encounter with Lucy and Marie, and when she'd finished, Beresford said, 'But we're overstretched already, boss.'

'Not nearly as overstretched as we'd be if Mr Kershaw's men hadn't come on board,' Paniatowski replied. 'And I really do think that there might be a clear connection between the two cases.'

If anyone was about to take a pot shot at the theory, she expected it to be Beresford, but, in fact, it was Crane who said, 'I'm not convinced, boss. Snatching two women on the same day would be almost impossibly complicated.'

'It would certainly be very complicated, I'll grant you that – but not impossibly so,' Paniatowski told him.

'Especially if there were two men involved,' Colin Beresford said, totally out of the blue.

'*Two* men?' Paniatowski repeated.

'One of my young DCs asked me this morning why we assumed there was only one intruder in the Kershaw house, when – for lack of any specific evidence pointing in that direction – there might just as easily have been two or even three,' Beresford explained. 'I had to admit that he had a point.'

'Go on,' Paniatowski said – welcoming the support but almost fearful of where Beresford might be leading them.

'What if we turn the constable's question on its head?' Beresford continued. 'What if, instead of asking ourselves if two men could have kidnapped Elaine Kershaw, we ask instead if it's possible that two men *were* involved, but that while one was snatching Elaine, the other – his partner – was snatching Grace Meade?'

And suddenly Paniatowski's mind was flung violently back down a long, dark, jagged, time tunnel – back to a kidnapping case which she and Charlie Woodend had investigated, where the very fact that they *hadn't* worked out earlier that more than one man was involved had almost cost the life of an innocent child.

'Dear God!' she said aloud.

'Are you all right, boss?' Crane asked worriedly.

'I'm fine,' Paniatowski lied. 'Denise Slater needs to be walked through the mug shot book, and, with any luck, she'll be able to identify her attacker,' she continued – more crisply, more in control, now. 'If she does manage to pick out a suspect, then the next thing we need to do is to find out if he crops up in any of Mr Kershaw's investigations.' She turned to Meadows. 'That'll be your job, Kate.'

'Got it, boss,' Meadows agreed.

Paniatowski looked up at the clock above the bar. 'That's probably about as far as we can get tonight,' she pronounced. 'See you all in the morning.'

As she stood up and turned towards the door, she felt a tap on her shoulder, and looking round, she saw that the tapper was Beresford.

'Did I miss something out?' she asked.

'Not really,' Beresford admitted. 'But I would like a quiet word in the car park, if that's all right with you.'

'It's all right with me,' Paniatowski told him – though she strongly suspected that it wouldn't be.

Paniatowski and Beresford walked to the far end of the Drum and Monkey's car park in uneasy silence. Even when they reached the boundary wall, they didn't speak, but instead both looked up at the night sky.

Finally, after perhaps half a minute of star gazing, Beresford said, 'I'm more than a bit concerned about the new direction that the investigation is suddenly taking, boss.'

Paniatowski, who had been expecting something like this, already had her answer prepared.

'Correct me if I'm wrong, but wasn't it you who said – not five minutes ago – that the two cases could easily be connected?' she asked.

'Yes, I said it,' Beresford conceded.

'Well, then?'

'The thing is, boss, my first instinct is *always* to support you, because I've learned to trust your judgement. But on this occasion . . .'

'On this occasion, you've decided that you *don't* trust it,' Paniatowski interrupted. 'And why is that, Colin? Could it be because you think that I hate Mr Kershaw so much that I don't really *want* to investigate his wife's abduction—'

'No, I—'

'—and that I'm desperately searching for a distraction – any kind of distraction – which will give me the excuse I need to avoid having to really try to get a result?'

'Of course not!'

'So just what point *are* you attempting to make?'

'I think that what's been happening has offended your sense of natural justice.'

'Sense of natural justice?' Paniatowski scoffed. 'That's a bit of airy-fairy, doesn't-actually-say-much, way of speaking, isn't it?'

'All right, let's put it in more concrete terms,' Beresford said firmly. 'I think it offends you that Elaine Kershaw's getting so much attention because of who she is – and Grace Meade's getting none at all, because of who *she* is.'

'There may be something in that,' Paniatowski admitted.

'But you're playing a very dangerous game – because if Grace turns up alive and well, and Elaine turns up dead, what do you think people are going to say?'

'What you really mean is, what will the great *Tom Kershaw* say?'

'No, I don't. I mean what will *everybody* – from the chief constable down – say?'

'They'll say that if I'd devoted more of my resources to Elaine, I might have been able to save her. Was that the answer you were looking for?'

'You know it was.'

'And what if it's Elaine who turns up safe and well, and Grace who turns up dead? What will people say then?'

'They'll probably say exactly the same thing as they would have if it had been the other way round.'

'Well, then?'

'But they won't say it half as critically, because . . .'

'Because, when all's said and done, Grace is only a prostitute!'

'If Grace dies, it will be no more than a footnote on your record,' Beresford said. 'If Elaine dies, it could cost you your career.'

'I'll just have to take that chance,' Paniatowski said.

Beresford nodded resignedly. 'I knew I'd be wasting my breath.'

They walked back to the middle of the car park – in silence again – and it was only when they reached Paniatowski's MGA that she broke that silence by saying, 'Where's your vehicle, Colin?'

'It's back at the station.'

'So would you like a lift home?'

'I don't think so, thanks. I'd prefer to walk. I need the exercise.'

Paniatowski laughed. 'Good idea. I was only noticing the other day just how fat you're getting.'

Beresford laughed, too. 'Isn't that a bit of a case of the kettle calling the pot bellied?'

They didn't mean it, either of them. They were two of the fittest people in the whole of the Whitebridge area. But it was their way of saying that though they might disagree from time to time – and though those disagreements could sometimes seem bitter – they were, and always would be, the best of mates.

Paniatowski watched Beresford walk off into the darkness. For a moment, she was almost certain that he was whistling, but Colin never whistled, so it must have been someone else.

She slipped the key into the ignition, but hesitated before turning it.

Colin had really been rather gentle in his criticism of the way she was handling the case, she thought – far gentler than he'd been during some of their other investigations. So why was it that, on this particular occasion, she'd felt anger bubbling up inside her even from the start?

Could it be – could it possibly be – because Colin's doubts and criticisms were no more than an echo of her own deep-down self-doubts and criticisms?

She didn't *think* that was the case, but she couldn't be *sure*.

She fired up the engine, slipped the car into gear, and drove out of the car park. She could see Beresford walking down the road, about a hundred yards away.

And she could also see that he was not alone.

ELEVEN

'Y ou're the first person I've invited to the house since I had to have my mother put in the home,' Colin Beresford told Kate Meadows, as he inserted the key in his front door.

You're the first person I've invited to the house since I had to have my mother put in the home, repeated a mocking voice from somewhere at the back of his brain. *Nice going, Colin!*

Nice going indeed, he thought. What better way to woo a girl than to let her know that your mother had lost her mind, and that you yourself were nothing but a sad loner?

He led her down the hallway into the living room.

'Very nice,' she said, unconvincingly.

It wasn't nice at all, he suddenly realized, as if seeing it for the first time himself.

In fact, it wasn't so much a lounge as a museum – frozen in time from the moment his mother had first shown signs of developing Alzheimer's disease.

There was nothing of his own personality in the room at all – and perhaps that was because, when he wasn't deeply involved in a case, he *had* no personality!

'I don't spend much of my time here,' he said awkwardly. 'Well, you know how it is, working for a boss like Monika Paniatowski.'

Meadows smiled at him. 'But you enjoy your work, don't you?' she asked.

'Oh yes,' he agreed, perhaps a little hastily.

And the mocking voice in his brain chuckled, *You enjoy it because it's all you've got.*

'Take a seat,' he said.

He cringed as he watched her lower herself on to an old-fashioned sofa he should have thrown out years ago.

'Can I get you a drink?' he asked.

Then he thought, Oh my God, why did I say that? I haven't got any drink – any *real* drink – in the house.

But that was all right, he remembered with relief, because Kate never touched booze.

'I'm fine,' she told him.

And she was. She was better than fine. She was beautiful – and growing more beautiful every time he looked at her.

'Are you going to sit down yourself?' she asked him.

He wondered if he should sit beside her, or in the armchair opposite her. Which of the two did *she* expect him to do? But it was impossible to work out, and, after some weak-willed prevarication, he chose the armchair.

'So tell me a bit about yourself,' he said – and the moment the words were out of his mouth, he thought, Jesus, I sound like a spotty kid making his first fumbling attempt to pick up a girl.

And apart from the spots, he accepted, that was a pretty fair description.

'There's really not much to tell,' Meadows said. 'My dad abandoned us when I was five, and my mother died a couple of years ago.'

I wish *my* mother had died, he thought. I wish that instead of sinking into a woolly, confused world of her own, she'd simply *died*. It wouldn't have bothered her – and it would have been so much better for me.

'You're either feeling sad or guilty,' Meadows said, noticing the expression on his face. 'Which is it?'

Both, he thought.

'Neither,' he said aloud. 'So before you transferred here, you were working in Stoke-on-Trent, weren't you?'

'That's right,' Meadows agreed.

And though her expression remained unchanged, he sensed that she was closing herself down.

'So what made you decide to move so far from home?' he asked, like the fool he was beginning to realize he was.

'I felt like a change,' Meadows said. 'Listen, Colin . . . it's all right if I call you Colin now we're not at work, isn't it?'

'Of course.'

'Then listen, Colin, we both know why we're here, don't we?'

He knew why he was there, but he didn't want to make any more mistakes, and so he said, 'Why do *you* think we're here?'

'I like a man to *be* a man,' Kate Meadows said. 'I like a man with rock-hard muscles, and a stomach that you could bounce tennis balls off – and you pretty much fit the bill.'

'I see,' he said, feeling vaguely disappointed – though he could not say exactly why.

'And I also like you as a *person*.'

'That's good.'

'So why don't we cut out all the unnecessary chit-chat and go straight upstairs.'

'There's something that you have to know,' Beresford blurted out. 'I'm a virgin.'

She could have laughed, or she could have looked shocked, but she did neither.

Instead, she nodded her head, and with a half-smile said, 'Do you know, I sort of suspected you might be.'

Fool! he told himself. You've let out your big secret to somebody you *work with* – and by tomorrow afternoon, at the latest, you'll be the laughing stock of police headquarters.

'I won't tell anybody, I promise,' Kate said. 'It really doesn't bother me that you've had no experience – and I'm rather hoping that it doesn't bother you that I *have*.'

'It doesn't bother me,' he said.

'Then, for goodness sake, let's go upstairs and get on with it.'

Lily Perkins, the housekeeper, met Paniatowski at the front door.

'That's another three hours overtime you owe me,' she said cheerfully. 'I'm really getting to be quite rich.'

'Well, I'm pleased that one of us is,' Paniatowski replied. 'Was Louisa any trouble?'

'None at all. I said she could stay up an extra half-hour in case you came home, and she said, "There's no point. Mum's on a major case. She won't be home for hours yet." And she was right, wasn't she?'

'Yes,' Paniatowski agreed tiredly, 'she was.'

She waited until Lily had left, then tiptoed upstairs to Louisa's room. Her daughter's long and luxurious black hair – her only legacy from her real mother, who'd been Spanish – was spread across the pillow, and Louisa was sound asleep.

She might not spend as much time with the girl as she should, Paniatowski thought – hell, there was no 'might' about it – but she loved her with all her heart. And if she never fell in love with a man again – if she lived like a nun until the day she died – it didn't matter, as long as she had her wonderful child.

No harm would ever come to Louisa – not if she could help it. She'd fight like a lioness to keep her safe. Louisa would never have to walk the streets and suffer the drunken embraces of men who cared nothing for her, but had the necessary money in their pockets.

Is that what this is all about? she asked herself.

When she thought about Grace, was she also thinking about Louisa, who was only a few years younger?

You can't protect every waif and stray who comes your way, just because you have a daughter, she thought.

'No, I can't,' she said aloud – though softly, so as not to wake Louisa. 'No, I most certainly can't – but at least I can bloody well *try*!'

Kate Meadows glanced around the bedroom, fixed the location of every piece of furniture in her mind, then switched off the light.

'Why did you do that?' Beresford asked.

'Maybe I'm shy,' Meadows said.

But she certainly didn't sound as if she were shy – and anyway, he had seen enough of her firm figure to know she had no reason for shyness.

'I want to look at you,' he said.

'Not now,' Kate told him.

'Then when?'

'Maybe later.'

'Later tonight, you mean?'

'Perhaps,' said Kate's disembodied voice, unconvincing, through the darkness.

'It won't be tonight, will it?' Beresford said.

'No,' Kate agreed. She paused. 'I have to learn to trust you a little more first. I have to be certain that when I do show you, it won't really matter.'

'*What* won't really matter?'

Kate didn't answer. Instead, all Beresford could hear was the rustling in the darkness, as she started to take off her clothes.

'Get undressed, then,' she said.

Beresford was worried. Something was wrong, his brain told him – something was *very* wrong.

But though his brain was advising caution, his body – especially that part of it between his legs – was not listening.

He unbuttoned his shirt and stripped it off.

He dropped his trousers.

He heard the bed creak, somewhere in the darkness.

'I'm waiting,' Kate said, in a soft, seductive voice.

Why won't she let me see her naked? he asked himself, and he discarded his underpants and peeled off his socks.

It was only as he was climbing into bed that the images of the 'shemales' who hung around the Boulevard were suddenly filling his head.

Oh God, no! he prayed. Please, no, not that!

But if it *was* that, wouldn't it explain all the things that, up to now, had made no sense?

She had transferred from Stoke-on-Trent to a town she'd had no previous connection with.

She had been the one who'd made all the running in getting them into bed together.

She hadn't minded that he was a virgin.

And she had insisted on getting undressed in the dark.

His hand brushed against Kate Meadows' right breast, and the breast felt as firm and as silky as he'd imagined it would be.

But perhaps the shemales on the Boulevard also had breasts like that.

How the hell would he know?

They was one way to find out for sure whether Kate was a real woman or not, and though his hand had never before made such a verifying journey, he knew the route it had to take clearly enough.

And yet he couldn't do it! He just couldn't summon up the courage necessary to establish once and for all whether this was a dream come true – or a complete bloody nightmare.

Then Kate Meadows took his hand in hers, and placed it where it refused to go under its own volition – and everything was all right.

The tea from the machine outside the now-closed canteen wasn't wonderful, but at least it was hot and wet, Sergeant Bill Lee thought, as he walked along the corridor with the flimsy plastic cup in his hand.

He was surprised to see there was a light on in Paniatowski's office, because he was a frugal man by nature and could almost have sworn he'd switched it off when he nipped out. But then, he supposed, his mind was so stuffed with the material in the files that he probably wouldn't have noticed if the ceiling had fallen in on him.

He opened the door, and saw Chief Superintendent Kershaw sitting at the desk, looking through one of the files.

Kershaw looked up, surprised, and said, 'I thought you'd have gone home by now, Bill.'

'I did think about it, boss,' Lee admitted. 'I even told DS Meadows that's what I would be doing,' he shrugged, 'but then I weighed up how many files there were still left to go through, and decided to give it another hour or two.'

'I'm convinced the solution's here,' Kershaw said. 'I really believe that if we can just find the right file, we'll know who kidnapped Elaine.'

'Aren't you doing just what you told us *never* to do, boss?' Lee asked.

'I don't know,' Kershaw replied. 'What *did* I tell you never to do?'

'You told us never to put all our faith in one line of inquiry. You said it was bit like betting all your money on one horse, as if that alone would automatically guarantee it would romp home first.'

Kershaw grinned, sheepishly. 'I did say that, didn't I?' Then, almost immediately, the weary and worried look was back. 'But I have a gut feeling about these files, Bill. I really do.'

'And all that aside, sir, I'm not sure you should be looking through the files at all,' Lee continued gravely.

'Why not? They're my files! I wrote the bloody things!'

'I know that, sir.'

'And why are you calling me "sir" all of a sudden?' Kershaw wondered. Then, without waiting for an answer, he continued, 'We have permission – from the chief constable himself – to look through these files, you know.'

'I'm calling you "sir" because I'm trying to sound official, sir,' Lee said. 'And *we* don't have permission to look through them – *I* do.'

'Now look here, Bill—' Kershaw began.

'It's only right and proper that some of your lads should have a toehold in this investigation,' Lee interrupted him. 'But not you, Tom,' he added almost pleadingly. 'You're too close to it. And because you're so close, you might make a disastrous mistake.'

'What do you mean, a "disastrous mistake"?' Kershaw demanded.

'You know what I mean,' Lee said levelly.

'Yes,' Kershaw admitted. 'Yes, I do.' He stood up. 'My coming here was no reflection on your abilities, Bill. I still have complete confidence in you.'

'I know that,' Lee said.

Kershaw walked over to the door. 'All I will ask is that if there are any developments . . .'

'You'll be the first to know,' Lee promised him.

It was going wonderfully, Beresford told himself.

They had kissed.

He had fondled her.

She had fondled him.

And now he was inside her, thrusting away, and determined not to reach his own climax before it became obvious that she had reached hers.

'Hurt me!' she groaned.

'What?'

'Not my face. Don't mark my face. But hurt me!'

He was losing his rhythm.

'I don't know . . .' he said. 'I'm not sure what you want me to do.'

'Twist my breasts,' she said.

He took her left breast in his right hand, and turned it slightly, as if he was cautiously opening a door.

'Not like that,' she said. 'Harder!'

He did as instructed.

'That's better!' she screamed. 'But harder still!'

She was reaching the climax he'd hoped to bring her to – he could hear it in her voice – but the harder he twisted the breast, the softer he was growing himself.

Grace Meade had spent much of her fifteen short years of life worrying.

She had been worried whenever her father had come home drunk, looking for the slightest excuse to knock his long-suffering wife about and cause his daughter other kinds of pain.

She had worried when – out of sheer desperation and misery – her mother had turned to the bottle herself, and very soon had become almost as violent as her husband.

She had worried when – coming home from one of her rare days attending school – she had found her mother in the bath, the water around her a swirling red stickiness.

She had worried when she'd first gone on the game, afraid that the police would arrest her and lock her up, or – even worse – send her back to her dad.

And she had worried every time she got into a punter's car, because – as good, kind, wise Lucy had warned her – there were some very bad men out there.

She had been less worried than usual when the man had picked her up the night before, because he had seemed almost fatherly – though not like *her* father, of course.

But as he'd driven into town, rather than out towards the moors (where most of her punters took her), the concern had started to return.

'Where are we going?' she'd asked.

'I've got a place,' he'd said, and now there was a hardness in his voice which had been absent earlier.

'A place?' she'd replied. 'What do you mean?'

'What do you think I mean? A house, you stupid little bitch – a place where I live!'

'Aren't you . . . aren't you married?' she asked, because most of her punters were, *whatever* they might say.

'Yes, I'm married,' he'd replied.

'Then won't your wife—'

'Don't you go worrying your tiny pathetic brain about my wife,' he'd said harshly.

They'd driven on, through streets she'd never seen before, past houses that she could only dream of living in one day.

'How tall are you?' he'd demanded suddenly.

'I don't know. It's a long time since I measured myself.'

'I'd say you were four feet ten. Is that about right?'

'I don't know.'

'Then how much do you weigh? You must surely know how much you weigh?'

'Why are you asking me all these questions?' she'd said, almost in tears.

'How much?' he'd insisted.

'About . . . about seven and a half stone.'

'Perfect,' the man had said.

And it was the *way* he said it which brought the worrying back, as strong as it had ever been – as strong as when her father had first pulled her knickers down, and her mother had been too frightened to say anything about it.

Yes, she had worried all her life, but she was not worried now. She would, in truth, never be worried again – because she had been dead for over twenty-four hours.

TWELVE

Sergeant Bill Lee had not finally abandoned the mountain of files until after one o'clock in the morning. Even then, he had not gone home to his wife and children – with the early start he was planning, there seemed little point in that – and instead had dossed down on his boss's sofa.

Exhausted though he was, sleep refused to come, and he spent the night tossing and turning.

This was the most important case that he'd ever worked on – or was ever *likely* to work on – he told himself at two o'clock, as he searched in vain for the elusively comfortable position on the sofa which might help him to slip into unconsciousness.

He desperately wanted to save Elaine Kershaw, he thought at four o'clock, as he became aware of a crick in his neck, which no amount of moving around would assuage. Of course he did! That was beyond question. But he would be lying if he said that she was his prime concern.

It was around half past four that images started to come into his mind, and however hard he fought against them, they refused to go away: Tom Kershaw standing by his wife's open grave, hardly able to see through the tears; Kershaw back at work, a shadow of his former self, his edge blunted, his mind wandering; another open grave, this time awaiting the arrival of one of the finest men who ever walked the earth.

At half past five, Lee gave up on his quest for sleep, and returned to Paniatowski's office.

At half past seven, when he had still made no more than a minor dent in his epic task, the door opened and Kate Meadows walked in.

He looked up at her, through tired, prickling eyes, and said, 'I've had a rough night, and you look like you've had one, too.'

'Do I?' Meadows replied. 'Well, all I can say is that, as far as I'm concerned, the night wasn't nearly rough enough.'

'What do you mean?' Lee asked.

'It doesn't matter,' Meadows said wistfully.

And then she sat down and reached across for the nearest file.

The little café was almost bursting at the seams with customers at that time of the morning, but Paniatowski managed to secure a table near the window for her meeting with Lucy.

As she sat there, smoking her fourth cigarette of the day – or was it her fifth? – she noticed that some of the other customers were staring at her. No, not staring, she corrected herself – giving her a quick sideways glance and then rapidly turning away.

She smiled inwardly. The lorry driver who'd tried to solicit her had not only made himself look a complete fool, but had helped to create a local legend which would continue to haunt him by being retold – and probably greatly embellished on – for years to come.

And serve the bastard right, she thought – because without men like him, there would not be girls like Grace and Marie.

She was being naïve and foolish, she told herself. There had always *been* prostitution, and there always *would be* prostitution.

But that still didn't mean she should give up getting angry about it.

The café door swung open, and Lucy walked in. She was not dressed as a walking advertisement for her trade that morning. Instead, she was wearing the sort of plain dress that a shop girl or a shorthand-typist might have chosen.

She wasn't wearing any make-up either, and her glistening skin gave her an aura of innocence which made it almost impossible to think of her as a prostitute.

Lucy walked over to the table, and sat down. 'I'm not used to being around and about at this time of the morning,' she said, with a grin. 'What's this all about?'

'I want you to introduce me to Denise Slater,' Paniatowski said.

'Introduce you!' Lucy repeated. 'Well, that sounds very la-di-da, doesn't it?'

'You do *know* why I want to meet her through you, don't you?' Paniatowski asked, ignoring the frivolity of the comment.

Lucy's face grew more serious – and perhaps a little

world-weary. 'Yes, I know,' she admitted. 'You want me to introduce you because Denise doesn't trust the police – especially since nothing happened after I made her report the attack – and you think that if I say you're all right, she'll believe me.'

'She *will* believe you, won't she?' Paniatowski said.

Lucy nodded. 'Oh yes, she'll believe me. All the girls trust good old Lucy.'

'So when can I meet her?'

'Not for two or three days.'

'You do realize how important it is that I talk to her, don't you?' Paniatowski asked urgently. 'You do understand that the man who attacked Denise might be the same man who's got Grace?'

'Yes, of course I understand that,' Lucy replied. 'And if I could just snap my fingers and make it happen, that's exactly what I would do. But I can't – and so you're going to have to wait until Denise gets back.'

Gets back!

Paniatowski felt the hairs on the back of her neck tingle.

'You can relax,' Lucy said. 'She's not been kidnapped – she's just gone off on a trip with a punter.'

'When did this happen?' Paniatowski demanded.

'It was the day before yesterday.'

'The same day that Grace disappeared?'

'That's right.'

'And you're not *worried* about her?'

'No, I'm not. Because I know for a fact that the punter she went off with is harmless enough.'

'*How* do you know? Is he one of *your* clients?'

'No, he isn't, but he's been with several of the other girls, and I've talked to them about him.' Lucy paused for a second. 'You surely don't think I'd have let her go if there'd been any danger, do you?'

'Could you have stopped her – even if you'd wanted to?' Paniatowski asked sceptically.

Lucy shrugged. 'I think so. As I said, the other girls trust me – and that includes trusting my judgement.'

'Tell me where Denise and this man have gone, and I'll send a car to pick her up,' Paniatowski said.

'I can't tell you – because I don't know.'

'So much for the girls trusting you,' Paniatowski scoffed.

And the moment the words were out of her mouth, she felt ashamed of herself – because Lucy was a good woman, a woman who cared for others, and she had no right to belittle her.

'I'm really so sorry, Lucy,' she said hastily. 'That was completely uncalled for.'

Lucy favoured her with a smile which was a gentle mixture of forgiveness and amusement.

'You don't know much about punters, do you?' she asked.

'Then enlighten me,' Paniatowski said humbly.

'The reason Denise didn't tell me where she was going is that she didn't know herself.'

'I see,' Paniatowski said.

Lucy was still smiling. 'No, you don't. Not yet. Most of the punters who take a girl away on a trip with them don't like to be asked where they're going – they have to go through daily interrogations from their wives, and it's nice, once in a while, to be with someone who isn't always questioning them. Besides, it would spoil the surprise.'

'The surprise?'

'There's a part of every punter who takes a girl away which knows that what he's in fact doing is hiring a prostitute for sex. But there's another part of him which likes to pretend he's romancing a girl who's not only prettier than the battleaxe he's left at home, but also seems to have no interest in trying to emasculate him. Punters like him want the girls to be happy. They want them to be thrilled. That's why they normally take them to the seaside.'

'And *are* the girls thrilled?'

'Not usually. They're not buying into the same dream as the man they're with – but if they've got any sense, from a business point of view, they at least *pretend* to be over the moon.'

'Tell me about the man,' Paniatowski said.

'He says his name is John Smith. You'd be surprised how many of the punters are called John Smith. He's very vague about what he does for a living, but I suspect he's some kind of travelling salesman.'

'When will they be back?'

'Again, he didn't say, and she didn't ask.'

'I'll want to know about it the moment they return to Whitebridge,' Paniatowski said.

'You will,' Lucy promised.

'Can I ask you a personal question?' Paniatowski said – knowing that she shouldn't.

'Why not?' Lucy replied – though there was a caution in her words which belied their apparent casualness.

'Are you a drug user?' Paniatowski said.

'Ah, I see!' Lucy replied, shaking her head disappointedly.

'See what?'

'I'm a reasonably bright, reasonably intelligent girl, so there's no reason for me to be on the game unless I'm a slave to some narcotic. Is that about it?'

'That's about it,' Paniatowski admitted guiltily.

'Everything has to be black and white, doesn't it?' Lucy demanded. 'You're as bad as the punters. In fact, you're worse – because you should know better.'

'I made a mistake – *another* mistake – and I'm sorry,' Paniatowski said contritely. 'I hope this won't affect our relationship.'

'It won't,' Lucy said, 'but only because I really do care about the other girls.' She stood up. 'I'm sure you were about to offer me a cup of tea, but if you don't mind, I think I'll pass.'

'Lucy . . .' Paniatowski said, almost pleadingly.

'I'll be in touch,' Lucy said, and then she turned and walked towards the door.

Crane considered bacon sandwiches – dripping with fat – to be bad for the body but good for the soul, and he was enjoying his early morning ration of this soul food in the police canteen when DI Beresford sat down opposite him.

'Morning, sir,' he said, between mouthfuls of gristle.

'I'm glad I caught you, because there's been something of a personal nature I've meaning to ask you about,' Beresford said.

The inspector's tone was serious and his face was grave, and despite his best efforts, Crane found himself slipping into a mild panic.

'A personal nature, you say?' he asked, to buy himself time.

'That's right,' Beresford agreed.

Has he found out about my degree? Crane wondered. Is he about to ask me why I kept it secret for so long?

Because the fact was that once he'd got to know Beresford

and Paniatowski – once he'd begun to trust them not to have the typical bobby's reaction to an 'egghead' – he'd always meant to tell them about his qualifications, and had only been waiting until the right moment arrived.

But somehow, the moment never had.

'What was it you wanted to ask, sir?' he said.

'A friend of mine came to me for advice recently,' Beresford said woodenly, 'and ever since I gave it, I've been a little concerned that it was the *right* advice.'

'Oh yes?' Crane said, non-committally.

'How many women have you slept with, Jack?'

'I've never kept count, sir.'

'Oh, come on, you must have!'

'I haven't,' Crane insisted. 'You see, when I first went up to uni—'

He stopped, suddenly, aware that he'd been on the point of revealing that he'd been to Oxford, and at a moment which – from the serious expression on Beresford's face – was very clearly *not* the right one.

He tried again. 'When I started my first job, which was a couple of years before I joined the police, I had a workmate called Eddie who was always bragging about the number of women he'd slept with.'

Or rather, I had rooms on the same staircase as a third year Classics student called Simon Smythe, who bragged about the number of women he slept with, he amended mentally. Simon Smythe! Brilliant mind! Prize shit!

'Go on,' Beresford said.

'I soon decided that the reason he went to bed with a woman was not so much for the pleasure he got at the time, as it was for the pleasure it gave him when he could carve another notch on his bedpost once it was all over,' Crane continued. 'It seemed to me that he was missing out on the main point of the whole process – and that was when I promised myself that when I finally starting sleeping with women, I wouldn't keep a tally.'

'But if you *wanted* to add them up, you probably could,' Beresford persisted.

'Probably,' Crane agreed.

'Which suggests to me that it's more than ten.'

'Oh yes, I think you could say it's definitely more than ten.'

A look came to Beresford's face which seemed very much like envy – though, of course, it couldn't possibly be that, Crane thought.

'This friend of mine doesn't have our experience, and that's why he came to me for advice,' Beresford said, awkwardly. 'You see, he's only ever slept with one woman – and even then, he's only done it once.'

'How old is he?' Crane asked.

'About my age,' Beresford said.

'Then he's a real marvel!' Crane said. 'They should put him in a cage, and charge people admission just to see him.'

'The thing is, the woman who he slept with wanted him to hurt her, and he wondered if that was normal,' Beresford ploughed on relentlessly. 'Now, of course, I told him that had never been my experience at all, but then I got to thinking that one person's experience isn't really enough to base advice on, and I'd better get a second opinion. And that's why I'm talking to you now, Jack. Have you ever come across a woman like that?'

No, but he thought he finally knew who the 'friend' was, Crane told himself, amazed that this strong, confident inspector – who he hoped to be like, some day – should have led such a sheltered life.

'I haven't come across one myself,' he said cautiously, 'but I believe it's quite common. If I was you, I'd tell my friend not to worry. If his girlfriend likes to be hurt – and he doesn't mind hurting her – then there's no reason on earth why they can't carry on just as they have been.'

'And what if my friend *doesn't* like to hurt her?' Beresford asked. 'What if all he wants to do is cuddle her and caress her and protect her from all harm?'

'Then I'm afraid the relationship is going nowhere fast, and the best thing he could do would be to break it off now,' Crane said.

'I think you're right,' Beresford replied heavily.

Lucy waited until she'd calmed down a little before finding a phone box and dialling a number she knew by heart.

Even so, when the person she was calling answered, she blurted out the first thing that came into her head, which was, 'I think she's on to me!'

'That would be DCI Paniatowski we're talking about, would it?' the man on the other end of the line asked calmly.

'Yes.'

'If you remember, I told you right from the start that there was a real danger in going to her.'

'I didn't have any choice in the matter.'

'There's always a choice.'

'You weren't here. You didn't see how insistent Marie was that I did something. If I'd turned her down, I wouldn't have been the "me" she thought she knew.'

'Let's go back a few steps,' the man suggested, still trying to calm her down. 'What exactly did DCI Paniatowski say to make you think that she was on to you?'

'She asked me if I used drugs.'

'Ah!' the man said pensively. 'And what did you say in response?'

'I pretended to be angry that she was being so simplistic – that she was looking for an easy answer to explain why the girls were on the street.'

'Clever,' the man said appreciatively. 'Very clever – especially since you were thinking on the hoof.'

He chuckled.

'What's so funny?' Lucy demanded.

'You said you "pretended" to be angry, but if I know you – and I do – at least a part of that anger wasn't pretence at all.'

'You're right, it wasn't,' Lucy admitted. 'So what do I do?'

'Nothing,' the man said.

'*Nothing?*'

'If you change your ways – if you suddenly become more like Paniatowski's picture of how a prostitute should be – it will seem very suspicious indeed to her. Far better to go on as you are – enigmatic and unfathomable.'

'I think something might really have happened to Grace,' Lucy said. 'I honestly do.'

'And possibly it has,' the man agreed. '"Something happening" is, as we've discussed before, an occupational hazard.'

'How can you be so calm?' Lucy asked.

'One of us has to be,' the man replied, with an edge of rebuke in his voice. 'You should be grateful that I'm not losing my head, as you obviously appear to be losing yours.'

'I am grateful,' Lucy said. 'I depend on you. You know that.'

The man chuckled again. 'Of course you depend on me,' he agreed. 'I'm your pimp, aren't I? And what's the point in having a pimp if you can't depend on him?'

The motto that Nathan Jones had suggested for the Whitebridge Over-Sixties Ramblers Association had been, 'Not one foot in the grave, but two feet on the ground'.

But though he got his way over most things concerning the association – like having the bus pick them up at an impossibly early hour of the morning – he had not prevailed on this occasion, and had been disgusted when most of the members had opted for the amazingly trite, 'Ramble with the Ramblers'.

The bus – 'Which was much too early, *whatever* Nathan says,' complained Ethel Hodge – had left them in the middle of the moors at around nine o'clock.

There had been no indications that snow was on its way in Whitebridge, but out on the moors there had been a light – unseasonal – fall, and a carpet of glistening whiteness was spread out before them.

'Behold, ladies and gentlemen – the true wonder of nature,' Nathan Jones said expansively.

'Huh, he's even claimin' credit for fixin' the weather for us now,' Ethel Hodge muttered.

It was nearly an hour before they reached the isolated low stone pub which rejoiced in the name of 'The Top o' the Moors', and by then what snow there had been on the pub's roof had all-but gone, and what there had been in the car park had already turned to slush.

Nathan Jones herded the walkers on to the car park, and formed them into a half-circle.

'I don't hear him claimin' any credit for this mess underfoot,' Ethel Hodge grumbled. 'It'll take me a good half-hour to clean these boots, once I get home.'

Nathan Jones inspected the gathering with the critical eye of a regimental sergeant major.

'Now remember,' he said, in the booming voice which had stood him in good stead when he'd been a mill foreman, 'the pub isn't open, so there's no point in knocking on the door and asking if you can have a bottle of lemonade.'

'He treats us like we were gaga,' Ethel Hodge complained to
her friend Doris Fielding, as they stood at the edge of the group.
'But if you want my opinion, *he's* the one who's not quite right
in the head.'

'However,' Nathan Jones continued, 'the landlord has kindly
agreed to let us use his outside toilets. But I needn't remind you
that this is something of a courtesy on his part . . .'

'If you needn't remind us, why are you reminding us?' Ethel
called out loudly.

'. . . and I would ask you to leave them as you find them,'
Jones continued, ignoring the interruption.

'Pity he said that,' Ethel told Doris. 'I was rather hopin' to
take the toilet bowl home with me.'

'Now as far as I know, there's only one stall in the ladies'
toilets, so I suggest that we work on the principle of age before
beauty – which means that we should probably let Ethel go first,'
Jones concluded.

'Bastard!' Ethel said under her breath.

But she was glad that – in an effort to score a point – Nathan
had put her first in line, because she was fairly bursting to go to
the lavvy.

She opened the outside door, and negotiated her broad hips
around the sink, so she was standing in front of the stall door.

She pushed, but the door refused to open.

Or rather, it would open so far and no further, which meant
that she could see the left-hand edge of the desired toilet, but
could not reach it.

She stepped out into the car park again, and saw Nathan
looking down at his watch, as if he were timing how long it took
each of them to have a tinkle – which was probably precisely
what he *was* doing.

'I can't open the lavvy door,' she told Nathan.

'Is it locked?' he asked.

'No, it's not locked. It's jammed. There's somethin' preventin'
it from openin' all the way.'

'And would you like me to do somethin' about that?' he
asked.

'Yes, please,' she said, hating herself for asking his help, but
now desperately in need of a pee.

Nathan stepped inside the toilet, and Ethel followed him.

'I see what you mean,' he said, when he'd given the door a tentative push. 'There *is* somethin' preventin' it from openin'. Somethin' quite solid, I'd say.'

'You're a bit of a genius, on the quiet, aren't you?' Ethel asked innocently.

'What I need to do is reach round the door with one hand, and try and shift whatever it is that's causing the obstruction, while using the other hand to push on the door,' Nathan said.

His left hand disappeared through the gap.

'It's something quite soft, but quite solid,' he said. 'To tell you the truth, it feels a little rubbery.'

'Maybe it's a very big door stop,' Ethel suggested.

'No, it's too high for that,' Nathan told her. Then he laughed – unconvincingly. 'Oh, I see, you were making a joke,' he continued.

'That's right,' Ethel agreed. 'I should be on the telly, shouldn't I?'

'Whatever it is, I think it's giving way,' Nathan said, visibly straining with the effort.

The door suddenly shot open – causing Nathan to almost lose his balance – then bounced back again.

'I believe I can get far enough inside to see what's causing the obstruction now,' Nathan said, squeezing into the gap between the door and the wall. 'Oh my God . . . it's . . . it's . . .' he gasped.

He jerked back through the gap.

'Well, *what* is it?' Ethel asked impatiently.

'It's . . . it's a woman,' Nathan said. 'I think she's dead.'

'Well, if she wasn't before, she will be now, after all that pushin' and shovin' you've done,' Ethel said, enjoying his discomfort.

'I have to go . . . I need to go outside before I . . .' Nathan said.

He just made it to the door before he doubled up and was violently sick.

Ethel watched him impassively.

Typical man – goin' to pieces in the face of death, she thought. Maybe if you'd laid out your granny, and two of your brothers – like I have – you wouldn't be quite so squeamish.

She had considerably more bulk to manoeuvre than Nathan

had, but eventually she managed to get her head around the door and could see what he had seen.

And then she understood why he had vomited.

THIRTEEN

'It's very fortunate for you the body was found by someone who knows how to keep his head in a crisis,' Nathan Jones told Detective Inspector Colin Beresford. 'I realized immediately, you see, that you needed to be informed as soon as possible, and, as chance would have it, just at that moment, a car appeared in the distance and I was able to flag it down. The driver, who you'll no doubt want to talk to, works for a company which manufactures surgical boots and . . .'

Beresford had stopped listening a long time ago. Instead, his eyes were following the drama which was being enacted around him, while his mind was processing the possible implications for the investigation that the discovery of the body carried in its wake.

There were a number of official vehicles already at the crime scene, including two patrol cars, an ambulance, Dr Shastri's Land Rover and the small lorry which had brought the heavy police barriers. And now the coach arrived, to take away the ramblers who had all been herded together in one corner of the car park, like lost sheep.

'Shouldn't you be taking all this down?' Nathan Jones asked, sounding aggrieved.

'I *am* taking it down,' Beresford lied. 'There's a small tape recorder in my pocket and a microphone behind my button-hole.'

'Damn clever!' Nathan Jones said. 'Isn't it amazing how small they can make things these days. When I started working in the mill—'

'I think your bus has just arrived,' Beresford interrupted him.

'So it has,' Jones agreed, looking vaguely towards the vehicle. 'But if you'd like me to stay behind . . .'

'That won't be necessary,' Beresford said.

'Are you sure?' Jones asked, with a hint of disappointment.

'You've been very helpful already, and if we need you again, we know where to find you,' Beresford said firmly.

As Jones made his way reluctantly towards the bus, Beresford looked first at the inn and then at the road which ran alongside it.

The nearest village – which, in practical terms, also meant the nearest *house* – was four miles to the south, he calculated. If you were going north, it would be at least six miles before you reached any sign of human habitation. And it was its very isolation which had once been the inn's fortune, he guessed, because in the olden days journeying from one village to the next would have been a protracted process, and by the time the weary traveller reached the Top o' the Moors, he would have been sorely in need of some liquid refreshment.

So why had the killer chosen this spot to dump his victim?

Why, with the whole of the moors to choose from, had he left her in the ladies' toilet of this pub?

And why was what happened last night, which should have been the start of a whole new life for you, such a disaster? asked a tiny, disappointed voice in the corner of his brain.

'I've no time to think about that now!' he muttered angrily. 'I've got a murder to investigate.'

And so he had.

But he couldn't entirely ignore the fact that now the investigation was picking up pace, the team would inevitably be spending more time together – and that meant, in turn, that *he* would spending more time with Kate Meadows.

A green Vauxhall Victor pulled up just beyond the police barrier, and a rotund man with a red face climbed out of it. One of the uniformed constables approached him and the two men exchanged a few words, then the constable pointed to Beresford, and the other man nodded.

The fat man walked around the barrier and up to where Beresford was standing.

'I'm the landlord,' he said, without preamble. 'What a bloody mess!'

'It is,' Beresford agreed. 'Since you've only just arrived, I take it you don't live over the pub.'

'Not at this time of year, no,' the landlord agreed. 'We're very busy in the late spring, the summer and early autumn – there's hundreds of people out on the moors for the day when the weather's nice – and that's when we use the flat over the pub. But when it gets towards the back end of the year, trade's sluggish at lunchtime and virtually non-existent at night, so we tend to sleep in our own home, which is in Honnerton.'

'You've been told the body was found in the ladies' toilets, have you?' Beresford asked.

'I have.'

'Before you left last night, did you lock it?'

'No, I didn't. I knew the Ramblers would be passing this way, you see – Nathan Jones has been reminding me of the fact every couple of days – so I left them open.'

'But you don't normally leave them unlocked?'

'I shouldn't,' the landlord said cagily.

'But you do?'

The landlord looked a little worried. 'This won't get back to the brewery, will it?'

'No,' Beresford assured him. 'It won't get back to the brewery.'

'I sometimes forget to lock the toilets,' the landlord admitted.

'Forget – or can't be bothered?' Beresford pressed him.

'Can't be bothered, I suppose,' the landlord admitted. 'I mean to say, this place is miles away from anywhere, and there's nobody here when I go home. I could probably leave the pub unlocked as well, for that matter. Not,' he added hastily, 'that I do.'

'Who's likely to know about your arrangements?' Beresford asked.

'I imagine it would be dozens of people,' the landlord said. 'Possibly even scores.'

And given that the landlord seemed to be such a chatty soul by nature, it probably *was* scores, Beresford decided.

'Why did the killer leave the body here?' the landlord asked. 'Why give me the aggravation?'

'Yes, that was very thoughtless of him,' Beresford agreed. 'But I think he probably chose this spot because it was so isolated – because he knew no one was likely to either see him or disturb him.'

'But why my ladies' toilet?' the landlord whined.

'Ah,' said Beresford, who had just worked it out, 'that's because he wanted to make sure that the body was found fairly quickly.'

'And why would he want that?' the landlord asked, now more curious than aggrieved.

'Now that *is* a good question,' Beresford said.

Paniatowski and Meadows had seen the ambulance arrive from their vantage point in the waiting room at the police morgue, and had watched the stretcher bearers carry the covered body into the dissecting room. As yet, though, they had not been allowed to take a look at the actual corpse itself.

'I shall require a few minutes alone with my latest companion, and only after that can I allow members of the constabulary the privilege of a viewing,' Dr Shastri had said.

And Paniatowski had merely nodded, for though the doctor looked as delicate as a soft summer flower, she was, in point of fact, as hard as nails – and in this morgue there was no question that her word was law.

'You may come through now,' Shastri said from the doorway. 'And if I were you, I would steel myself beforehand, because it is not a pretty sight.'

The girl – and it was definitely a *girl* – was lying naked on the dissection table. Her legs and arms were scarred with an extensive criss-cross pattern of paper-thin cuts. The girl's breasts had suffered a similar fate, yet, strangely, the rest of her trunk displayed absolutely no sign of injury.

'Jesus!' Paniatowski said.

She gazed at the dead girl's face – she'd been so young! – and her mind began to play tricks with her, moving the girl's jawline a little, making the eyes slightly larger and the nose a little less pointed, until the face had been transformed into Louisa's.

That was just the sort of thing that Charlie Woodend, her old boss, had done, she remembered. He, too, had been unable to view a corpse impersonally, but had, in his mind, transformed the slab of dead meat lying before him into a person he might have known. He'd told Paniatowski that this trick – which was, in reality, not a trick at all, since he had no choice about performing it – was nothing but a curse on him. But he would not have had it cast off even if he could have, because he knew it made him a better policeman.

And I wouldn't give it up, either, Paniatowski told herself. Because it makes *me* a better bobby, too.

She looked down at the dead girl again. She knew it *wasn't* her daughter. Louisa was safely in school, struggling with her French verbs or licking the corner of her mouth as she grappled with a particularly difficult equation.

So of course it wasn't Louisa – but it could have been!

Paniatowski felt the bile rising in her throat. It wouldn't do to spew up her guts in front of her new sergeant, she thought – but it was going to take a real effort of will to avoid it.

She forced herself to focus her mind on the girl who was dead, rather than the girl who could have been. If this was Grace, then she had walked the same streets as Denise, who had been attacked with a razor by a man who the other girls now called the Ripper.

Had the same man done this?

Had he found the courage, on his own territory, that he had lacked on the street?

'These could be razor wounds, couldn't they?' she asked.

'No, they couldn't,' Shastri replied. 'If they had been made by a razor, they would have been fairly uniform, whereas most of these wounds are deeper in the middle than they are at their edges. And by applying the same logic, we can virtually rule out knives.'

'So if they weren't made by a razor and they weren't made by a knife, what in God's name were they made by?'

'I think that they're whip marks.'

'You can do all that with a *whip*?' Paniatowski asked.

'If you have the right *kind* of whip, and know exactly how to handle it,' Shastri said, matter-of-factly. 'Her tormentor's job was made easier, of course, by manacles, evidence of which you can clearly see in the abrasions on her wrists and ankles. The skin has been scraped away, not so much by the manacles themselves as by the twisting and turning she did in an effort to escape. But, of course, there was no escape.'

'I want to chain your hands above your head so tightly that you are forced to stand on tiptoe,' the man with the razor had told Denise. *'I want to see your naked skin glistening in the candle light. And then I want to whip you!'*

Meadows moved closer to the cadaver, and bent over so far that her face was no more than a few inches away from it.

'Would you say that all these wounds were made within a short space of time – say, a few hours – Doc?' she said.

'What makes you ask that, Kate?' Paniatowski wondered.

'I don't know, boss – it was just the first question that came into my head,' Meadows told her. '*Were* they inflicted in one session, Doc?'

'I wouldn't want to commit myself without a more detailed examination, but my instinct tells me that is certainly the case,' Shastri said.

Paniatowski paced up and down. She should be used to this kind of thing by now, she thought. After all that she had seen during her years with the Mid Lancs police, she should be prepared for any example of human cruelty, however depraved. Yet it always came as a shock.

She stopped, and lit up a cigarette. When she inhaled, she tasted the by-now all-too-familiar mixture of cancerous smoke and formaldehyde.

She needed to think clearly, she told herself.

She needed to make herself as cold and analytical as her new sergeant seemed to be.

But, of course, it was easier for Meadows – because Meadows didn't have a teenage daughter.

'What I don't understand,' she said, turning to face Dr Shastri, 'is how the victim avoided injury to most of her trunk.'

'She was wearing some sort of costume while she was being whipped, wasn't she, Doc?' Kate Meadows asked.

'She was indeed,' the doctor agreed.

'*I have all kinds of costumes at home,*' the demented punter had told Denise. '*Tight corsets, masks, shoes which are so high they are almost stilts . . .*'

'If she was wearing a costume, how did her breasts get so scarred?' Paniatowski wondered.

'Ah, that is because of the *kind* of costume that she was wearing while she was being tortured,' Shastri replied. 'And is it precisely that costume, I believe, that she was still wearing when her body was discovered.'

'Can I see it?' Paniatowski asked.

'Of course,' Shastri agreed.

She walked over to a sterile cupboard, and returned with what looked rather like a high-necked swimming costume.

'It is made of high-quality rubber, and it is very thick,' the doctor said. 'If the whip had struck any part of her covered by this costume, it would not even have left a bruise.'

'But the breasts?' Paniatowski persisted. 'How did they get damaged?'

Shastri held up the costume, and Paniatowski could see the almost-circular holes cut in it at breast level.

'It's a beautiful piece of work,' the doctor said clinically. 'Carefully cut and very carefully sewn. The holes are perhaps a little too small, but I suspect that was deliberate, since it would squeeze the breast and make them plump up.'

She turned the costume round, to display the fact that it did not reach the neck, as the front did, but had been cut away almost to the buttocks.

'It will not surprise you to learn that there are lash marks on the victim's back, too,' Shastri said. 'The fact that her face was unmarked would suggest she was wearing some kind of hood. If it *is* the case, I should certainly find some traces of the hood during the autopsy.'

'How long has she been dead?' Meadows asked.

'I would guess that she died some time last evening, but, once again, I will be able to be more precise once I have conducted the post-mortem.'

'So the poor girl was literally whipped to death, was she?' Paniatowski said, sadly.

'No, boss, she wasn't,' Meadows said. 'The whipping would have hurt, but it wouldn't have killed her.'

The look of calm competence that Meadows had been wearing since she entered the morgue was suddenly gone, and in its place was something that could almost have been called horror.

Paniatowski wondered what could have brought about this instant change of expression, but before she had time to examine her sergeant's face more thoroughly, Meadows had turned quickly away and was addressing Shastri.

'I'm sorry, Doc,' Kate Meadows said. 'You're the expert here, and I should just keep my big mouth shut.'

Shastri smiled. 'Quite possibly so, Sergeant. But you are undoubtedly right – it was not the whipping which killed her. It is most likely that she was smothered, and I suspect the method used was a plastic bag over her head.'

'Did she have anything on her feet?' Paniatowski asked.

'Yes, she was wearing shoes.'

'Can I see them?' Paniatowski said.

And she was praying, 'Let them not be what I think they are
. . . let them not be what I think they are . . .'

Shastri made a second journey to the cupboard, and returned
with a pair of red shoes.

The heels were identical to the one found at the bottom of
Elaine Kershaw's garden.

FOURTEEN

WPC Crowther was directing the passing traffic away
from the crime scene when she became aware that
DI Beresford was standing next to her and eyeing
her speculatively.

'How tall are you, June?' Beresford asked.

Crowther gestured impatiently at a blue van which had slowed
down to almost a halt.

'There's nothing to see, so you'd best be on your way,' she
called out to the driver.

The van reluctantly accelerated away, and June Crowther turned
to face Beresford.

'Some of the people who have driven past here in the last
half-hour are worse than bloody vampires,' she said, in disgust.
'How tall am I, sir? I'm five-feet-five in flat shoes.'

'Five-five,' Beresford mused. 'That's much too tall.'

'Is it? Well, pardon me for breathing, sir,' Crowther said.

'Still, you're the shortest woman here, so I suppose you'll just
have to do,' Beresford said.

Crowther smiled. 'You really do know how to sweep a girl
off her feet, don't you, sir?'

Apparently not, if the previous night was anything to go by,
Beresford thought.

But aloud, he said, 'I've assigned somebody else to take over
this job, and I'd like you to come with me to the ladies' bog.'

'That's where the body was found, isn't it, sir?'

'That's right.'

'Why would you want me to go there with you?'

Beresford grinned. 'Because, just as you've always dreamed

might happen, I want to sweep you off your feet. And I mean that literally!'

'I don't think I quite understand what you're on about, sir?' Crowther admitted.

'You will, soon enough,' Beresford told her.

The police patrol car pulled up in front of the morgue, and Lucy got out of it. She was wearing a long dress and had a headscarf covering her hair. She was very pale, yet seemed surprisingly calm.

'Thank you for coming,' Paniatowski said.

'If it is poor little Grace in there, then it's only right she should be identified by someone who really cared for her,' Lucy said simply. 'And you *do* think it's her, don't you?'

'It's always possible that it's someone else, but she's the right age, and no one else has been reported missing,' Paniatowski replied.

'It's her,' Lucy said, stoically. 'I always knew it would end tragically. After the life she's had, how could it end any other way?'

Shastri appeared in the doorway. 'I'll talk you through what will happen once we're inside,' she told Lucy, in a soft, caring voice which was totally free of both her usual humour and her usual cynicism.

'Thank you,' Lucy said.

'There are two rooms inside, right next to one another,' Shastri continued. 'You will be in the first one, and the trolley with the person you have come to identify will be in the other. Do you understand?'

'Yes.'

'You will be able to see the trolley through a window. The person will be completely covered with a sheet, but when you give the signal that you are ready, the sheet will be folded back so that you can see that person's head.'

'I don't want to see her through a window. I want to be in the same room as her,' Lucy said.

'These procedures are designed to minimize the shock and distress you will experience,' Shastri explained. 'I don't think you quite realize—'

'I'm strong enough to take it,' Lucy said firmly. 'And if you won't do it that way, you'll have to get somebody else to identify her.'

Paniatowski and Shastri exchanged glances.

'Very well, but you do so at your own risk,' Shastri said.

'Dying is as natural – and as ordained – as being born,' Lucy told her. 'I can handle it.'

All three of them went to the room where the trolley had been left, and Shastri peeled back the sheet.

'It's her,' Lucy said, and crossed herself.

'Thank you for coming,' Paniatowski said again, and started to shepherd her towards the door.

But Lucy was not to be moved. 'I'd like to spend a few minutes alone with my friend,' she said.

'I'm afraid that is not possible,' Shastri told her. 'There are certain legal requirements that I must—'

'Please!' Lucy begged.

Shastri weakened. 'If I do allow it, you must not touch the body in *any way*,' she said severely.

'I promise I won't.'

The doctor nodded. 'Very well. You have five minutes.'

Shastri and Paniatowski left the room, closing the door softly behind them.

'I can't think what made me agree to that,' Shastri admitted, as they walked down the corridor. 'It is certainly something I have never permitted before. Perhaps I did it because I had a feeling that Lucy had the *right* to be there.'

'I know what you mean,' Paniatowski said – and wondered if she should mention the fact that she had half-turned as they were leaving the room, and had seen Lucy sinking to her knees.

Beresford and Crowther stood in front of the ladies' toilet.

'Forensics have given this place the all-clear, so I'm going to conduct a little experiment,' Beresford said.

'What kind of experiment?'

'I'm going to pick you up and carry you into the loo. And *when* I pick you up, I want you to make yourself as lifeless as you possibly can.'

'Because I'm the body,' Crowther said.

'That's right,' Beresford agreed. 'And I'm the killer.'

It wasn't that easy to manoeuvre the "lifeless" Crowther through the space between the wall and the wash basin, but it wasn't impossibly difficult either, and once they had passed that obstacle, Beresford opened the stall with his foot, edged his way in, and lowered his burden down on to the pedestal.

Beresford stepped out of the stall and closed the door.

'Don't move your backside, but let your upper torso slump forward as far as it will go,' he said. 'Got that?'

'Got it,' Crowther agreed.

Beresford pushed the door open, and heard a banging sound as it connected with Crowther's head.

'No, that's not right,' he said.

'You're telling me it's not right,' Crowther complained. 'I've probably got concussion.'

'The thing is, Nathan Jones had to push really hard before he could open the door,' Beresford mused, 'so the victim can't have been on the toilet, she had to be behind the door. Now how did the killer manage that?' He scratched his head thoughtfully. 'Are you still slumped forward, June?'

'No, I'm bloody well not,' Crowther said.

'Then I'm opening the door again,' Beresford told her. He pushed it open, and looked down at the glowering Crowther. 'I'm going to pick you up,' he continued, 'and then I'm going to let you go again. And when I do, I want you to fall down.'

'I want danger money for this job,' Crowther said.

Beresford hoisted her to her feet, and leaned her slightly towards him. Then he released his grip at the same time as he stepped backwards and tried to pull the door closed.

It didn't work. Crowther's falling body filled the gap, and the door was blocked.

'We'll try again,' Beresford said.

'Do we have to?' Crowther asked. 'I've got a date tonight, and if it works out as I'm expecting it to, I'd like the feller to gasp at the beauty of my flawless skin, rather than look at my bruises and wonder if I'm a professional rugby prop forward.'

'If you do take him to bed, you could always make love with the lights off,' Beresford suggested.

The words, unexpectedly, began to bounce around his brain.

You could always make love with the lights off! You could always make love with the lights off!

'Are you all right, sir?' Crowther asked.

'I'm fine,' Beresford assured her. 'Look, June, if you *really* don't want to do it again, I suppose I could always ask one of the other WPCs to take your place.'

'I'll do it,' Crowther said, resignedly. 'But I'd just like you to bear in mind that when I joined the police force, it wasn't to be bounced around in some ladies' loo in the arse-end of nowhere.'

'Duly noted,' Beresford said with a smile.

It took him another two attempts to get the dropping and retreating just right, but when he did, Beresford found as much difficulty opening the door as Nathan Jones had done.

'So that's *how* he did it,' he said. 'Now the only question, WPC Crowther, is *why* he did it.'

The blue Vauxhall Victor screeched to a halt in front of the morgue just as Paniatowski and Shastri were standing on the steps, saying their farewells.

If he goes on driving like that, he'll end up wrecking another bloody car, Paniatowski thought.

She turned to Shastri. 'This isn't good,' she said, as she watched Chief Superintendent Kershaw climbing out of the car and sprinting towards them. 'This isn't good at all.'

'I think I could have worked that out for myself,' Shastri replied.

For a moment, it looked as if Kershaw would completely ignore the two women and storm straight into the morgue, then he seemed to have second thoughts and came to a halt directly in front of Shastri.

'They told me at headquarters that a woman's body has been discovered,' he said to the doctor.

'That's true,' Shastri agreed.

'I want to see her,' Kershaw said.

'It isn't Elaine,' Paniatowski told him.

'How would *you* know whether it's Elaine or not?' Kershaw demanded angrily. 'You've never even met her – I made sure of that!'

'It's a much younger woman,' Paniatowski said.

The anger drained from Kershaw's face, and was replaced by a strange mixture of hope and fear.

'I need to see her,' he said. 'I need to be sure.'

'She's already been identified,' Paniatowski said. 'She was a prostitute called Grace Meade.'

'I'd like you to give me your permission to look at her, Dr

Shastri,' Kershaw said, ignoring Paniatowski now, 'but if you won't give it, I'm going to see her anyway – and to hell with the consequences.'

'You may see her,' Shastri said, 'but as DCI Paniatowski has already informed you, it is not your wife.'

Shastri peeled back the sheet to reveal the dead girl's head.

'It isn't her,' Kershaw gasped. 'Thank God – it isn't her!'

'Perhaps you would like to leave now,' Shastri suggested.

But Kershaw didn't move. Instead, he just stood there, deep in thought.

'Mr Kershaw . . .' Shastri said tentatively.

'What are you doing here, DCI Paniatowski?' Kershaw demanded. 'You're supposed to be looking for Elaine.'

'We *are* looking for Elaine,' Paniatowski promised him. 'We're doing everything we can.'

But even as she was speaking, she could almost hear the wheels turning in the chief superintendent's head.

'How did this girl die?' he asked.

'She was murdered,' Shastri said.

'You think her death has something to do with Elaine's disappearance, don't you, Monika?' Kershaw said.

She was almost *certain* that it had, Paniatowski thought.

'I can't reveal the details of an investigation to anyone not directly involved in it, Tom,' she told Kershaw. 'You should know that better than anyone.'

'Was it a surprise to you when this girl's body happened to turn up?'

'I can't discuss it.'

'It wasn't, was it? Or, at least, not much of one – because you'd been *half-expecting* it to happen.'

Paniatowski said nothing – because there was nothing she could say.

'How long have you been looking for this girl?' Kershaw asked.

'Why don't you make an appointment to see the chief constable?' Paniatowski suggested. 'He can probably tell you more than I'm allowed to.'

'*When* did you start looking for her?' Kershaw asked, his rage growing by the second. 'Was it *before* Elaine disappeared? Or was it *after*?'

'This is pointless,' Paniatowski said.

'It was *after*, wasn't it?'

He took two steps closer, and towered over her. His fists were clenched into tight balls, and a vein on his forehead was throbbing madly.

He's going to take a swing at me, Paniatowski thought, preparing herself to meet the attack.

'*Wasn't* it?' Kershaw screamed.

Paniatowski sighed.

'Yes, it was after Elaine disappeared,' she admitted, because there was no point in denying it when he'd so obviously worked everything out for himself.

The admission seemed to relax the chief superintendent a little, and his hands unclenched.

'It was your job to find my wonderful, beautiful wife – and that was your *only* job,' he said, and now there was a coldness to his voice which would have frozen blood. 'I want her back. That's all that matters to me. And if a dozen worthless whores – or a hundred, for that matter – die in the process, I won't lose a minute's sleep over it.'

'You're a good policeman, Tom, – a caring policeman – so I know you don't really mean that,' Paniatowski said.

'But I do,' Kershaw replied. 'And I'll tell you something else, *Detective Chief Inspector Paniatowski*. If I don't get my Elaine safely back home – and if I find out the reason for that is you've been wasting your time protecting prostitutes – then I'll . . . then I'll . . .'

'Then you'll what?' Paniatowski asked, her own temper finally snapping. 'Go on! Say it! Let's get it out into the open.'

'If I find it's your fault, then I'll kill you,' Kershaw said.

FIFTEEN

'I feel like I'm letting you down,' Kate Meadows said, as she watched Bill Lee place one file on the desk and immediately reach for another one from the stack.

'Letting me down?' Lee replied. 'In what way?'

'We're supposed to be working together on these reports,' Meadows said, 'but I've been missing for most of the morning, and I'm afraid I'm going to have to leave again soon.'

'I see what you mean,' Lee said seriously. 'Here I am, working my arse off reading all these files, and what are *you* doing?' He grinned. 'You're nipping out every five minutes to attend cocktail parties or have dress fittings!'

Meadows laughed. 'If only I was,' she said.

'You're DCI Paniatowski's bagman,' Lee reminded her. 'Your most important function is to be there when your boss needs you.'

'You're a good friend,' Meadows said gratefully. She shook her head in irritation at herself. 'I'm sorry, I shouldn't have said that. It was very presumptuous of me, considering we hardly know each other.'

'If you're looking for a friend, you've got one,' Lee said. 'And you shouldn't feel guilty about not being here to help me, because there's no point in both of us wasting our time.'

'I didn't know you thought it was a waste of time.'

'I *didn't* when I started – I wouldn't have given up my holiday in Spain if I'd thought it would be a waste of time – but the more I consider the matter, the more it seems to me to be exactly that. You see, Kate, most of the men in these files are career criminals.'

'Yes, I know that, but what—'

'And a career criminal is a professional, just as much as we are. He knows the rules. His job is to break the law, and our job is to catch him. And if we do catch him, he accepts it. He doesn't think about taking revenge on the feller who caught him, because he knows it's not personal. But if the reason Elaine was kidnapped was to get at my boss – and it is still an "if" – then it *is* personal.'

'Then why haven't you given up already?' Meadows wondered.

'I daren't.'

'Daren't?'

'That's right. There's just a very small chance that one of these fellers *did* take it personally, you see. And if his name *is* in these files, and I don't find it because I couldn't be bothered to go on looking, I don't think I'd ever be able to forgive myself.'

Meadows was silent for perhaps a minute, then she said, 'I'd like to ask your advice, if you don't mind, Bill.'

'Go on,' Lee encouraged.

'I've got a secret, and I've been wondering whether or not to tell my boss about it.'

'What kind of secret?'

'I'd rather not go into details.'

'Then you're making it very difficult for me to give you advice,' Lee pointed out.

Meadows waved her hands helplessly in the air. 'Let's just say it's a secret about something I do.'

Lee nodded. 'Something you do,' he repeated.

'It doesn't hurt anybody else, and as far as I'm concerned, there's nothing wrong with it and so I've nothing to be ashamed of. But my boss may not take the same view, and if I tell her, she might start looking at me differently. She might not even like the idea of me working as her bagman any more – and I want that job, Bill, I really do.'

Lee sat deep in thought for a while. 'Say you were a compulsive gambler,' he said, finally.

'That's not it. That isn't it at all.'

'I'm just giving an example.'

'All right.'

'You're a gambler. You know it's stupid, because you never have any money to spend – *and* because you know your boss would disapprove – but you just can't stop. But when you're at work, you put all that behind you. You don't slip off to place bets when you should be questioning witnesses. You don't fiddle money from the petty cash to cover your debts. You see what I'm saying – as long as whatever your weakness is—'

'I never said it was a weakness,' Meadows interrupted fiercely.

'All right, then, what shall we call it?' Lee asked. 'Your foible?'

'Foible is fine.'

'As long as your *foible* doesn't affect the way you do the job, it's nobody's business but your own.'

'And it *hasn't* affected the way I do the job,' Meadows said.

'Well, there you are then.'

'But I think it may be affecting this particular case.'

'This particular case? You're talking about Mrs Kershaw's disappearance, are you?'

'No, not at all. I'm talking about Grace Meade's murder. I think I know something that Monika Paniatowski doesn't, but

I can't tell her *what* I know without telling her *how* I know it.
And I don't want to do that.'

'If it's a vital piece of information that you're holding, then I
think you really have to—' Lee began.

'It's not as clear-cut as that,' Meadows interrupted again. 'It's
more of a vague feeling – a hunch based on my own experience.
But it could be wide of the mark – and I might be wrecking my
career for nothing.'

'Hold off for a while, then,' Lee said. 'But if the feeling gets
any stronger, you simply have to tell your boss.'

'I know I do,' Meadows said miserably.

When people asked Roger Hardcastle what it was like to run the
local news programmes on Northern TV, he would inevitably say
it was a grand life, and the odd thing was that though he would
almost invariably twist his lips into a sneer around the word
'grand', he really *did* enjoy it.

What he *didn't* like – as a veteran producer who had been
with Northern TV since its early days – was having to work with
some of the idiots that the company's management were always
foisting on him.

The anchorman, Gary Pound – who he was watching through
the control room window at that very moment – was a prime
example of what he was talking about.

'Gary! What kind of a name is that for an Englishman?'
Hardcastle muttered grumpily to himself.

And *Pound* wasn't much better!

Why couldn't he have had a decent, honest surname like
Hebden or Ramsbottom?

Pound began looking down into the small mirror he always
carried with him, and, with a snort of disgust, Hardcastle
swung round in his chair so that he was facing Ted, his assistant,
who was a bit gormless, but at least had the *makings* of a
newsman.

'Just look at yon Gary – preening himself,' he said. 'He's
a bloody man, not a budgerigar, though, come to think of it, a
budgie would probably make a better job of reading the news.'

'Do you want one of your pills, Mr Hardcastle?' Ted asked
helpfully.

'No, I don't want one of my bloody pills,' Hardcastle replied.

'Do you know what the managing director told me when he first hired Pound?'

'No, I don't,' Ted replied dutifully.

'He said that Gary had the kind of contemporary face that our viewers would love, which, as far as I'm concerned, just means that he's got poncy hair that drives the make-up girl to distraction, and teeth that look like they've been coated with fluorescent white paint!'

'I really do think a pill might help,' Ted said tentatively.

'Bugger that!' Hardcastle replied. He swung his chair round again, so he was over the microphone. 'We're on the air in one minute, Gary,' he told the anchorman. 'As you can see from your running order, we've got the murder as the lead story, so you do the introduction, and then—'

'There's not much meat on the story, is there?' Pound interrupted.

'No, there isn't,' Hardcastle agreed. 'You'll just have to make up for the lack of detail by looking *contemporary*.'

Pound slipped the mirror back into its case, and the case back into his jacket pocket.

'Why can't we use all that detail that the police have given us?' he asked.

Hardcastle sighed. 'Because, in case you've forgotten, most of the briefing was off the record.'

'But there's ways and ways of going about things, aren't there? If we did it sneakily, we could sort of imply—'

'We could "sort of imply" nothing,' Hardcastle told him. 'If we don't play it exactly the way the police want us to, they won't even give us the time of day when next there's a major crime.' He ran his fingers through his rapidly thinning hair. 'Now where was I? Oh yes, you do the introduction that we agreed on, and then we cut to Lynda Jenkins at the scene of the crime. Got that?'

'I suppose so,' the anchorman said, sulkily.

'We're on air in five seconds,' the floor manager said. 'Five . . . four . . . three . . .'

'Bitch!' Hardcastle said, almost to himself.

'Who's a bitch?' Ted asked.

'Lynda Jenkins. She was on local radio until two months ago, but now – just because she's waggled her tits at our ever-gullible managing director once or twice – she's on regional television. That's a big leap for anybody, and most people would show a bit of humility. But not our Lynda! She thinks she knows all there is to know already.'

'*A corpse has been discovered in the ladies' toilet at Top of the Moors Inn, midway between Whitebridge and Honnerton,*' the anchorman said. '*The police have released very few details, but have confirmed that it is the body of a young woman, and that foul play is suspected . . .*'

Satisfied that the idiot with the poncy hair was sticking to the agreed script, Hardcastle switched his attention to the second monitor.

'Can you hear me, Lynda, love?' he asked.

Lynda Jenkins nodded. 'Yes, I can hear you.'

'You've got two minutes to fill. I suggest you concentrate on general stuff . . . famous local landmark, scene of many happy family picnics, now transformed into the scene of a tragic death, blah blah blah.'

The corners of Lynda Jenkins' mouth drooped. 'Do I have to keep it as general as that?' she asked. 'I'd much rather talk to my witness.'

'You've got a witness!' Hardcastle exclaimed. 'Somebody who actually *saw* the murder?'

'Well, no, maybe "witness" was not exactly the right word,' Jenkins admitted. 'I've got the man who discovered the body. Can I talk to him?'

Hardcastle felt a warning stab from his ulcer. 'You have read the guidelines, haven't you?' he asked.

'The guidelines?' Jenkins repeated, blankly.

'They're in one of the files you were given – the one that has the word "guidelines" written on the front. They tell you what you can say on air, and when you can say it.'

'Oh, them!' Jenkins said. 'Yes, of course I've read *them.*'

I shouldn't be doing this, Hardcastle thought. I really shouldn't. But if it works, it will be good television.

'All right, you can talk to him,' he heard himself say. 'But for God's sake, keep him under control.'

'No worries, chief,' Lynda Jenkins said cheerfully.

'No worries, chief,' the producer repeated scornfully to Ted. 'Is it really any wonder I can't keep my food down?'

'*And now we go over to our reporter, live outside the Top of the Moors Inn,*' the anchorman said.

'Top *o'* the Moors,' Hardcastle grumbled to himself. 'It's Top *o'* the Moors, you ignorant southern bastard!'

Lynda Jenkins' complacent face filled the screen. '*I'm talking to Mr Nathan Jones, the man who discovered the body,*' she said. '*Could you tell us what actually happened, Mr Jones?*'

The camera panned back to Jones, who was looking very full of himself indeed.

'*I was leading a hike of the Whitebridge Over-Sixties Ramblers, an organization of which I was one of the founding . . .*' Jones began.

'*Yes, yes, tell us about the body,*' Jenkins said impatiently.

'No details!' the producer warned her in her earpiece. 'Keep him off the details.'

'*One of the ladies in my party was desirous of using the facilities, but she couldn't get the toilet door open, so naturally she called on my assistance. It wasn't easy to open the door, because the body was jammed behind it.*'

'That's it, Lynda,' Hardcastle said. 'That's more than enough. Cut him off now.'

'*When I looked behind the door, I saw the girl. She was wearing some kind of corset, and her legs were slashed to ribbons.*'

'You stupid cow!' the producer screamed into Lynda Jenkins' earpiece. 'Cut the mad bitch off,' he told his assistant. 'Cut her off now!'

Though Lennie Brown could be a bit annoying sometimes – and, once in a while, could be *very* annoying – he was still Timmy Holland's best mate, and Timmy couldn't even imagine a life in which Lennie didn't play a central part.

The two of them had been lying on their stomachs in front of the television, watching the cartoons, but now Elmer Fudd had made his last attempt to shoot Bugs Bunny, the cartoons had ended, and the news had come on.

Neither of the boys had had high expectations of the news – it was always about boring people doing boring things – and the report on the murder had come as an unexpected, and thoroughly delightful, surprise.

'Legs slashed to ribbons,' Lennie said, with obvious relish.

'There must have been blood all over the place,' Timmy replied. 'I bet there was enough of it to fill a bath.'

'I bet there was enough of it to fill a swimming pool,' said Lennie, who always had to go one better.

Timmy tried to think of something even bigger than a swimming pool, but quickly gave up.

'What's a corset?' he asked.

Lennie snorted. 'Fancy you not knowing that!' he said. 'It's something that grannies wear.'

That was the problem with Lennie, Timmy thought. If he knew something, he made you feel a fool for *not* knowing it – and if he didn't know, he pretended to.

And he was pretending this time – Timmy was sure of that.

'If it's something that grannies wear, why had this girl got one on?' he asked.

Lennie said nothing.

'Well?' Timmy demanded.

'I can't tell you,' Lennie said finally.

'Because you don't know yourself!' Timmy jeered, thinking he had finally scored a point.

'I do, too, know,' Lennie said, partly angry, partly defensive. 'But if I told you, you wouldn't understand – because you're too young.'

That hurt – that really hurt. 'I'm only four months younger than you,' Timmy protested.

'You can do a lot of growing up in four months,' Lennie countered. 'And anyway, I'm cleverer than what you are.'

'Are you saying I'm thick?' Timmy asked, almost in tears.

'Not thick, no,' Lennie said hastily, sensing he'd gone too far. 'You're a very smart lad.' He should have left it there – he knew he should – but he just couldn't. 'Very smart,' he repeated, 'but not as smart as me.'

'I am so,' Timmy said, rolling on to his side, so that he had his back to the boy who had once been his best friend.

And when he'd done that, of course, Lennie had no choice but to do the same.

The silence was almost intolerable right from the start, but they both held out for more than a minute, before Lennie cracked and said, 'Do you know what?'

'What?' Timmy asked sulkily.

'If we found a dead body, we'd be on the telly, too.'

'Do you think so?' asked Timmy, all feelings of hostility slipping away.

'Forced to be,' Lennie assured him.

It all sounded very good, Timmy thought, but he could see one fatal flaw in his friend's plan.

'Where would we find a dead body?' he asked.

'In the woods,' Lennie said. 'There's bound to be a body somewhere in the woods.'

Of course there was, Timmy agreed, and wondered if Lennie was stating no more than the truth when he said he was the smarter of the pair.

The sign outside the seedy-looking shop said its owner was the purveyor of surgical supplies, but that was a convenient fiction which fooled no one but the most gullible, and when Kate Meadows entered she was immediately confronted by a series of corsets which plainly had very little orthopaedic value.

'So what can I do for you, my dear?' asked the owner, who *wasn't* in fact wearing a dirty raincoat, but certainly should have been.

'I don't see any magazines,' Meadows said.

'Why would you?' the owner wondered. 'This isn't a newsagent's shop, now is it?'

'Perhaps I didn't express myself very well,' Meadows conceded. 'I'm looking for instructional manuals in the art of unusual love-making.'

The owner licked his lips, as if he could clearly imagine her making unusual love, but erring on the side of caution, he said, 'What exactly are we talking about here?'

Meadows stood on tiptoe, then clasped her hands and held them over her head.

'Are you getting the picture?' she asked.

The owner licked his lips again. 'I'm sorry, I still haven't grasped your meaning,' he said.

Meadows sighed, and produced her warrant card.

'Show me your dirty books,' she demanded.

'I don't have any dirty books,' the owner said.

'I could come back with a search warrant,' Meadows threatened.

'No, you couldn't,' the owner told her confidently. 'You don't have any reason to get one sworn out, because I've always kept my nose clean. And even if you did get a warrant, any dirty books there might have been would be long gone by the time you came back.'

Meadows sighed again. 'You're making me do things the hard way,' she said. 'I really hate that.'

She walked over to the door and flicked the open sign over to closed. Then she turned the key in the lock.

'What are you up to?' the owner asked, starting to sound slightly worried.

'I told you, I'm doing it the hard way,' Meadows replied.

Slowly, she undid the top buttons of her blouse, until her brassiere was exposed.

'Very nice,' the owner said, in a voice which had almost become a wheeze. 'But I'm still not going to . . .'

Meadows took the flesh at the top of her left breast between her finger and thumb, and gave it a hard twist.

'That'll be a nasty bruise in an hour or two,' she said, as she calmly buttoned up the blouse again. 'You really shouldn't have done that to me, you know.'

'You're trying to stitch me up,' the owner gasped.

'There's not much *trying* about it,' Meadows said. 'In fact, I think I've done a really good job.'

'I'll deny it,' the owner said.

'Of course you will,' Meadows agreed. 'But who do you think is most likely to be believed – a police officer with a spotless record, or a real piece of dog shit like you?'

'What do you want?' the owner asked.

'You know what I want,' Meadows said.

'Then you'd better come in the back,' the owner told her, defeated.

'Chief Superintendent Kershaw suspects that Grace's death is connected to his wife's kidnapping,' Paniatowski told Crane and Beresford, across the table in the Drum and Monkey.

'Only *suspects*!' Beresford exclaimed.

'That's what I said.'

'You haven't told him about the red shoes, have you?'

'No, I haven't. There'd be no point.'

'He has the *right* to know,' Beresford argued.

'So you're in favour of telling all victims' relatives how an investigation is progressing, are you?' Paniatowski asked.

'Of course not, but . . .'

'Because that's what he is – a victim's relative. If I turn his suspicions into certainties by telling him about the shoes, can you imagine what hell he'll go through? And it may be *unnecessary* hell – because it's still possible we can save Elaine.'

'The boss is right, you know, sir,' Jack Crane said to Beresford.

'Besides, the more desperate he becomes, the more he's going to want to take over the investigation,' Paniatowski said.

'He's a good bobby – he could be useful,' Beresford told her.

'So you think he *should* take over the investigation?'

'Not take it over. Of course not. But maybe we could use a bit of his help and experience.'

'He may be a good bobby but he's also a very desperate man,' Paniatowski countered. 'And desperate men make mistakes – desperate men believe the wrong things because they *need* to believe them.'

'And I suppose you're going to tell me she's right about that, too,' Beresford said to Crane.

'Yes, sir, she is,' Crane said firmly. 'And you *know* she is.'

'Yes,' Beresford admitted. 'I *do* know that.' He turned to Paniatowski. 'Sorry, boss, maybe I'm a bit too involved myself, because while I don't know Elaine well, I do really like her.'

'And you really *admire* her husband,' Paniatowski said, with a hint of envy in her voice.

'I don't understand why the killer left Grace behind the bog door,' Beresford said, keen to change the subject. 'It wasn't an easy thing to do. I know that, from my own experiments. So what does it mean?'

'I don't think it was meant to mean anything,' Crane said.

'And what leads you to that conclusion?' Beresford asked.

'The very fact that he didn't have enough control over the positioning of the corpse.'

'Come again?'

'Ritual is a precise business. If you study the history of human sacrifice, for example, you'll find that everything involved in the ritual was laid down, and had to be present in exactly the form that had been specified.'

'I don't see how looking at ancient history will help us,' Beresford said.

'Then let's not look at ancient history,' Crane suggested. 'We arrested a serial killer a couple of months ago, didn't we?'

Indeed they had, and even the thought of it was enough to make all three of them shudder.

'He posed all victims naked and on all fours – and the keywords are *posed them*. Because what he did had a meaning – at least to him. But there's no possible meaning to what this killer did – because he couldn't control exactly how Grace fell or exactly how she looked when she was found.'

'So, if there was no meaning to it, why did he do it at all?' Beresford asked sceptically.

'I think he did it because he hoped we'd waste our time searching for a meaning, instead of directing our energy at any other leads we might come up with. And it worked out perfectly for him, didn't it – because that's exactly what we *have* been doing.'

'What do you think, Colin?' Paniatowski asked.

'Crane might be right,' Beresford admitted. 'In fact, it's the only thing that makes any sense. But exactly what kind of man would even think that way? It's almost as if —'

'Found them!' called a triumphant voice from across the bar.

Beresford, Crane and Paniatowski turned, and saw Meadows walking towards them and waving a glossy magazine above her head.

'Found what?' Paniatowski asked.

'The shoes,' Meadows said, slamming the magazine down on the table. 'The bloody shoes!'

The magazine was called *The Joy of Pain* and it was full of pictures of women being hung in the air, beaten and branded.

'Is this filth legal?' Beresford asked, disgusted.

'That's not been clearly established, one way or the other,' Meadows said. 'Magazines like this are sold very discreetly, so they hardly ever end up in court. And the publishers do claim that all the acts shown are simulated, rather than real.'

'And are they?' Beresford asked.

'They may be,' Meadows said, almost indifferently. 'But I didn't bring the magazine here to titillate your jaded fancies, sir, I brought it to show you these.'

She opened the magazine to the middle, where there was a double-page advertisement. Two of the articles offered had been ringed by Meadows. One was a rubber suit with holes where the breasts were, and the other was a pair of red, extremely high-heeled shoes.

'He bought both items from the same company,' Meadows said, with a hint of excitement in her voice. 'And maybe he bought other stuff as well. Maybe he bought so much that we just might have a chance of tracing it back to him.'

'Where's the company based?' Paniatowski asked.

'Bolton, boss.'

'I want you to go there this afternoon, Kate,' Paniatowski said. 'And take Jack with you. Say you want full access to their records, and if they won't give it . . .'

'They'll give it,' Meadows said confidently. 'I've got a trick or two up my sleeve which will leave them with no choice.'

'I don't want you do anything illegal,' Beresford said, more harshly than he intended.

'Of course not, sir,' Meadows replied. 'I'll take your own high standards as my guide, and that way there's no chance I'll ever step over the line.'

I wish I'd never gone to bed with you, Beresford thought.

But even as the idea flashed across his mind, he knew that what he really meant was, I wish I'd gone to bed with you and it had been *different*.

The outside door opened, and Lucy walked into the bar. She looked around, then waved to Paniatowski to join her.

'What's happened?' Paniatowski asked.

'Denise is back in Whitebridge,' Lucy said.

Paniatowski felt her heart speed up. 'And where exactly is she at this moment?' she asked.

'She's in the car park outside,' Lucy said. 'Waiting for you.'

SIXTEEN

Denise Slater was standing at the far end of the car park, huddled in what – if there'd been any sun on that cold November day – would have been the shadow of a builder and decorator's van.

'I don't want to do this,' she said as soon as Paniatowski and
Lucy were close enough to hear her.

'I know,' Lucy said softly.

'I don't like police stations.'

'Of course you don't,' Lucy agreed. 'Neither do I. But that's
because we normally only go to them when we've been arrested.
This time it's different – you're a witness, a visitor. Isn't that
right, Monika?'

'That's right,' Paniatowski agreed, wondering how Lucy knew
her first name – and how many other prostitutes there were who
would have dared to use it, even if they had.

There was not room for three of them in Paniatowski's MGA,
and they took Inspector Beresford's car instead, with Paniatowski
driving and Lucy and Denise hugging each other in the back.

The closer that they got to police headquarters, the more
agitated Denise became.

'Do I have to do this?' Paniatowski heard the young prostitute
ask.

'No, of course you don't,' Lucy replied.

Of course she bloody *does*! Paniatowski thought. She's doing
it whatever it takes – because she's our best chance of getting
Elaine Kershaw back alive!

But then she surprised herself by saying nothing and letting
Lucy handle the situation.

'No, of course you don't have to do it,' Lucy repeated. 'But
you'll be letting yourself and the other girls down if you don't . . .'

'I don't care!'

'. . . and I'll be very disappointed in you, too,' Lucy concluded.

There was a short silence, and then Denise said, 'You won't
leave me once we're in there, will you?'

'No,' Lucy promised. 'I'll be with you every step of the way.'

Five minutes earlier, there had been a couple of dozen officers
– sitting in groups of two or three – spread out around the police
canteen, but a phone call from DI Beresford had soon changed
all that. Now, all the policemen were together at the far corner
of the room – and no doubt complaining to each other about the
fact.

But that was the way it had to be, Paniatowski thought, as she
led the two prostitutes into the emptied end of the canteen – because

just *being* in the interview room would have terrified Denise, and even the DCI's own office might have seemed daunting to her.

'This is WPC Crowther, but I'm sure she won't mind if you call her June,' Paniatowski told Denise, pointing to the one officer who *hadn't* been herded into the corner, and so had a long table entirely to herself.

Crowther smiled. 'I won't mind at all,' she said. 'Why don't you take the seat next to mine, Denise?'

The prostitute looked to her companion for guidance, and when Lucy nodded, she said, 'Will you sit down as well?'

'Of course I will,' Lucy assured her.

'We'd like you to look through the photographs in this book,' Paniatowski said, tapping the ledger which lay on the table. 'There are a lot of them, but you shouldn't let that worry you. All right?'

'All right,' Denise replied, uncertainly.

'What we want you to do is to tell us if any of the men looks like the one with the razor,' Paniatowski continued. 'Can you do that?'

'She can do it,' Lucy said, putting her arm protectively around Denise's shoulder.

'I'll leave you to it, then,' Paniatowski said cheerily, and walked across the room to another table, where Crowther had left a second ledger – this one contained mug shots of all the women who had been arrested on soliciting charges.

It did not take her long to find Denise's picture, and the details that accompanied it told a depressingly predictable story.

Denise Slater had been arrested four times. The first three times, she had been fined. The fourth, she had been locked up for a week.

And no doubt the magistrate had given her a stern warning that next time she'd get a longer sentence, Paniatowski thought.

But had it had any effect?

Had it hell!

She'd probably no sooner been released than she was back on the street.

Grace Meade had been arrested twice. The first time – possibly because she was obviously so young – she'd been let off with a caution, but the second time she'd been fined.

And if she'd lived, Paniatowski told herself, there was no doubt she would have followed the same depressing path as Denise had.

But it was not Denise or Grace who she was really interested in, Paniatowski admitted to herself. She wanted to find out about Lucy.

And there was nothing in the ledger about her.

Not a single mention.

So either she had been very clever, or . . .

'Denise thinks she's found the man, boss,' WPC Crowther said, from somewhere behind her.

'I'll be right there,' Paniatowski told her.

Mug shots were a bit like passport photographs, Paniatowski had long ago decided. You clearly recognize the man from the picture, but in some ways the picture didn't really look like the man at all, because it was characterless and sterile.

But not this one, she thought, looking at the picture.

The man that Denise had picked out was in his late twenties or early thirties, and his character shone through despite the harsh lighting and hostile circumstances in which the photograph had been taken. He did not look the least intimidated. In fact, he seemed to be almost enjoying the process – perhaps because it gave him the opportunity to show just how superior to his surroundings he felt.

From the corner of her eye, she saw Denise lean over and whisper something in Lucy's ear.

'Denise is having second thoughts about him,' Lucy said.

'But you picked him out immediately you saw him,' June Crowther said. 'There wasn't a moment's hesitation.'

Denise shrugged. 'I know, but . . .'

'So what's happened to make you change your mind?' Paniatowski pressured.

'This man looks younger than the one that attacked me.'

'A lot younger?'

'No, not a lot.'

'Well, you have to remember that the picture will have been taken when he was charged, which may have been several years ago now.'

'It's not just his age,' Denise said. 'This man seems like he hasn't got a care in the world, but the one who attacked me looked like . . . looked like the shipyard had closed down for him.'

'What do you mean by that?'

'I'm from the north-east. We lived near the shipyard when I was growing up,' Denise said. 'And one day, the owners said there weren't enough orders on the books, and shut the place up.'

'Go on,' Paniatowski encouraged.

'A lot of the men who lived on our street worked in the yard. They were big, strappin', confident men until the day they got that pink slip in their pay packets. And then they just seemed to shrink. They walked slower, like it was a real effort. And when they spoke, it was like they weren't sure they were worth listening to any more.' Denise paused for a moment. 'I'm explaining it very badly.'

'You're explaining it beautifully,' Paniatowski assured her. 'What you're saying is that the man in the photograph looks like he still had his job, and the one who attacked you didn't.'

'That's right,' Denise agreed. 'When he went for me with the razor, he really *did* want to hurt me – I'm sure of that – but I think the *reason* he wanted to do it was because he was even more frightened than I was.'

Chief Superintendent Kershaw was sitting at his desk. There was paperwork spread out in front of him, but Paniatowski was willing to bet that he had read it at least ten times and still had no idea what it was about.

'Have you found her?' he asked, in a voice that seemed filled with hope and dread in about equal proportions.

'Not yet, sir,' Paniatowski admitted.

'Then why are you here?' Kershaw exploded. 'Why aren't you still out looking for her?'

'I've got a mug shot that I'd like you to look at, sir.'

'Is it that man who you think kidnapped Elaine? Do you think he did it because of something I once did to him?'

'You can't carry on like this,' Paniatowski said. 'You've got to stop thinking like a policeman and start thinking like a witness. It's the only way we'll make any progress in this investigation – and you know it!'

Kershaw sighed. 'You're right,' he agreed. 'Show me the picture.'

Paniatowski slid it across the desk. Kershaw devoured it with his eyes, and then a look of disappointment filled his whole face.

'I thought I'd know him immediately,' he said. 'I thought he was bound to be one of the toerags I'd banged up over the years. But I *don't* know him. He does look vaguely familiar – but I don't actually *know* him.'

'You tried your best,' Paniatowski said, reaching out her hand for the photograph.

But Kershaw was not prepared to relinquish it yet.

'Wait a minute,' he said. 'I *do* know him. I couldn't place him at first because he wasn't one of my cases.'

'You're not doing yourself or the investigation any good here, Tom,' Paniatowski advised.

'But I *do* know him!' Kershaw insisted. 'His name's Taylor Jones – or something like that, anyway.'

'Taylor Brown.'

'That's right. His name's Taylor Brown – and the only reason he went to jail was because of me!'

Kershaw is taking a break in the police canteen when DI Mortimer sits down next to him.

'Do you know what I most hate about this job, Tom?' Mortimer asks, without any preamble. 'It's that, for a lot of the time, we have to do it with our hands tied behind our bloody backs.'

Kershaw smiles. 'Are you just having a general rant, Walter, or have you got a specific case in mind?'

'I've got the Honourable Reginald George Taylor Brown in mind,' Mortimer says.

'An Honourable!' Kershaw says, with mock awe. 'Well, you certainly seem to be dealing with a better class of criminal than I do.'

'Class?' Mortimer repeats in disgust. 'Taylor Brown's got no class. Money, yes – his family owns two breweries and half the pubs in Lancashire – but no class. The man's a real scumbag.'

'So what's he done?'

'Tortured his housekeeper!'

'You've got to be joking!' Kershaw says.

'I wish I was. It's been going on for months. You wouldn't believe the things he's done to her. He's whipped her, he's stubbed

out his cigarettes on her – he's even cut her with a razor. And in the end, when she couldn't take it any more, she came to us.'

'Seems like an open and shut case, then,' Kershaw said.

'It would be, if she hadn't withdrawn her statement.'

'Whatever made her do that?'

'His family have got at her. She's Russian, a political refugee, and I think – though I can't prove it – that the family have told her that if she testifies, they'll see to it that she's sent back home. And they probably could do that, you know, because the Taylor Browns have a lot of influence.'

'So you had to let him go?'

'Not yet. I'm going to have one last crack at him, but that's just stubbornness on my part, because I don't really expect to get anywhere.'

'Who's his lawyer?' Kershaw asks. 'Some expensive brief from Manchester, I expect.'

'He doesn't have a lawyer.'

'What?'

'He's such an arrogant little shit that he doesn't think he needs one. He's laughing at us, Tom! He's laughing at me!'

Kershaw looks at his watch. 'I've got an hour or so to spare,' he says. 'Why don't you let me talk to him?'

Reginald Taylor Brown has an aristocratic nose and a naturally contemptuous curl to his lip. He looks up with interest when the man in overalls enters the interview room, and says, 'You seem to have forgotten your bucket and mop.'

Ignoring him, Kershaw turns to the uniformed constable standing by the door, and says, 'Go and have a cup of tea, son. Don't hurry back.'

Taylor Brown chuckles. 'I knew this country had gone to the dogs since the War, but I never thought I'd live to see the day when a mere cleaner would be issuing orders to a copper – even a lowly one.'

'I'm not a cleaner, I'm a chief superintendent,' Kershaw tells him.

'Then why are you wearing overalls?'

'That should become clear later. Tell me about what you did to this girl. Sonia, wasn't it?'

'I did nothing to her.'

'Oh, come on, Reg, she's got whip marks on her back, cigarette burns on her legs and razor slashes on her arms. How did she get them?'

'I don't know. Perhaps her boyfriend liked to treat her roughly.'

'She didn't have a boyfriend. You kept her a virtual prisoner. It's all in her statement.'

'Which she has since retracted.'

Kershaw sits down opposite Taylor Brown.

'I hear you're a big fan of the Marquis de Sade,' he says.

'And I am not alone in that,' Taylor Brown replies. 'Simone de Beauvoir has claimed that his writings are the earliest examples of existentialism, and Guillaume Apollinaire said he was the freest spirit who ever lived.'

'And who's this Guy . . . Guy . . .?' Kershaw asks.

'Guillaume Apollinaire,' Taylor Brown repeats condescendingly. 'He was a French poet and literary critic, who invented surrealism and died in 1919. And in case you don't know what surrealism is—'

'He didn't invent surrealism, he only coined the term which describes it,' Kershaw interrupts him. 'And he didn't die in 1919, he died in 1918.'

'You're playing games with me,' Taylor Brown says accusingly.

'That's right,' Kershaw agrees. 'But then I'm only taking a leaf out of your own book, aren't I?' He pauses for a moment. 'So you think it's all right to hurt people, even if they don't want to be hurt. Is that correct?'

'A man must be true to himself, and seek the liberation of his soul in whatever way is open to him,' Taylor Brown says.

'Interesting,' Kershaw muses. Then he takes a piece of paper out of his pocket, and slaps it down on the table. 'Sign this.'

'What is it?''

'It's your confession. It's not in your words, exactly, but it is based on the statement Sonia made, so it should be accurate enough.'

'You must be insane if you think I'll sign that.'

Something heavy falls on to the floor, and Kershaw picks it up.

'Oh look,' he says, 'it's your razor – the one you cut Sonia with. How very remiss of the officers not to take it off you when they arrested you.'

'They did take it off me,' Taylor Brown says.

'They can't have, or it wouldn't be here.'

'You brought it with you.'

'I most certainly did not.' Kershaw opens the razor and holds it up to the light. 'Very nasty, this blade.'

'Are you . . . are you threatening me?' Taylor Brown asks.

'Between you and me, yes, I am,' Kershaw admits. 'But that isn't the story I'll be telling later.'

'Then what story will you be telling?' Taylor Brown asks, as his concern mounts.

'I'll say you confessed everything, and said you were very sorry for what you'd done. I may even add that you were weeping tears of remorse. Then I'll say that I left you alone to contemplate your wickedness, and that while I was out of the room, you took out the razor you had secreted in your clothing.'

'Are you saying that you're planning to fake my suicide?' Taylor Brown asks, visibly relaxing because he knows this just has to be a bluff. 'You wouldn't dare.'

'You're right,' Kershaw agrees. 'Besides, I have a moral objection to execution, even for scum like you. But that's not the story I was halfway through telling you.'

'Then what is?'

'You're so eaten up by remorse – so determined never to do anything like that again – that you drop your pants and cut your own balls off.'

'You couldn't . . . you wouldn't . . .'

'You wondered why I was wearing overalls, and now you know,' Kershaw says. 'Ten minutes from now, these overalls will be burning away merrily in the furnace, I'll be back in uniform – and you'll be in the hospital.'

'You'd never get away with it,' Taylor Brown gasps.

'Of course I will,' Kershaw says confidently. 'I'm a senior police officer with an exemplary record. Nobody would believe I'd ever be mad enough to risk my career by castrating a suspect.' He pauses again. 'Why don't you sign the statement, Reg? It'll save an awful lot of mess.'

'It's him, isn't it?' Kershaw said. 'He's the one.'

'He might be,' Paniatowski admitted, cautiously.

'I have to talk to him! I have to make him tell me what he's done with her!'

'No!' Paniatowski said firmly.

'For God's sake, woman, it's my wife we're talking about – and I outrank you.'

'If you try to get anywhere near the suspect, I'll have you locked up,' Paniatowski said. 'You know I can do it – and you know the chief constable will back me.'

'He needs to be arrested,' Kershaw said.

'That's already in hand.'

'He might have an accomplice. You need to check on that.'

'I will,' Paniatowski said. 'Listen, Tom, you have to promise me that you won't try to interfere with the investigation. I need your word on that.'

For a few seconds, Kershaw said nothing, then he looked Paniatowski straight in the eyes and said, 'You have my word – but you'd better make damn sure you get it right!'

With Beresford driving the lead car, and Paniatowski in the passenger seat, the convoy of five police vehicles shot along the narrow moorland road which led to the village of Lower Yatton.

'At his trial, Taylor Brown's brief claimed Kershaw forced his confession out of him,' Paniatowski said. 'Police records, on the other hand, state that Kershaw wasn't even in the building at the time.'

'So maybe Taylor Brown was lying,' Beresford suggested.

Paniatowski snorted. 'It was a serious charge, but the judge only gave him two years – which suggests to me that while the jury might have swallowed the police version of events hook, line and sinker, his honour had serious doubts.'

The signpost said they were now only three miles from Lower Yatton. Paniatowski switched off the siren, and the cars behind them followed suit.

'There's no chance that Taylor Brown was innocent, is there?' Beresford asked.

'What are you suggesting? Surely not that your great hero – Chief Superintendent St Thomas Kershaw – would actually fit up an *innocent* man?'

'That was uncalled for, Monika,' Beresford said.

'You're right, and I'm sorry I said it. But to answer your question, no, I don't think there's much doubt that Taylor Brown was guilty as charged.'

'So if Mr Kershaw *did* force a confession out of him . . .'

'I think we can take that as read.'

'. . . then Taylor Brown must know that, without Kershaw's intervention, he'd never have gone to jail.'

'Yes, he must.'

'And that's a powerful motive for revenge.'

It was, Paniatowski agreed silently.

The village was now less than half a mile away, and they could clearly see the large old house on the edge of it, which had been the vicarage in the days when the Church of England was still a thriving concern.

'That's where he lives,' Beresford said. 'It must be at least a hundred yards away from any of the other houses.'

'At least,' Paniatowski agreed.

'And that gives him all the privacy he needs to do whatever he wants,' Beresford said.

'Yes,' Paniatowski replied.

And she was thinking, if Elaine Kershaw *is* in there, please God let her still be alive.

SEVENTEEN

From the end of the driveway, they could see the whole of the old vicarage through the windscreen, but as they drew ever closer – Beresford's foot still hard down on the accelerator and the speedometer needle hovering at around sixty miles an hour – the panorama narrowed, and their eyes became focussed on the front door.

There was an old carriage turning circle just yards from the house, and the moment his front wheels crossed on to it, Beresford stamped down on the brake. The car juddered, rocked, and slewed to the right. Gravel chips flew in all directions, some disappearing harmlessly into the undergrowth, some hitting the cars behind with a dull metallic thud.

And as the rest of the convey screeched to a halt behind them, Beresford and Paniatowski were already out of their own vehicle and sprinting desperately towards the house.

The front door resisted the first assault from the heel of Beresford's shoe, but at the second, the wood around the keyhole splintered, and it swung complainingly open.

The large hallway lay ahead of them – the place where, in times gone by, the vicar would have received his guests. There was an elaborate staircase ascending to the left, and a much narrower set of stairs descending to the right. Beyond the stairs was a series of doors.

The first wave of officers from the other cars had already arrived in the hall.

'Target?' Paniatowski shouted.

'Basement, ma'am!' the sergeant bellowed back.

'It's down those stairs! And for Christ's sake be careful – because the man we're after is a really vicious bastard!'

More officers appeared in the doorway.

The second team had already been given the ground floor, and the third – led by Beresford – was soon thundering up the staircase.

Alone in a hall which, seconds earlier, had been pandemonium – and now was eerily still – Paniatowski looked around her.

The place was a real mess, she thought. The carpet was encrusted with years of filth, and the walls were stained with the vomit of someone who hadn't quite made it to the toilet. It looked more like a squat than the home of a member of an aristocratic brewing family.

A constable appeared in one of doorways.

'The kitchen is clear, ma'am,' he said.

So what? Paniatowski thought.

She'd never expected the kitchen to play a significant part in the search anyway.

But what about the rest of the house?

Was it about to divulge some good news – or was there only the *worst* kind of news waiting for her lads to find?

She crossed the hall and entered the kitchen. It was a big room, filled with expensive equipment, but, once again, it was the dirt which made the strongest impression.

Plates were piled up in the sink, encrusted with barely touched food which was now covered in mould. Aluminium trays, which had once contained takeaway food, were scattered haphazardly across the floor. Cigarette ends – carelessly dropped without even being extinguished – had left brown burn marks on the glazed tiles. And the whole place stank.

It was all wrong, Paniatowski thought, on the verge of despair. The house that the man they were looking for lived in shouldn't have been anything like this.

The leaders of the search teams began to filter into the kitchen. 'Nothing in the basement, ma'am,' one of them said.

'The ground floor's clear, ma'am,' a second reported.

Wrong, Paniatowski told herself. It's all bloody wrong!

Finally, Beresford arrived. 'We've found Taylor Brown, boss,' he said. 'He's upstairs.'

'Just him?' Paniatowski asked, knowing even as she spoke that she was wasting her breath. 'Not her?'

'No,' Beresford said heavily. 'Not her. I'm afraid there's absolutely no trace of her at all.'

The Ajax Novelty Company was based in an industrial unit on the edge of Bolton. It was divided into four parts, the workshop and warehouse being the larger two, with the dispatching and office sections looking as if they'd been squeezed – with some effort – into what space was left.

The managing director, Geoff Combes, looked more like a department store Santa Claus than a purveyor of somewhat dubious merchandise, but he seemed relaxed enough about being visited by the police and warmly invited Meadows and Crane into his tiny office.

'It's a business like any other business,' he explained when they'd sat down, jamming their knees under the visitors' side of the desk. 'We saw a need, and we filled it.' He rubbed his hands across his Father Christmas belly. 'Now, how can I help you, officers?'

Meadows slid the pictures of the shoes and the corset across the desk.

'What can you tell me about these?' she asked.

'The Lady Zelda and the Bride of Dracula,' Combes said, with obvious pleasure. 'They're both the top of the range, and they're both custom-made.'

'And if I wanted to buy either of these items, how would I go about it?' Meadows asked.

'They'd suit you,' Combes said, instinctively running his eyes up and down her body. 'You've got just the right build to show them off to their best advantage.' He checked himself. 'Sorry, what was the question again?'

'Where would I buy them from?'

'Well, you'd have three choices. You could buy them directly by mail order from us, you could go to one of the stores we stock, or you could ask one of our travelling salesmen to call.'

'You're joking, aren't you?' Crane said.

'What about?' Combes wondered.

'That you actually have travelling salesmen?'

'And why wouldn't we?'

Crane looked stuck for a tactful answer.

'Well, it's just that, given what you sell, I'd have thought your customers would want to be as anonymous as possible,' he said lamely.

Combes chuckled. 'Some do, some don't. But you're right that the majority of our customers would prefer their friends and neighbours not to know what they get up to behind closed doors. And that's exactly where those salesmen of ours come into their own.'

'I'm not following,' Crane admitted.

'Most men wouldn't be seen dead in a sex shop. And having something sent in a plain wrapper through the post has its disadvantages too – because not only does it seem a little sordid to some people, but the postman might actually guess what it is he's delivering. On the other hand, buying from one of our salesmen is an entirely different matter. He's well dressed, and when he visits you at your home or your office, he's carrying a smart attaché case. He can show you leather bonds, and make it sound as if what he's actually offering you is *gilt-edged* bonds. And yet, at the same time, and on an entirely different level, both the salesman and the customer know that the transaction they're involved in is just a little bit dirty – and there's a real thrill for the customer in that.'

'You're quite the little psychologist on the sly, aren't you, Mr Combes?' Kate Meadows said drily.

'I like to think so,' Combes replied, complacently.

'So your customers are mainly men?' Meadows said.

'That's right,' Combes agreed. 'Occasionally, one of our salesmen will sell to a couple – or even a woman on her own – but it's mostly men. They buy these things as a surprise for their wives and girlfriends, you see.' He chuckled again. 'My wife would certainly be *surprised* if I took any of our products home. And then she'd *surprise* me out of the front door – with my suitcase following shortly afterwards.'

'You mentioned that both the shoes and corset were made-to-measure,' Meadows said.

'That's right,' Combes agreed. 'For some of our clients, it's very important to get *exactly* the right fit.'

'So you'll have records of where the goods were sent?'

'We certainly will. But I'm afraid I can't show them to you. Client confidentiality and all that, you know.'

'I quite understand,' Meadows said sweetly. 'I'm not in the business of asking people to betray their professional confidences.'

'Good, because—'

'But I *am* in the business of making sure that anyone who stops me doing my job suffers for it,' Meadows continued, with a hardness and certainty to her voice that made even Crane feel uneasy. 'And I do *mean* suffers.'

'I'll . . . I'll get the ledger,' Combes said shakily.

'Will you? That would be *very* kind of you,' Meadows replied, all sweetness and light again.

Paniatowski felt an overwhelming urge to get out into the fresh air – away from both the stink of the house itself and from the smell of her own failure – so she opened the kitchen door, and stepped out in the back garden.

It was a big garden and, like the house itself, it must once have been ordered and attractive. But nothing had been done to it for a long time – probably since Taylor Brown had been sent to prison for torturing his housekeeper – and now it was a wilderness, the paths overgrown, the flower beds buried in weeds, the trees covered in fungi and other unpleasant infestations.

'I know what's going through your mind,' said a voice from behind her, 'but it still *could be* him that we're looking for.'

She spun round to face Beresford.

'For God's sake, Colin, give it up!' she said angrily. 'The man can't even manage to feed himself properly, let alone kidnap two women!'

'We've always thought it was possible that he might have had a partner,' Beresford pointed out. 'Maybe it was the partner who did the kidnapping.'

'And why would anybody want to go into partnership with a man like that? What the hell has *he* got that he could bring to any partnership?'

'He's got the experience. And maybe the partner was afraid to do it alone – maybe he needed the moral support.'

'You're clutching at straws.'

'Or perhaps, given that Mrs Kershaw was one of the victims, it wasn't really a partnership at all,' Beresford speculated. 'Perhaps Taylor Brown simply paid the other man to do what he was unable to do himself.'

'That's ridiculous!' Paniatowski said.

'I don't think it is,' Beresford argued. 'Taylor Brown must still have money in the bank, and he's certainly got enough reason to hate Mr Kershaw.'

'Then if this is all about revenge, why kidnap and torture poor little Grace Meade?'

'I never said it was *all* about revenge. Taylor Brown likes torturing women just for the sheer pleasure of it. Or maybe it was his assistant – or his partner, or whatever you want to call him – who insisted on kidnapping two women instead of one. Maybe they enjoy it more if they're torturing two women at the same time. I don't know, Monika, I really don't – because I can't get my mind around things in the same way that they must.'

'No, I don't suppose you can,' Paniatowski agreed. 'All you *can* do is to offer me a long list of maybes.'

'Come on, Monika, you can't rule Taylor Brown out, just because everything about him doesn't fall as neatly into place as you'd like it to,' Beresford pleaded.

'You're right,' Paniatowski agreed. 'Where is he?'

'He's still up in his bedroom. He said he's not coming out unless he's arrested.'

'Then I suppose I'd better go and talk to him,' Paniatowski said, without enthusiasm.

'Only two pairs of the Madame Zelda were ever made in anything like the size you've given me,' Combes said, consulting his ledger.

'And what happened to them?' Meadows asked.

'The order was placed with one of our salesmen, a chap called Brian Waites.' Combes turned a page in the ledger. 'He was also the one who ordered the Bride of Dracula corset, so maybe that was for the same client.'

'And what's this client's name?'

'Ah, there I'm afraid I can't help you.'

'Remember what I was saying earlier – about getting upset when someone stops me doing my job?' Meadows asked.

'I mean I *really* can't help you,' Combes said hastily. 'We have records of the order from our tailoring department, of course, but we won't have any for the actual transaction.'

'No records at all?'

'Well, the name and address of the client will have been written down in the salesman's order book . . .'

'Then show us that!'

'I don't have it.'

'Why not?'

'We *never* get to see the salesmen's order books. They work on a commission basis, you see, and they feel – wrongly, of course – that if we had the addresses of their clients, we'd hand those clients over to another salesman, who'd work for a smaller commission.'

'Now wherever would they have got that idea from?' Meadows mused.

Combes looked distinctly uncomfortable. 'There was a misunderstanding once,' he admitted. 'You see, we did have this particular salesman who—'

'I need to speak to the salesman who placed the order,' Meadows interrupted him. 'You said his name was Brian Waites, didn't you?'

'Err . . . talking to Brian might prove a little difficult,' Combes admitted. 'You see, he ran up rather a lot of debts and, in the end, he decided that the easiest way to pay them off would be to help himself to the money we keep in the safe. The moment we found out, of course, we had to inform the police. We really had no other option.'

'So he's in jail, is he?' Meadows asked impatiently.

'Regrettably not. He did what you might call "a runner", and the local police have no idea where he might be.'

'Which means you've no idea where his order book might be, either?' Meadows asked.

'Just so,' Combes agreed.

Taylor Brown's bedroom was in as bad a state – if not a worse one – as the rest of the house. The sheets were filthy, the windows were coated in grime, and the floor was littered with bottles.

The Honourable Reginald George Taylor Brown himself was sitting in an armchair, wrapped in a bathrobe which it was just possible to discern had once been white. He was a shadow of a man – far too shrunken and insignificant to fill his posh name. With his claw-like right hand, he was picking at threads in the arm of the chair, and had almost stripped away the fabric down to the wood. His left eye was flickering uncontrollably, and there was spittle at the corner of his mouth.

'Why won't you just leave me alone?' he moaned, when he saw Paniatowski standing over him.

It would be a kindness to both of them if she did, Paniatowski thought, but she supposed she had better go through the motions.

'Tell me about Elaine Kershaw,' she said.

Taylor Brown looked up at her blankly.

'Who?'

'Or better yet, tell me about Grace Meade.'

'I . . . I don't know what you're talking about.'

'Don't play the innocent with me,' Paniatowski said harshly. 'Even if you'd had absolutely nothing to do with Grace's abduction, you'd still have read about it in the newspapers.'

'I don't read newspapers,' Taylor Brown said. 'I don't read anything any more.' Then, a sudden sign of life flashed across his dead eyes, and he asked, 'Is the first woman you mentioned related to Chief Superintendent Kershaw?'

'She's his wife.'

Taylor Brown began to cry. 'He fitted me up,' he said. 'He sent me into the jaws of hell.'

The garden was an ugly testament to what neglect could do. Actually, it was more than that, Beresford thought – it was a savage reminder of how thin the line really was between chaos and order. But even so, faced with the choice of battling with the undergrowth or returning to the house, he chose to battle through the undergrowth.

He had not been expecting his expedition to turn up anything of real interest, which was why, when he reached the bottom of the garden and actually *did* find something in front of the rickety, rotting shed, he paid more attention to his discovery than he might otherwise have done.

The *something* in question was the remains of a small fire which had been set inside a metal box. As fires went, it had not been entirely successful, he noted, for though there were ashes enough, he could also see bits of charred newspaper sticking out.

He bent down, and touched the ashes with the back of his hand. They were cold, but damp.

It was obvious what had happened. The fire had not been burning strongly enough to resist a sudden November downpour of rain, and had gone out before it had completed its work.

But he was not so much interested in the actual fire itself as he was in who had lit it.

Could Taylor Brown have started it?

Given both the state of the house and the state of the man, it was hard to imagine him battling his way through the under-growth in order to do it. And why should he *want* a fire, anyway?

Could it have been one of the neighbours?

Beresford walked over to the back wall. The problem with that theory was that the vicarage was separated from the nearest neighbour by a field. And while the wall was low enough for any reasonably agile man to climb over without much difficulty, why would anyone make the effort, when it would be just as easy to start a fire in their own back garden?

He broke off a twig from a sad-looking tree, and started to poke through the ashes of the fire.

And that was when he discovered that the newspaper was not the only thing that had failed to burn properly.

'Prison completely destroyed me,' Taylor Brown whined. 'It was no place for a gentleman, and you can't imagine what I had to endure while I was there.' He ran the back of his hand across his nose to clear away the mucus. 'The rabble I was

locked up with hated me because I was better than them. They
beat me, they scalded me with hot water, they . . . they made
me eat food that I'd seen them urinate in. They took my life
away from me.'

'Well, that's the way it goes,' Paniatowski said, unsympathetic-
ally. 'I wouldn't think Sonia, your ex-housekeeper, has quite the
same rosy a view of life as she once had, either.'

'My family tried their best to keep me out of prison,' Taylor
Brown said, 'but once I'd been convicted, they didn't want
anything to do with me. They still don't. They're *ashamed*
of me!'

'Fancy that,' Paniatowski said. 'Some people are just so
unreasonable, aren't they?'

Wrapped up in his own self-pity, it was doubtful if Taylor
Brown even heard her.

'Kershaw *made me* sign the confession,' he said. 'It's all his
fault. Everything that has happened to me is *his* fault.'

'He wasn't the one who tortured Sonia,' Paniatowski pointed
out. 'That was you.'

'She liked it,' Taylor Brown said, unconvincingly.

'And did Denise like it, as well?' Paniatowski asked.

'Who?'

'The girl you slashed with your razor on Market Street, a
couple of weeks ago. Did *she* like it?'

'That was her own fault.'

'Everything seems to be somebody else's fault, doesn't it?'
Paniatowski asked. 'So tell me, how is Denise to blame for what
happened to her?'

'It was her fault because she wouldn't help me.'

'She wouldn't do *what*?'

'Do you realize how much courage it took for me to even
approach her, after everything that's happened to me?' Taylor
Brown asked. 'But I did it. I was very brave. And if she'd only
done what I wanted her to, I might have started to get my confidence back. But she wouldn't. She *laughed* at me. If she hadn't
moved when she did, I'd have slashed her face until there was
nothing left of it. That's what she deserved.'

It was hopeless, Paniatowski thought. Taylor Brown was one
of the vilest creatures she'd ever met. And no doubt he would
have been more than delighted to torture Grace Meade and Elaine

Kershaw if he'd had the opportunity. But he could never have accomplished such a thing alone.

And even the possibility that he had a partner – an idea which had never shone very brightly – was growing dimmer and dimmer by the minute, because if someone else *had been* involved, Taylor Brown would surely have tried to shift the entire blame on to him by now.

It had all been a complete waste of time.

'*You'd better make damn sure you get it right!*' Chief Superintendent Kershaw had said, threateningly.

And she hadn't. Whichever way she looked at it, she bloody hadn't!

Beresford appeared in the doorway, and said, 'Can you spare me a minute, boss?'

Paniatowski stepped out in the corridor.

'We can charge this bastard with the assault on Denise – which will at least ensure he's back in prison – but that's it,' she said despondently.

Beresford smiled. It was not quite a smile of triumph – that would have been putting it far too strongly – but it was at least a smile of relief.

'I wouldn't be too sure that's all we can do, Monika,' he said. 'Somebody lit a fire in the garden – I suspect it was Taylor Brown's accomplice – but he didn't quite manage to burn everything he intended to burn. And the thing he *didn't* quite burn was this.'

He reached into his pocket and produced a transparent evidence envelope. Inside it was a piece of cloth, irregularly shaped and charred at the edges. It was not large – no more than two inches in one direction and three in the other – but it was a big enough sample for Paniatowski to see that it was a blue, silky, translucent material.

'That matches the description of the nightdress Elaine Kershaw was probably wearing when she was abducted!' Paniatowski said.

'Yes, it does, doesn't it?' Beresford agreed.

EIGHTEEN

I f the Pride of Bolton public house really *was* the pride of Bolton, then the town was in deep trouble, Jack Crane thought, as he surveyed the tobacco-stained ceiling and peeling wallpaper from his strategic position at the bar. Still, it did have the advantage of being the closest pub to the Ajax Novelty Company, and the pint of bitter the barman was currently pulling for him looked inviting enough.

He took his pint – and Meadows' tonic water – over to the table where the sergeant was sitting, deep in thought.

'Thanks,' Meadows said, absently, when he placed her glass down in front of her.

'So what do you think we've learned from our visit to Mr Combes' cosy little establishment, Sarge?' Crane asked.

'I think we learned that our killer's been planning this whole operation of his for a long time,' Kate Meadows replied.

'And you're not just talking about Mrs Kershaw being kidnapped, are you?'

'No, I'm not. I'm almost certain that it was always his intention to kidnap Grace Meade, too – or, if not Grace herself, then someone very like her.'

'And what's brought you to this conclusion? The shoes?'

'Yes, the shoes. He had *two* pairs of shoes made-to-measure – and that means he had *two* victims in mind, right from the start.'

'It bothers me that he's been so careless – especially when you consider that he's never put a foot wrong before,' Crane admitted.

'Careless?'

'If Brian Waites hadn't decided to steal the cash from the safe and then do a runner, he'd already have given us a description of the man he sold the shoes to, wouldn't he?'

'Yes.'

'But the killer couldn't possibly have known what Waites was going to do, so he was taking a huge – and unnecessary – risk.'

'It was certainly a risk, but as far as he was concerned, it wasn't an unnecessary one,' Meadows said. 'In fact, it was *very* necessary.'

'I don't understand.'

'Everything about the whole business had to be *right* – whatever danger that might put him in.'

'I'm still not there,' Crane admitted.

'No, of course you're not,' Meadows replied. 'How could you be?' She paused for a moment. 'You're not a virgin, are you, Jack?'

Crane felt himself flush. 'Why do you ask?' he said. 'Do I look like one? Do I *act* like one?'

'I'd have said not,' Meadows replied. 'But appearances can sometimes be deceptive. So, how would you describe your career as a *non-virgin*? Has it been successful?'

This was getting to sound eerily like his early morning conversation with DI Beresford, Crane thought.

'Are you asking me if I've slept with a lot of girls?' he asked.

'Yes.'

'That's not really relevant to the matter in hand, now is it?' Crane asked, a little huffily.

Meadows smiled. 'That's where you're wrong,' she told him. 'I'm about to explain something quite complicated, and I need to know if you're in a position to really understand it.'

'And how can that – whatever it is – possibly relate to my sex life?'

Meadows' smile widened. 'Just answer the question, Jack.'

'I've . . . er . . . had my share of successes,' Crane admitted, reluctantly.

Meadows nodded. 'Good! And tell me, Jack, have you ever taken a girl to bed when you knew you shouldn't have – when you knew, in fact, that you'd only be building up trouble for yourself?'

'Oh yes,' Crane said, with real feeling. 'Oh yes, indeed.'

Her name is Lisa. He knows she is not his soulmate and never will be, but she certainly has a very strong thing for him.

For months, she has been pestering him. He has tried being kind and sympathetic, and he has tried being downright rude – and nothing has worked. Then, one night, she visits him in his rooms at college.

*'I know you don't love me, but that doesn't matter any more,'
she says. 'I just want to sleep with you.'*

'It's not a good idea,' he tells her.

'Most men would jump at the offer,' she says.

*And so they would, he thinks. She is a very attractive girl. She
is a very nice girl. She is just not for him.*

*'I don't expect it to change anything between us,' she says. 'I
just want to feel you between my legs.'*

*She might believe that now, but she won't believe it in the
morning, he thinks. In the morning, things will look very different.*

*He paces the room. If he wants a woman – a woman without
complications – he can get one easily enough, he tells himself.
So there is no need for this.*

And still she is sitting on his bed.

'Please!' she says.

*And that should have been warning enough – that should have
said, in capital letters, that this was a BAD IDEA.*

'If it's what you want,' he says.

He wakes up in the morning with her snuggling up to him.

'Well?' she says. 'I was right, wasn't I?'

'About what?'

'About us. And now you can see it, too.'

There is a scene – an inevitable scene.

But it does not stop there.

She writes him desperate notes.

*She is waiting in ambush for him every time he leaves his
room.*

*And then, towards the end of the Trinity Term, she slits her
wrists.*

*It was never a serious attempt at suicide. He knows that. But
he is weighed down by guilt for a long time.*

*And not just guilt, but anger with himself – because the whole
thing could so easily have been avoided.*

'So you knew it was a mistake from the start,' Meadows said,
half-amused, half-serious. 'So why did you do it?'

'Because I just couldn't help myself,' Crane confessed.

'Then you have some idea of what it's like to be a fetishist,'
Meadows continued, her voice suddenly much deeper – much

more intense. 'A reason a lot of women submit to pain is not for the pleasure it brings them – though the pleasure is undoubtedly there – but because they *have to*, because there is something inside them driving them to it. So they run the risk of being shunned by the friends they've known all their lives – and of being ridiculed by people who are not fit to lick their boots – because they have no choice in the matter!'

'I still don't see where you're going with this,' Crane said.

And he didn't – though it did cast a certain light on the conversation he'd had with Beresford.

'The killer's in exactly the same situation,' Meadows continued. 'He has a vision of how this whole grisly business should be carried out – and those red shoes are part of it. They're in his head. He didn't consciously put them there, but they won't go away. He has to have them – whatever the consequences.'

'Jesus!' Crane said.

'Well, it's a theory, anyway,' Meadows said, sounding much more like her normal self now. She stood up. 'I suppose I'd better check in with headquarters, hadn't I?'

'Good idea,' Crane replied shakily.

The Pride of Bolton's payphone, like most pub payphones, was in the corridor next to the toilets, and when Meadows was connected to Whitebridge Police HQ, she asked to speak to Monika Paniatowski.

'The DCI's left word she's in interrogation and is not to be disturbed for the rest of the day,' the switchboard operator said. 'But I can put you through to DI Beresford, if you like.'

I don't like, Meadows thought – I don't like at all!

'That would be fine,' she said aloud.

'It's me, Meadows,' she told Beresford, when he came on to the line. 'We've developed what we think might turn out to be a really good lead here, sir.'

'What sort of lead?' Beresford asked.

'We know who provided the killer with the shoes, but we haven't been able to trace him yet, so we'd like to stay in Bolton for a little longer.'

'Would you?' Beresford asked, in a cold, distant voice. 'And how much longer is a *little* longer?'

'We don't know. Until we find him, I suppose.'

'So it could be a *lot* longer, couldn't it?'

'That's a possibility,' Meadows conceded. 'But it is a *good* lead, sir.'

'It may well be,' Beresford agreed. 'It may even be an excellent one – but I've got other priorities at the moment, and I want you back here within the hour.'

'Is this personal, sir?'

'Personal?' Beresford repeated. 'What do you mean?'

'Does the fact that you won't let me follow up on my lead have anything to do with what happened between us last night?'

'No, it doesn't,' Beresford replied angrily. 'It has nothing to do with that at all!'

'I'm not sure I believe that, sir,' Meadows said.

'I don't give a toss about what you believe. I want you back in Whitebridge, Sergeant Meadows – and the *reason* I want you back is that the shit's about to hit the fan.'

Reginald Taylor Brown sat hunched up at the interview table, his hands clasped so tightly that they could have been welded together.

'I'm cold,' he moaned. 'I'm very cold.'

So am I, Paniatowski thought. That's what happens when you turn the heating off in the middle of November.

She stood up and stripped off her jacket. 'It's not cold at all, Reg – not for someone with a clear conscience.'

'Could I have a blanket, please?' Taylor Brown asked.

'Of course,' Paniatowski agreed. 'But you have to earn it by answering a few questions first. All right?'

'All right.'

He looked so pathetic – so helpless – she thought. And if she'd been watching someone else conduct this interrogation, she'd have been convinced they were questioning the wrong man.

But it was all an act he was putting on. A good act, admittedly, and one that had been completely convincing back at the old vicarage. But once Beresford had found the remnant of the nightdress in the garden, she'd seen right through that act – and she wasn't about to be fooled again.

'You're a mess,' she said. 'You could never have organized two kidnappings and one murder.'

'That's . . . that's what I've been telling you all along.'

'In fact, the more I think about it, the more I'm convinced that the whole thing was your partner's idea.'

She said it – but she didn't believe that for a second. It had been Taylor Brown who had wanted Elaine kidnapped – Taylor Brown who had yearned for revenge on Kershaw.

The suspect said nothing.

'It's even possible that you didn't *want* to do it at all,' she continued. 'That you only went along with it because he threatened to hurt you if you didn't.'

There was no logic behind that statement, and she knew it.

If Taylor Brown hadn't been behind the kidnapping, it would never have happened at all.

But this wasn't about logic – it was about offering him the illusion that there was still a chance he could escape from the consequences of his own evil actions.

'Is that what happened?' she asked. '*Did* he threaten you?'

'I . . . I don't have a partner,' Taylor Brown mumbled.

There could be only one reason why he was holding back, Paniatowski told herself, and that was because he didn't want his partner caught before he had completed the task that he'd been set.

And what that meant, in turn, was that it was more than likely that Elaine Kershaw was still alive!

'What do you think he's going to say when we catch him?' she asked. 'And we *will* catch him – have no doubts about that.'

'Don't know what you're talking about,' Taylor Brown told her.

'He'll say that it was all your idea – that he'd never have done it if you hadn't talked him into it. Then it will be too late for you to tell the truth – because everybody will already have accepted his version of events. So he'll get off with a short sentence, and you'll never see the light of day again. Is that what you want?'

It was an effective argument. She'd sat across the table from guilty men a score of times and had seen it work – had been able to follow every twist and turn of their thinking.

Why should I take most of the blame? they'd asked themselves.

And in no time at all, they'd be convinced that the policewoman was right – that they were almost entirely innocent of the crime, and the fault lay with their partners.

But it wasn't going to work with this man, because he'd abandoned any hope for the future, and all that was keeping him going was his desire for revenge.

'Tell me where you're keeping Elaine Kershaw,' she coaxed. 'Just give me a hint. Is it in a house? A barn? A shed?'

'I don't know where she is.'

'So your partner didn't tell you,' Paniatowski jeered. 'He didn't even trust you enough to let you know where he'd taken her! You're not *really* his partner at all, are you? You're nothing but his dupe. And while you're in here, cold and miserable, he's out there – laughing at you!'

'I don't have a partner,' Taylor Brown sobbed. 'Please believe me, I don't have a partner!'

'I'll bet he didn't even trust you to light the fire,' Paniatowski mocked. 'I'll bet he even did that simple job himself.'

'What fire?' Taylor Brown asked.

'The one at the bottom of your garden. You remember? The one you tried to burn Elaine's nightdress on?'

'I . . . don't . . . know . . . anything . . . about . . . a . . . fire,' Taylor Brown said.

He was good, Paniatowski admitted. Driven by a hatred that was stronger than any love he might ever have felt – stronger than even the instinct for self-preservation – he was *very* good.

She did not think he would crack, but she had to go on trying.

'Can I . . . can I have that blanket now?' he asked.

'You won't need it,' she told him. 'I'm turning up the heat.'

Beresford was sitting at his desk, a mug of strong tea within easy reach of his left hand, a cigarette – burned almost down to the filter – in his right.

'Any progress?' Paniatowski asked.

The inspector shook his head despondently. 'Not really. I've got some of my lads checking on Brown's background – who his friends were when he was at school, who he might have met when he was in prison, whether or not he belongs to any clubs or associations . . . you know the drill.'

'Yes,' Paniatowski agreed. 'I know the drill.'

'I've put the rest of the team on door-to-door. They've been told to ask the neighbours what visitors he's had, and whether they've seen any strangers around. But, as you know yourself, his house is a fair distance from the rest of the village – and if *I* had a neighbour like him, I know I'd do my level best to ignore him completely.'

'What about the search of the house?' Paniatowski asked. 'Has that turned up anything that might conceivably give us a lead?'

'No, all it's done is to confirm what we all already know about him. There were some masks and whips – though they didn't look like they'd been used for years – and there were some fairly recent magazines.'

'What kind of magazines?'

'The kind you'd have expected us to find –' Beresford slid an evidence envelope across the desk to her – 'including an old favourite.'

'And if either Grace or Elaine were ever there, there's no evidence of that now?' Paniatowski asked – though she already knew that if there had been, it would have been the first thing that Beresford mentioned.

'It's possible we will find some trace of them when we've sifted through all the filth,' Beresford said, 'but I'm not holding my breath while I'm waiting. Taylor Brown might be a complete bloody nutter, but he was clever enough to put on that act for us – an act that had us completely fooled for a while – and I think he was also clever enough to have the women taken to somewhere that has no connection with him.'

'Keep plugging away at it,' Paniatowski said – because there was nothing more positive she *could* say.

'I will,' Beresford told her. 'What about you, boss? Are you planning to have another go at Taylor Brown?'

Paniatowski nodded. 'Cold hasn't worked on him, so I've had the thermostat adjusted to make it like an oven in there. And I'll stay with him all night, if that's what it takes.'

'Or until he asks for a lawyer,' Beresford said.

'He won't ask for a lawyer.'

Why should he? No lawyer would be able to save him, and he knew that. And by fighting off the interrogation on his own – by holding out until what he needed to happen *had* actually happened – he was probably rebuilding a little of his self-respect.

'Elaine could already be dead, you know,' Paniatowski said – because *somebody* had to say it.

'Yes, I do know that,' Beresford agreed gravely.

It had been dark in the woods for some time, but Lennie and Timmy had thought of that in advance, and had brought their torches with them.

At first, the darkness had only added spice to their mission – making it even more mysterious and exciting. Now, however, both the mystery and excitement were wearing thin, at least for Timmy.

If they were ever going to find a body, he told himself, they would have found it by now, because they had been searching for at least an hour. Besides, it was getting cold, he was hungry, and though the darkness didn't scare him – of course it didn't! – he would have felt much more comfortable on a well-lit street.

'I think we should pack it in,' he said.

'What's the matter?' Lennie asked. 'You're surely not frightened of the bogie men, are you?'

'Course not.'

'Then we'll give it another five minutes.'

Since neither of them had a watch, Timmy knew that the five minutes would be *Lennie's* five minutes – and that Lennie's five minutes could be at least half an hour – but he didn't see how he could turn down such a reasonable request without seeming chicken.

'All right,' he agreed. 'Five minutes. But I'm counting them,' he added, searching for a compromise which would avoid either of them losing face.

'We'll *both* count them,' Lennie said.

They wandered along, both chanting, 'One . . . two . . . three . . . four . . . five . . . six . . .' though at considerably different speeds.

It was as they were reaching the edge of the woods, and were navigating their way through a clump of bushes, that Lennie suddenly took a dive.

'Stop messing about!' Timmy called to him, starting to feel really scared now.

'I've fallen over something!' Lennie said excitedly. 'Come and look!'

It was a sack he'd fallen over – a long thinnish sack tied at the top.

'It pongs a bit!' Lennie said.

'It pongs a lot!' Timmy corrected him.

Lennie climbed to his feet. He poked the sack with his stick, and it yielded to the pressure.

Maybe they had found a body, Timmy thought. He'd never *really* believed they would – but maybe they had.

'There's not much more we can do in the dark,' Lennie said, in a thin squeaky voice which was not his own.

'No, we'd best be getting off home,' Timmy agreed, eagerly.

They walked the first few paces, then, abandoning all pretence, their walk became a run, and eventually a gallop.

The temperature in the interview room was almost unbearable, and Paniatowski could feel sweat running down her back in half a dozen hot little streams.

Taylor Brown looked uncomfortable, too, but he did not complain about the heat, as he had about the cold.

Maybe he thought he needed to get used to it, since he was probably expecting to spend an eternity in Hell, Paniatowski thought.

You're so tired that you're getting whimsical! she told herself angrily. And you can't afford that.

She looked up at the clock.

Twenty minutes to ten!

They had been sitting in this room facing each other – she and Taylor Brown – for well over six hours.

She'd have to take a break from it soon.

She *needed* to take a break soon.

Besides, she'd arranged to meet the team at half past ten.

She'd make one last attempt to crack the suspect, and then someone else would just have to take over for a while, she thought.

She reached into her handbag, and took out a small package.

'What's that?' Taylor Brown asked.

'Now isn't that interesting?' Paniatowski mused.

'Isn't what interesting?'

'You want to know what I've taken out of my handbag, yet you've shown no curiosity at all about the envelope that's lying on the table.'

Nor had he. She had placed the envelope midway between them at the start of this last leg of the interrogation, and he had not so much as glanced at it.

But then, why should he be curious, when he'd probably already guessed what it contained?

She opened the packet and took out a pair of sterilized gloves.

Her hands were so sticky with sweat that slipping the gloves on wasn't an easy task at all, but – given the fascinated horror with which Taylor Brown was watching the whole process – that could only work to her advantage.

'You're . . . you're not going to touch me, are you?' the suspect asked worriedly. 'I don't like being touched by women.'

'Trust me, Reg, I wouldn't touch you if my life depended on it,' Paniatowski said, opening the envelope. 'But what I am going to do is show you some of the evidence against you.' She pulled out the glossy magazine. 'This is called *The Joy of Pain*, Reg. We found it in your house.'

'It's not mine,' Taylor Brown mumbled.

'Of course it's yours,' Paniatowski said dismissively. 'It's got your fingerprints all over it. We're going to look at it together, Reg. What particular page would you like me to turn to?'

'Doesn't matter. Don't care.'

'Then let's start in the middle,' Paniatowski suggested. She opened the magazine. 'Oh look, Reg, it's a double-page advert for the Ajax Novelty Company. Have you seen that advertisement before, Reg?'

'I don't know,' Taylor Brown said.

'Of course you know,' Paniatowski said, her voice hardening. 'Have you seen it or not?'

'I've seen it.'

'So you'll have noticed the snazzy red shoes, won't you? Take another look at them.'

'Don't want to.'

'Do it – or maybe I will decide to touch you, after all!'

Slowly and reluctantly, Taylor Brown lowered his eyes so that they were focussed on the advertisement.

'I can tell what's going through your mind, Reg,' Paniatowski said. 'You're imagining what it would feel like to slip one of those shoes on to the foot of a small, delicate woman, aren't you?'

'You know I am,' Taylor Brown gasped.

And no doubt it was giving him a huge erection, Paniatowski thought in disgust – though thankfully that was hidden by the table.

'But I've never done more than imagine it,' Taylor Brown said. 'I didn't buy the shoes and I didn't put them on any woman's foot. I haven't been near a woman since I came out of prison.'

'Except for Denise Slater,' Paniatowski said.

'And I even made a mess of that, didn't I?' Taylor Brown countered, and began crying again.

Paniatowski turned to the uniformed constable who was standing silently and patiently by the door.

'Could you go and find Sergeant Lee?' she said. 'I'd like him to take over from me for a while.'

'That would mean leaving you alone with the suspect, ma'am,' the constable pointed out.

'That's no problem,' Paniatowski assured him. 'Reg here only attacks *helpless* women. Isn't that right, Reg?'

Taylor Brown, who – even through the tears – was still fixated on the magazine, said nothing.

The constable opened the door, and stepped out into the corridor.

I've failed again, Paniatowski thought miserably.

The three of them – Beresford, Meadows and Crane – had been sitting in silence at the usual table in the Drum and Monkey for quite a while.

And it wasn't a *companionable* silence, Crane thought – the sort of silence there sometimes was within a group of people who knew each other so well that there was no real need to talk. No, it was an *uncomfortable* silence, made worse by the fact that DS Meadows and DI Beresford seemed barely willing to make eye contact with each other.

What was going on between them would have to be sorted out, he told himself – if not for their own good, then for the good of the team.

But *who* would sort it out? That was the question!

He wasn't about to alert the boss to their difficulties, and he doubted that either of them would, either.

And *he* couldn't sort it out, because the problem with taking on the role of kindly Uncle Jack was that they were both older than him, and both outranked him.

At twenty-five to eleven, Paniatowski arrived.

'Let's hear it, then,' she said, the moment that she'd sat down.

'Taylor Brown seems to have been a particularly nasty piece of work even when he was at school,' Beresford said. 'He had his own little gang, which picked on the weaker kids.'

'And has he stayed in touch with any of them?'

'We don't believe so. We spoke to one of his old mates, and he said – and I quote exactly – "The problem with Reginald is that, while the rest of us put aside childish things eventually, he never quite seemed able to. And it reached the point, to be perfectly honest, where I was embarrassed to even be seen talking to him."'

'What about the friends he made at work?'

'He's never held down a job for more than a few weeks. He doesn't really need to, because he's got a trust fund from his grandfather. He doesn't seem to have developed any close friends since he left school, either. Before he went to prison, he got some kind of companionship from his family, who at least tolerated him, but now he's lost that as well.'

'How about close associates in prison?'

'They despised him as much he despised them – maybe even more so. As far as they were concerned, a day on which they didn't torture Taylor Brown was a day wasted.'

'He must have found his partner from *somewhere*,' Paniatowski said.

'Perhaps he used the contact advertisements in one of those dirty magazines we found in his house,' Beresford said. 'And if he did do that, it'll be virtually untraceable.'

'So, to sum up, we've no idea who his partner is, where Grace was killed, or where Elaine is now,' Paniatowski said. 'We're doing a bloody marvellous job of investigating this case, aren't we?'

'We're doing the best we can, boss – which is probably considerably better than most of the teams who might have been assigned to the case could have done,' Beresford said.

'So what you're telling me is that though we've got *nothing*, it's a *better* nothing than any other team could have come up with?' Paniatowski demanded. Then her expression softened a little. 'I'm sorry, Colin. You say we're doing our best, and I know we are – but our best just doesn't seem to be good enough.'

It was at seven minutes past eleven that the drunk staggered up to the bar and said, 'Give me another double whisky, can you?'

'I'm sorry, sir, but you're too late,' the landlord said firmly. He pointed to the clock on the wall. 'It's well past closing time.'

'Nobody would notice,' the drunk persisted.

'That's where you're wrong,' the landlord said. 'There's four bobbies sitting there behind you, and they'd notice.'

'If you . . . if you just slipped it to me . . .' the drunk suggested.

It had been a long day, and the landlord's patience was wearing thin.

'You're too late!' he said, raising his voice, in the hope that if he really shouted, the information might finally penetrate the drunk's whisky sodden brain. 'You're too bloody late!'

'*You're too late. You're too bloody late,*' the four bobbies at the table heard the landlord roar.

It seemed like a message aimed at them, and though none of them actually nodded their heads in agreement, it was only by an effort of will.

NINETEEN

*T*immy has no memory of arriving at the edge of the woods, *but that is definitely where he is – and what he is doing there is standing by the bushes, looking down at the long narrow sack which Lennie fell over.*

Things have changed since the last time he was here.

It is light, but it is a peculiar light, not like daytime at all.

And the sack doesn't smell any more. He is sure of that.

In fact, nothing smells.

Not the dark earth, drenched in morning dew.

Not the trees.

Not the air.

Nothing!

And though he has eyes – or how could he be watching now? – he doesn't think he has anything else.

It would be easy enough to find out if he's wrong about that, of course.

He could attempt to raise his hand and cover his eyes.

He could try to pinch himself.

But he doesn't want to do either of those things.

He is afraid to do them.

The sack begins to shake – gently at first, then with much more violence. And suddenly, something sticks out through the sacking. It is a long fingernail which is painted bright red, just like his mum paints hers when she has finished the washing up and is getting ready to go out.

But this one is longer than his mum's nails – and stronger, too, because now it starts to rip its way through the sack.

He wants to run, but he is now certain that he has no legs, and so he just stays where he is.

A line has been slashed along the whole length of the sacking from top to bottom, the two halves part, and SHE rises out of it. She has a face as pale as death, and yellow eyes that seem to glow. She is grinning, a terrible frightening grin which reveals sharp teeth as yellow as the eyes.

But what she does next is even worse. She crooks her little finger – which is just like the ones the skeletons have in the cartoons – and wags it in his direction.

She wants him to come to her, and he knows he will – because he must.

But before he steps forward to his certain doom, he opens his mouth and screams as loudly as he can.

By a quarter past three in the morning, Paniatowski's eyes had stopped focussing properly, and she was forced to accept that even if Taylor Brown did suddenly decide to tell her everything she wanted to know – and more – it would probably just slip by her unnoticed.

She turned to the uniformed constable standing by the door – the third officer to occupy the post since this marathon began – and said, 'That's it. Take him down to the cells.'

She sat, watching through bleary eyes, as the constable escorted the suspect from the room – Taylor Brown offered no resistance – and when she stood up she found that her legs had turned to water.

Climbing the stairs from the interview room to her office was an epic journey, and when she had finally completed it, she sank down on to her couch with a gasp of relief.

But though her mind was at least as exhausted as her body, it would not be still.

Could Tom Kershaw have made a better job of running this investigation than she had? she asked herself.

It would have been totally *inappropriate* for him to be in charge, of course – *but could he have made a better job of it?*

I don't know, she thought. I'll *never* know – and that's a very heavy burden to have to carry through the rest of my life.

Then her mind, finally overloaded, shut down, and she fell into a troubled sleep.

Colin Beresford had gone home to catch a little rest, but that wasn't working out for him, and as he paced the bedroom he had slept in all his life – which was next to the bedroom in which his mother had quietly lost her grip on reality – he was replaying the previous day's events in his head.

When he'd ordered Meadows to leave Bolton and return to Whitebridge, she asked him if it was personal – if it had anything to do with what had happened the night before.

'*No, it doesn't,*' he'd said angrily. '*It has nothing to do with what happened at all.*'

The anger had been real enough. He was convinced at that.

But had he been angry at her for making the suggestion that he would ever allow his personal life to spill over into his professional? Or had he been angry with himself, because he'd suddenly realized that that was exactly what had happened?

'I called her back because I needed all the manpower I could lay my hands on,' he argued to himself.

And that was true enough.

But had he really given enough consideration to the possibility that Meadows might have found the missing salesman, and that the salesman might have given them the name of Taylor Brown's partner?

'I made a command decision,' he said aloud, to the empty

room in which his first and only attempt at love-making had been such a dismal failure. 'I did what I thought was right.'

But still the nagging doubts would not go away – still, he caught himself wondering if he would have made the *same* command decision if the fiasco with Meadows had never happened.

He looked at his watch and saw that it was nearly half past six. There was really no point in going back to bed now – he might as well take a very cold, very long, shower.

'You were rather disturbed last night, weren't you, old chap?' Timmy's father said at the breakfast table. 'Mum was up for hours, comforting you, you know. She almost brought you into our bed, and we haven't had to do that for years.'

'I'm sorry, Mum,' Timmy said.

'We don't want you to be sorry,' his father said, with that mixture of firmness and understanding which he had perfected over the years. 'We want to know what upset you so much. Was it something that happened at school?'

'No.'

'Well, there must be *some* reason for it.'

If this was happening to Lennie, he would find a way to talk his way out of it, Timmy thought miserably. But he was *not* Lennie. His parents would make him tell the truth in the end – they always did – and so he might as well just come clean now.

'Me and Lennie . . .' he began.

'Lennie and I . . .' his father said.

'Oh, for goodness' sake, Philip, why must you always be correcting him?' Timmy's mum asked. 'Just let him tell the story.'

'Sorry, old chap, go ahead,' his father said, contritely.

'Lennie and I were watching the telly yesterday, and there was this story about a woman who'd been murdered. The lady on the telly said that there was blood everywhere, and—'

'I've told you a dozen times, you shouldn't watch things like that,' his father said.

'Philip!' Timmy's mother warned.

'So me and Lennie . . . Lennie and I . . . went to the woods, to see if we could find a body,' Timmy continued.

His father chuckled. 'And did you?'

'Yes.'

For a moment, both parents were silent, then Timmy's dad said, 'Are you sure it was a body?'

'Yes.'

'Then you'd better describe it to me.'

'It was wrapped up in this big sack, and it was just lying there.'

'Could you . . . could you see its arms and legs? Could you see its face?'

'Course not,' Timmy said, surprised that his dad could be so stupid. 'Like I told you, it was in a sack.'

He sensed – though did not understand – a lowering of the tension which had enveloped the room.

'Then how do you know it was a body?' his dad asked.

'Because it ponged!'

His father leant across the table, and took Timmy's small hands in his own large hands.

'It wasn't a body, old chap,' he said softly.

'It was!' Timmy protested. 'Honest, it was.'

His father turned to his mother.

'The only way I'm going to convince him it wasn't a body is to go there with him myself,' he said. 'In fact, I think we'll do it straight after breakfast.'

'But he's got school!' Timmy's mother said.

'It won't do him any harm to miss an hour's school,' his dad said. 'Come to that, it won't do *me* any harm to miss an hour's work.'

He really liked his bedsit, Jack Crane decided, as he stood in front of the mirror in the communal bathroom, shaving. It was true that it consisted of little more than a bed and table and chair, but the bed was comfortable, and the table was the ideal place at which to think and read, so it served his simple needs well enough.

And this particular bedsit had an added advantage, which was that the widowed landlady, Mrs Ophelia Danvers, didn't mind him entertaining what she called 'young ladies' overnight.

In fact, she positively encouraged it.

'Get your fun while you're young, Jack,' she'd advised when he moved in. 'Lord knows, I did – and I've never regretted it.'

His shave completed, he returned to his bedsit, slipped on his tie, and then headed for the stairs.

He was surprised to see an envelope lying on the mat under the letterbox, because it was much too early for the post to have arrived, but he bent down and picked it up anyway.

'Jesus!' he said, when he examined it.

There was no stamp, no address, and the name had been painstakingly constructed from bits cut out of magazines.

Chief Inspector PannyatovSKI, it said.

Finding the word 'inspector' had presented the sender with no problems, and 'chief' was made up of only two different typefaces, but even if he'd spelled 'Paniatowski' correctly, he'd have been struggling to get more than three letters from one source.

Paniatowski got a lot of crank letters, he reminded himself – most senior police officers did – but they were normally sent through the regular mail, whereas this sender had gone to the trouble of finding out where one of her underlings lived and delivered it personally.

He wondered if he should open it, and decided against doing so. It was, after all, addressed to the boss, and even if it had been written by a nutter, that gave her the right to look at it first.

He slipped the letter into his overcoat pocket, and opened the front door.

Timmy was not afraid as long as he was with his big strong dad, and he was almost skipping as they reached the bushes at the end of the woods.

'There!' he said, triumphantly.

'Well, you were certainly right about it ponging,' his father admitted. 'But it's not a body.'

'Then what is it?'

'It's just rubbish that some irresponsible person couldn't even be bothered to take to the tip.'

But even as he said the words, Philip was wondering *why* that person had done it, because surely there was more effort involved in dumping it here than there'd ever have been in taking it to the municipal facility.

'Well, I still think it's a dead body,' Timmy said stubbornly.

His father sighed. 'You're going to make your poor old dad stand over that stinking sack and slit it open, aren't you?' he asked.

'Yes,' said Timmy, realizing that, for once, he had the upper hand.

'Well, if it saves your mum having to get up in the middle of the night, I suppose it's worth it,' Timmy's dad said.

He took his penknife out of his pocket, pulled out a blade, and gingerly bent over the sack. He inserted it at the top end of the sacking, and began to draw downwards.

It was not a difficult task. The sack had rotted almost as much as its contents, which soon began to spill out.

'Yuk!' Timmy said.

'Yuk indeed,' his father agreed, looking down at the rotting, scaly bodies. 'There must be at least a hundredweight of fish in there.'

When Paniatowski arrived in the custody area, the duty sergeant was sitting at his table, eating a sausage sandwich he'd had sent down from the canteen, but the moment he saw her, he jumped smartly to his feet.

'Have you come to see the prisoner, ma'am?' he asked.

'That's right,' Paniatowski agreed.

'Do you want me to accompany you?'

Paniatowski shook her head. 'You finish your butty in peace. Just give me the key and tell me where he is.'

The sergeant handed the key across the desk. 'He's in the cell at the end, ma'am.'

Perhaps a night under lock and key would have loosened Taylor Brown's tongue, Paniatowski thought, as she walked along the row of cells.

But she doubted it. The man's sole remaining purpose in life, it seemed to her, was to keep quiet until his aim had been achieved. Then, and only then, he'd tell her everything she wanted to know – because it wouldn't really matter any more.

She reached the cell door and slid back the peephole – and that was when she saw the pair of legs suspended in mid-air.

'Call Dr Shastri,' she shouted over her shoulder, as she slid the key in the lock. 'Tell her I want her here, right now.'

She wrenched open the door. Taylor Brown was hanging from one of the heating pipes which ran close to the ceiling. He was naked to the waist, but that was because the 'rope' he had fashioned had been made from his shirt.

Paniatowski stood on the same chair that Taylor Brown had kicked over when he'd launched himself into what he must have hoped was oblivion, and felt his neck for a pulse. There was none.

'Bloody hell – he's gone and hanged himself!' she heard the sergeant say behind her.

'Brilliant deduction, Sergeant,' Paniatowski said, stepping down off the chair.

'Shall we cut him down, ma'am?'

'It's too late for that. We'll leave him there until the doctor arrives.' Paniatowski lit up a cigarette, and sucked the smoke in greedily. 'When was the last time you saw the prisoner alive?'

'Let me see,' the sergeant said shakily. 'It was about half past five that Mr—' He stopped, abruptly. 'Seven o'clock, ma'am,' he continued. 'I make my rounds every hour, on the hour.'

Paniatowski looked up at the hanged man. His face was bloated, as such faces always were, but there was a bruise under his left eye, and another on his chin, which had nothing to do with his suicide.

'Who was it that came to see him at half past five?' she demanded.

The sergeant looked at the floor. 'No one, ma'am.'

'You're in enough trouble as it is, without making things any worse,' Paniatowski said gravely.

The sergeant raised his eyes. 'It was Mr Kershaw, ma'am.'

'You allowed Mr Kershaw to see the prisoner?'

'Yes, ma'am.'

'But you went into the cell with him, didn't you?'

'Not at first, ma'am.'

'And what the hell do you mean by that?'

'He said he was very worried about his wife, and he thought that if he appealed to the prisoner, man-to-man, he might get him to talk.'

'So you just said, "Fine! Go ahead."?'

'No, ma'am, it wasn't like that at all. I knew it was against regulations, and I almost refused to give him the keys. But he looked so desperate that, in the end, I handed them over. But I did make him promise not to lay a hand on the prisoner while he was in the cell.'

'And a lot of good *that* did, didn't it?'

'He did promise, ma'am, and I think he meant it at the time. But when Taylor Brown wouldn't help him, he just lost control.'

'So how long did you allow Kershaw to beat up Taylor Brown before you finally decided the time had come to intervene?'

'It couldn't have been more than a couple of seconds, ma'am. I was right outside the cell all the time, and the moment I heard Taylor Brown scream, I went straight in. I don't think Mr Kershaw could have hit him more than twice.'

'No more than twice! Well, that's all right, then,' Paniatowski said sarcastically. 'What happened next?'

'I told Mr Kershaw to stand clear of the prisoner, and got him out of there as quickly as I could, ma'am. He didn't resist. He was as quiet as a lamb. I think he knew he'd done wrong.'

'Of course he knew he'd done wrong! He'd have to have been a complete bloody imbecile *not* to know he'd done wrong! What did you do once Mr Kershaw had left?'

'I went back to the cell, and patched Taylor Brown up a bit.'

'And how did you plan to explain his bruises to me this morning?'

'I don't know, ma'am.'

'Yes, you bloody well do!'

'I was going to say Taylor Brown had attacked me, and I'd only been defending myself.'

'And what would have happened when Taylor Brown told *me* that it was Kershaw who'd done it?'

'I'd have said he was lying, and that Mr Kershaw had never been near the cells.'

'That would be the second time that Kershaw had a meeting with Taylor when he wasn't even officially in the building, wouldn't it? The first time was when he got him to sign his confession.'

'Look, ma'am, Taylor Brown was guilty then and he was guilty now,' the sergeant said. 'I'm sorry I let Mr Kershaw into the cell. I know it was wrong. But I'm not going to apologize for trying to cover for him, because he'd do the same for me – or for any other bobby on this force.'

'Yes, you're probably right,' Paniatowski agreed.

'So what happens now, ma'am?'

'To Reginald Taylor Brown? He'll be taken down to the morgue – which is what always happens to prisoners who die in police custody!'

'I don't mean that, ma'am.'

'Then what *do* you mean?'

'What happens to me and Mr Kershaw?'

'I'll need time to think about that,' Paniatowski said. 'But if I was you, I wouldn't be planning on collecting any long service medals.'

She turned and headed for the stairs.

Why had Taylor Brown hanged himself? she wondered.

It seemed unlikely that it was because Kershaw had frightened him so much that death looked like the easy way out, because the beating Kershaw had given him was nothing compared to what he would have received in prison.

So perhaps it was because, seeing what a state Kershaw was in, he had decided he'd achieved all he'd wanted to, and was happy to die.

But it was also possible that Kershaw's present state of mind was of little consequence – that it was the Chief Superintendent's *future* state of mind which was important to Taylor Brown.

And if that was true, then when the prisoner hanged himself, at sometime after seven o'clock, he was already certain of what Kershaw's future state of mind would be – because he was also certain that, by that time, Elaine would be dead.

'Is the boss not here, Sarge?' Jack Crane asked when he arrived at Paniatowski's office.

Meadows made an elaborate show of examining the room. 'No, I don't think so,' she said, with a grin. 'Somebody said she'd gone down to the cells to talk to Taylor Brown.'

'The thing is, I've got a letter for her,' Crane said.

'And what is it – your resignation?' Meadows replied, the grin still firmly in place.

'No, as a matter of fact, it's an anonymous letter. It's addressed to her, but it was posted through my letterbox.'

Meadows' grin froze. 'What did it say?' she demanded.

'I don't know. I haven't looked at it. Like I said, it wasn't addressed to me – it had the boss's name on it.'

'You bloody fool!' Meadows exploded. 'We're knee-deep in shit and the clock's ticking – and you didn't bother to look at what might turn out to be a lead simply because it's addressed to the boss?'

'Well, no – I mean, yes . . . I think.'

'Give it to me!' Meadows ordered, and when Crane handed her the letter, she ripped it open without ceremony.

There were only a few words pasted to the sheet inside in the envelope. Crane could see that for himself. But only Meadows was close enough to read them.

And read them she did.

Once, twice, and then a third time – as if she wanted to make really sure they actually said what she'd *thought* they'd said the first time through.

When she looked up again, she seemed much paler than she had been a few moments earlier.

'Well, if this letter's telling the truth, we can stop looking for Mrs Kershaw,' she said.

TWENTY

The old mill stood alone, in the middle of an industrial wasteland – like a decaying corpse that someone had forgotten to bury. It was framed, that early morning, against a slate-grey sky, and assaulted by a harsh wind which howled like a mad dog and cut like a knife

A casual observer of the dismal scene might have wondered why, suddenly, so many vehicles – six police cars, the ambulance, and Dr Shastri's Land Rover – should have drawn up in front of the mill's loading bay. But there *was* no casual observer, and the tragedy was about to be played out without the benefit of an audience.

Paniatowski got out of the car, turned up the collar of her coat, and watched as the other vehicles spilled their occupants.

None of the people gathered there could know – with any degree of certainty – whether their presence was actually necessary, she thought. But, from the general air of gloom which enveloped them, it was obvious that most of them thought it would be.

She lit up a cigarette, contemplated the building for a moment, then turned to Beresford and said, 'Let's do it.'

'Do you want me to organize the lads into search parties?' her inspector asked.

Paniatowski shook her head.

'We don't need them for the moment. They might as well get back in their cars and take a cigarette break.'

'Right, boss,' Beresford replied.

And he was thinking, *if anybody's going to find anything in there, it has to be you, doesn't it, Monika. In a way, that's your penance.*

They had brought a police locksmith with them, but he was not necessary. The owners of the mill had long ago given up having any hopes of a future life for their property, and when a window was smashed or a padlock cut through, no attempt had been made to replace them.

Beresford pushed at the small door inset into the bigger loading bay door, and it swung creakily open.

Paniatowski, Beresford, Meadows and Shastri stepped through the gap. A little light from outside followed them in, but they still needed their torches to pick their way through the semi-gloom.

The loading bay floor was strewn with empty bottles, used contraceptive sheaths, and old newspapers which had once served as tramps' bedding – but there was no sign of the body that the anonymous letter had promised them.

'Shall we split up, boss?' Beresford asked.

'What would be the point of that?' Paniatowski replied. 'However things turn out, there's no hurry now.'

They climbed the few short steps to the platform at the far end of the loading bay, and went through the connecting door to the main warehouse.

There was nothing there, either.

They found her in the main weaving shed, where the winter light streamed in through tall windows which had been installed so the weavers could see to do their job properly.

She was lying on a folding picnic table in the centre of the shed, and was covered from head to toe with a white sheet.

It was Dr Shastri who assumed the responsibility of peeling back the sheet to reveal the dead woman's face.

'That's her,' Beresford said, looking down at the dead sightless eyes. 'There's no doubt about it – that's Elaine Kershaw.'

They had all been expecting it, yet it still came as a shock.

Shastri pulled back the rest of the sheet. Elaine Kershaw was naked except for a pair of bright red shoes – one of which had the heel missing – but unlike Grace's body, hers appeared unmarked.

'Steady the table, please, Inspector Beresford, I'm going to turn her over,' Shastri said.

With the practised ease of someone who had handled dozens of cadavers, Shastri turned Elaine Kershaw so she was lying on her front.

'Oh shit!' Beresford moaned.

Elaine's back was like a churned up battlefield. Deep gashes cut into her flesh, almost to the bone.

'Who could do that to another human being?' Beresford wondered.

And when did it *happen*? Paniatowski asked herself silently. Could I have prevented it if I'd handled Taylor Brown just a little more skilfully?

'How long has she been dead?' she said aloud.

'I can't give you an accurate time, but it's certainly not more than a few hours,' Shastri replied.

So there's your answer, Monika, Paniatowski thought miserably. There's your *bloody* answer!

Paniatowski had never seen the chief constable pace up and down his office before, but now he was certainly making up for all the times he hadn't.

'This is a disaster,' he said. 'On so many levels, it's a disaster.'

'I know,' Paniatowski agreed.

'It's not an ordinary murder,' Baxter said, as if she didn't already understand that. 'Elaine Kershaw was the wife of a high-ranking police officer. The press will crucify us. I can see the headline now – If the force can't protect its own, what chances are there that it can protect us?'

'They won't actually say that,' Paniatowski told him.

'No, they won't,' Baxter agreed. 'Not in so many words. But they'll drop enough hints that even my dogs will be able to read between the lines. And then there's the morale of the Mid Lancs Constabulary to consider. How do you think Tom's brother officers will feel about it? Not to mention Tom Kershaw himself.'

'Ah,' Paniatowski said, 'I was wondering when you'd get round to him.'

'Don't get smart with me, Chief Inspector,' Baxter said angrily. 'If I haven't mentioned Tom Kershaw's personal sorrow – and indeed, my own – before, it's because I'm trying to be professional, and put the interests of the service above all else.'

'How is he taking it?' Paniatowski asked – dreading the answer.

'How would *you* take it?' Baxter asked harshly.

'I'd be devastated.'

'And that's exactly what *he* is. He's under very heavy sedation at the moment, but once he's back on his feet, he's going to want his revenge – and not just on the man who killed his wife.'

'I appreciate that,' Paniatowski said. 'And can I rely on your support in that area?'

'I've always supported you, Monika,' Baxter said, ambiguously. 'I know you're a fine officer, and you've always done everything you could to get a result – but I'm afraid that, on this occasion, I'm going to have to launch an internal inquiry.'

'Does that mean I'm off the case?'

'Not for the moment. In a situation like this, it's better to take things one step at a time, and avoid hasty decisions.'

'Meaning I am still on it – but it could be yanked from under me with no warning?'

'As I said, I'm not about to take any hasty decisions,' Baxter told her. He looked at his watch. 'There's one more point I'd like clearing up. I've seen the preliminary autopsy report on Taylor Brown, and apparently there was some bruising on his face which was not consistent with hanging. Could you explain that?'

It was her chance – and probably her *only* chance – to put the boot into Kershaw before he put the boot into her, she realized.

But, for God's sake, the man had just lost his wife!

'I've already investigated that,' she said. 'Taylor Brown attacked the duty sergeant, and the sergeant himself used no more force than was necessary to restrain him. I'll be writing a report on it, but I'd appreciate it if you'd give me a couple of days.'

'That shouldn't be a problem,' Baxter said. He checked his watch again. 'And now if you'll excuse me, Chief Inspector, in half an hour I've got a press conference at which I'll try my hardest to create the impression that we actually know what we're bloody well doing.'

'Would you like me to be there?' Paniatowski asked.

Baxter shook his head firmly. 'No, I really don't think that would be a good idea.'

Of course he didn't, Paniatowski thought. She walked to the door, almost stepped out into the corridor, then turned around.

'Could I ask you one more question, sir?' she asked.

'What is it?' Baxter replied, irritated.

'I'd like to know if you, *personally*, have confidence in the way I've conducted this investigation.'

'I have no reason not to, at the present time,' Baxter told her. 'But there is something that's been bothering me.'

'And what's that?'

'You spent over two days looking for Elaine. You had at your disposal every officer we could spare from other duties – and some we couldn't. She might have been anywhere in the country, but she wasn't. We know now that she was right here in Whitebridge all the time.'

'Is there a question hidden somewhere in all that?' Paniatowski said.

'You know damn well there is.'

'Then ask it – *put it into words!*'

'All right, I will,' Baxter said. 'Why couldn't you find her, Monika?'

'I don't know,' Paniatowski admitted.

Only hours earlier, Paniatowski's desk had been groaning under the weight of all Kershaw's files – a testament to five years of successful police work. Now the files were gone, and in their place stood a bottle of whisky and a bottle of vodka – testaments to the general sense of gloom and failure which had enveloped the team since the discovery of Elaine Kershaw's body.

'Apart from the shoes, there's no pattern to the two killings,' Beresford said. 'Grace Meade was wearing a kinky costume when we found her, Elaine Kershaw was naked. Meade was dumped in a ladies' toilet, Elaine was laid out in an old mill. Grace was whipped all over. Elaine was given a much worse beating – though only on her back. Grace was smothered. We don't know what killed Elaine yet, but it wouldn't surprise me at all if it was the shock from the beating.'

'And while the killer was content to have Grace found by anybody at all, he wanted *us* to find Elaine, which is why he sent the anonymous letter,' Paniatowski added. 'I agree with you, Colin, there *should be* a pattern – but if it's there, I simply can't see it.'

Meadows coughed, and when Paniatowski turned to look at her, she was astonished by the change that had come over her sergeant.

The expression on Kate Meadows' face was that of a woman forced to take a journey through her own personal hell. Her mouth was clamped tightly shut, as if she didn't dare to speak for fear of what she might say. Her eyes flickered uncertainly.

'What's the matter, Kate?' Paniatowski asked.

Was it seeing the body that had got to her bagman, she wondered. That was possible – it had certainly been a horrific sight – but Meadows had seemed perfectly calm when examining Grace Meade's corpse.

'Kate?' Paniatowski repeated.

Meadows took a deep breath. 'I need to have a word with you in private, ma'am,' she said, with effort.

'Is it about the case?'

'Yes, ma'am.'

'Then I'd like Inspector Beresford to stay, if you don't mind.'

'I *do* mind,' Meadows told her. 'I won't talk while he's here.'

'Maybe you don't quite understand this yet, Sergeant Meadows, but we work as a *team*,' Beresford said angrily.

He turned to Paniatowski, expecting her to back him – and was shocked to read in her eyes that she wasn't going to.

'Just give us ten minutes, Colin,' Paniatowski said softly.

There was no point in arguing, Beresford thought. None at all.

And perhaps he deserved this, he told himself – perhaps the way he had constantly jumped to Chief Superintendent Kershaw's defence whenever Paniatowski had tried to exclude him from the case had led her to believe that she didn't have *his* full backing.

It wasn't true, of course – at least, he didn't *think* it was true – but he could see how it might seem like that.

'I'll go and have a cup of tea,' he said, standing up.

Paniatowski kept silent until he'd closed the door behind him, and his footsteps had receded down the corridor, before turning to Meadows and saying, 'You've just put me in a position in which I had to side with my bagman against someone who's not only my inspector, but also my best friend, Sergeant. This had better be worth it.'

Meadows walked over to the door, and turned the key in the lock. Then she began to unbutton her blouse.

'What the hell do you think you're doing?' Paniatowski demanded.

'I'm establishing my credentials,' Meadows told her.

She finished unbuttoning the blouse, and took it off. She had been facing Paniatowski up until this point, but now she turned round to give the DCI a view of her back.

'What in God's name happened to you!' Paniatowski asked, seeing the line of small scars which ran from one side of Meadows' body to the other.

'I was whipped,' the sergeant said, slipping on the blouse again.

'How did it happen? Were *you* abducted?'

'No, boss. I *asked* to be whipped. I enjoy it.'

'I see,' Paniatowski said.

Meadows sat down again. 'I didn't want to show you that, boss – really I didn't – but I had to, if you were ever going to take what I have to say about the whippings seriously.'

'I'm listening,' Paniatowski said.

'Grace was whipped too much, too quickly.'

'I'm not sure she'd agree with you – if she could.'

'You don't understand,' Meadows said. 'Anyone whipping her for his own pleasure would have taken his time about it – even if he'd been meaning to kill her in the end.'

'Go on,' Paniatowski said.

'It's a bit like having a box of your favourite chocolates,' Meadows said. She made a fist, and hit her own forehead in exasperation. 'No, it's not like that at all – but it's the closest I can come to describing it.'

'Understood.'

'You love all the chocolates in the box, and you want to eat them all straight away. But you don't. Why is that?'

'Because you know that by the fourth or fifth chocolate, you won't be enjoying the experience half as much as you should.'

'Exactly. So you pad it out. You have one or two now, then you leave them alone for a while. And in some ways, it's the *anticipation* of the next chocolate which is the greatest pleasure.'

'But all Grace's injuries were sustained over a very short period.'

'That's right.'

'So what you're saying is that whoever killed her wasn't really interested in torturing her at all?'

'I wouldn't go that far – but it certainly wasn't his primary concern.'

'So what *was* his primary concern?'

'I've no idea.'

'Tell me about Elaine's injuries.'

'They were too extreme.'

'What do you mean?'

'The chances are that she would have fainted after the first or second blow.' Meadows paused for a second. 'Trust me on this, boss – I know.'

'You've fainted yourself?'

Meadows shrugged. 'It wasn't my partner's fault – he just miscalculated. But, yes, I was out cold. And that's not what a man who's into whipping wants. He wants the woman to be conscious – wants her completely aware of everything that's happening to her.'

'And Elaine won't have been?'

'Dr Shastri may tell you different, boss, but I don't see how she could have been.'

'I am going to have to give Inspector Beresford the gist of this conversation, you know,' Paniatowski said.

'I *do* know that, ma'am. But does it have to go any further?'

'What do you mean?'

'I don't want to find crude cartoons taped to my locker, boss. I don't want my colleagues making whipping sounds when I walk past.'

Paniatowski remembered the photographs which had been taped to her own locker, and which – in her naivety – she'd imagined Inspector Kershaw would do something about.

'You need have no worries on that score,' she promised. 'What you've told me goes as far as Colin – and no further.'

'And how does it affect my place on the team?' Meadows asked.

'It doesn't,' Paniatowski said – though she was thinking, if there *is* still a team for you to have a place on.

'Oh, come on, boss!' Meadows said. 'I've been honest with you – can't you be honest with me?'

'All right, I will be,' Paniatowski replied. 'I've had a lover who not only had a baby daughter but also a blind wife. I've had a lover who is now our chief constable – and I'm not above using that fact, if it will help my investigation. And once – when I was working with my old boss, Charlie Woodend, on a case far away from Whitebridge – I slashed through the tyres of a murderer's car, knowing he'd probably kill himself if he tried to escape. Most of the time, I don't regret any of those things, but occasionally, when the memory of them sneaks up on me unawares, I *do* feel ashamed.' She paused. 'From what I've learned about you so far, Kate, I wouldn't think *you've* got anything to be ashamed of.'

'Thanks, boss,' Meadows said, her voice brimming over with gratitude.

'For what?' Paniatowski asked innocently.

Lynda Jenkins cornered Hardcastle the moment the producer entered the studio.

'The chief constable's just given a news conference,' she said.

'Fancy that,' Hardcastle replied.

'It was to announce that the body of Chief Superintendent Kershaw's wife has been found in an old mill.'

'Really! You'd have thought I'd have known about that already, wouldn't you – what with me being in the media and everything.'

'I want the story, chief,' Lynda Jenkins said, failing to notice that, at the word 'chief', the producer visibly winced. 'I *really* want it.'

'And I want to be twenty-five again – with a full head of hair,' Hardcastle told her. 'But I won't get my wish, and you won't get yours – because I'm giving that particular assignment to Barry.'

'I thought you said you knew nothing about it,' Lynda Jenkins said, accusingly.

'I lied,' Hardcastle told her. 'But you shouldn't start worrying your pretty little head that I might actually know what I'm doing *most of the time*. Finding out about the murder and the press conference was just a fluke – and I promise it won't happen again.'

The comment went right above Linda Jenkins' head.

'It's not fair that the assignment should go to Barry,' she whined.

'Of course it's not fair,' Hardcastle agreed wholeheartedly. 'It's totally unjust and totally inappropriate.'

'Well, then . . . ?'

'And there's absolutely nothing you can do about it.' Hardcastle
smiled. 'Welcome to the wonderful world of television, Lynda!'

'Just because I messed up the tiniest little bit on the story of
that dead prostitute—' Jenkins began.

'You messed up *a lot*,' the producer interrupted harshly. 'But
I'm not a vindictive man by nature,' he continued, softening his
tone to that of a kindly uncle, 'and that's why I'm giving you
an even better story than Mrs Kershaw's murder.'

'An even better story?' Jenkins repeated, disbelievingly.

'Certainly,' the producer assured her. 'Barry will be reporting
on only one dead body, while you'll be reporting on dozens –
possibly even hundreds.'

'What . . . what is the story?' Jenkins asked.

'The editor's got the details,' Hardcastle replied.

And as he walked away, he was chuckling softly to himself.

It came as no surprise at all to Meadows that Beresford should
be waiting for her in the corridor outside Paniatowski's office.
Nor was she surprised that he looked both troubled and angry.

'I don't know what you've told the boss—' he began.

'You will,' Meadows interrupted him. 'She made it quite plain
to me from the outset that whatever I told her, she'd tell you.'

'. . . but if it was anything about me . . .' Beresford continued,
ploughing on with the speech that he'd probably already run
through his mind a dozen times.

'It wasn't,' Meadows said firmly.

'It wasn't?'

'No!'

'Oh!' Beresford said, as he felt the whole foundation on which
he'd planned this argument slip from under him.

Meadows put her hand on his shoulder. 'I really think we need
to talk, sir,' she said. 'Do you fancy a cup of tea?'

'All right,' Beresford agreed numbly.

They said no more until they were sitting opposite one another
in the police canteen, each holding a large mug of industrial
strength tea.

It was Meadows – inevitably – who took the lead.

'Let's get personal matters out of the way first?' she suggested.
'What happened the night before last was a mistake.'

'You can say that again.'

'But it doesn't have to affect the way we get on as colleagues – and perhaps even as friends – in the future.'

'No, it doesn't,' Beresford agreed.

'And look on the bright side,' Meadows said.

'Is there one?'

'Oh yes, there most certainly is. The whole thing might have been a complete disaster from both our points of view – but at least it means that you're not a virgin any more.'

Beresford grinned. He didn't want to – but he couldn't help himself.

'So it does,' he said.

'Now let's move on to what's *really* eating away at you – even if you're not entirely aware that's what it's doing,' Meadows said. 'You're worried that it was a mistake to pull us out of Bolton yesterday afternoon, aren't you?'

'Are you going to tell me it *wasn't* a mistake?' Beresford asked hopefully.

'No, I can't do that,' Meadows told him. 'If we'd stayed, it's *possible* we'd have found the ex-salesman, it's *possible* he'd have given us the name of Taylor Brown's partner, and it's *possible* we'd have been able to save Mrs Kershaw.'

'You're a *great* source of comfort to me,' Beresford said gloomily.

'Oh, I can give you comfort if that's what you want, sir,' Meadows said. 'I can give you positively oodles of it. But I rather thought that you'd prefer to hear the truth as I see it.'

'And you were right.'

'OK, then we're back on track. I said it was *possible* those things might have happened, but it's also possible they wouldn't have. We'll never know.'

'No, we won't.'

'But what I *do* know is that when I accused you of bringing me back for personal reasons, I wasn't being honest – either with you or myself. The fact is that I was so excited at the thought of cracking the case entirely on my own that I really didn't care about anything else. But I've got over that now, and I have to say that if I'd been in your position, then – rightly or wrongly – I'd have done exactly what you did.'

Beresford nodded gratefully.

'You need to pick up that line of inquiry again,' he said, all crisp and efficient now. 'As soon as you've finished your tea, I'd like you to get straight back to Bolton. And don't worry – I'll clear it with the boss.'

'Thank you, sir,' said Meadows – who already *had* cleared it with Paniatowski. 'The third thing we need to talk about is the boss herself. After what happened this morning, her career is on a knife-edge, and we need to do everything we can to protect her.'

'I'd go through fire and water for that woman,' Beresford said.

And it took him by surprise when Meadows said, 'And so would I,' with such obvious conviction.

TWENTY-ONE

Kate Meadows was wearing a tight black skirt, a lemon blouse, a lilac jacket and high-heeled patent-leather shoes. It was not the kind of outfit which suggested the wearer was out conducting serious police business, Crane thought as they walked across the police car park together, but then, he reminded himself, she was the sergeant and he was the constable, and so he said nothing.

A brand new Volkswagen convertible was sitting at the edge of the car park, and Crane whistled appreciatively.

'I wonder who owns that,' he said.

'We do,' Meadows told him. 'Or rather, we've hired it for the day. It's part of the disguise.'

'So we're in disguise, are we?'

Meadows ran her eyes up and down Crane's sober second-best suit. 'Well, one of us is, at any rate,' she said.

'*Why* are you in disguise?' Crane wondered.

'Because, if we adopt the conventional approach, it could take days – or maybe even weeks – to find our missing salesman. But we don't have that luxury – so we're going to have to be sneaky.'

'Sneaky?' Crane repeated.

'Sneaky,' Meadows confirmed, climbing into the driver's seat of the Volkswagen.

She was not as fast a driver as Paniatowski – very few people were – but she was certainly fast enough, Crane thought, as they pulled out of the car park and headed for Whitebridge High Street.

'You can stop worrying about my relationship with Inspector Beresford, Jack,' Meadows told him, as they overtook a van on what was not *quite* a blind corner. 'That's all sorted out.'

'Who said I was worrying about it?' Crane asked.

'I did.'

'Oh?'

'From the way you were watching both of us in the Drum last night, I could tell that Colin had confided in you about his little problem. I don't suppose he mentioned my name in your cosy man-to-man chat – he probably didn't even mention his own, just said was that he was asking for a friend – but you weren't fooled, were you? You might not have known immediately what he was talking about, but it didn't take you long to make some kind of sense out of it.'

'And you could really work all that out just by looking at me?' Crane asked.

'Yes.'

'That's scary.'

Meadows shrugged – no mean feat when sliding into a gap in the traffic which was only slightly bigger than the Volkswagen.

'I'm a good observer,' she said. 'People like me have to be – because when you're surrounded by a hostile world, you always have to be on the lookout for your own kind.'

'Your own kind?'

'Come on, Jack, don't play the dummy,' Meadows said, with a hint of exasperation. 'You've been to university, and—'

'Who told you I'd been to university?'

'Nobody did, but we've already agreed that I'm a good observer. You *did* go to university, didn't you?'

'Yes.'

'Cambridge?'

'Oxford.'

'Funny,' Meadows mused, 'from your little idiosyncrasies, I'd have put my money on you being a Cambridge man. But no matter. You really do know what I mean when I say, "my own kind", don't you? Or at least, if you don't know, you can probably take an Oxford-educated guess.'

'Yes, I probably can,' Crane agreed.

'That's settled, then,' Meadows said, pulling up in front of one of Whitebridge's trendiest – and most expensive – boutiques. 'Now let's get you your disguise.'

Meadows swept through the boutique like a tornado, and within fifteen minutes, Crane found himself dressed in an expensive leather jacket, and trousers that a Hollywood star would not have been ashamed to be seen in.

He blanched when he saw the bill.

'Is the force paying for this?' he asked tremulously.

'Of course not,' Meadows replied.

'Then who is?'

'I am.'

'I don't see how you can possibly afford to do that on a sergeant's pay,' Crane said.

'On a sergeant's pay, I obviously couldn't,' Kate Meadows replied, enigmatically.

Chief Constable George Baxter's broad ginger face filled the television screen.

'*Are there any questions?*' he asked.

'*You say that Mrs Kershaw was missing for three days before her body was discovered,*' said the deep-but-disembodied voice of one of the reporters at the press conference.

'*That is correct.*'

'*So why wasn't any appeal made to the general public for help?*'

'*It was felt that the investigation could proceed more smoothly if the public wasn't involved.*'

'*And in the light of what's happened, do you still think that was the right decision?*'

Baxter hesitated for a second, then said, '*I can't possibly answer that question without revealing more about the investigation than is judged to be prudent at the moment.*'

'That's scarcely a ringing endorsement of the DCI in charge of the investigation,' Paniatowski said, watching the conference on the portable television in her office.

'It could have been worse,' Colin Beresford replied, without any real conviction.

'They're getting ready to tip me off the sleigh, Colin,' Paniatowski said. 'I'll do my best to make sure you're not thrown to the wolves as well, but given how low my stock is at the moment, there's no guarantee it'll have any effect.'

'What the hell? Who wanted to be a bobby, anyway?' Beresford asked.

Baxter disappeared from the screen, and was replaced by an earnest-looking young man with a microphone, standing outside police headquarters.

'*So it is not yet clear why Mrs Kershaw was killed or even* how *she was killed,*' he said. '*However, this reporter can reveal that sources close to the investigation feel that mistakes were made, and that perhaps if Chief Superintendent Kershaw – one of the most respected policemen in the force – had been allowed to participate in the hunt for his wife himself, there might have been quite another result. This is Barry Burns, returning you to the studio.*'

'Now *that's* how it should be done,' Hardcastle told his assistant. 'A little sincerity, a little insinuation – the soupçon of a suggestion that the reporter knows more than he's telling – and sign off, leaving them wanting more.' He leaned across to his microphone. 'Do the lead-in to Jenkins' story, Gary.'

The anchorman gave a barely perceptible nod.

'*On a lighter note, we ask why you might need a gas mask the next time you go for a walk through Waverton Woods,*' he said to the camera. '*Lynda Jenkins has the story.*'

'Cut to Jenkins,' Hardcastle said.

A smiling Lynda Jenkins appeared on the screen, with the woods behind her as a backdrop.

'She's pissed off with me, but she doesn't want to show it, because she realizes I'm even more pissed off with her,' Hardcastle said to his assistant. 'But however she feels, she'll make a good job of this – as would anybody who knew her career was hanging by a thread.'

'*It's often said you should never cry stinking fish in your own backyard, but out here in the countryside it would be almost impossible not to,*' Lynda Jenkins said, on-screen. '*And it's all because of this!*'

The camera panned to the sack on the ground.

'*There's a lot of stinking fish here,*' Jenkins continued, as the camera dwelt lovingly on the rotting perch and trout. '*How many? I don't know – because I'm certainly not going to count them, let alone weigh them. They were discovered yesterday by our intrepid fish detective, Timmy Holland.*'

'Cut to the kid – give it five seconds,' Hardcastle said.

Timmy's grinning face filled the screen briefly, and then was gone.

'*Why were the fish dumped here?*' Lynda Jenkins, now back on camera, asked. '*Nobody seems to know.*'

'Get ready for the fish puns,' Hardcastle said.

'Will there be some?' his assistant asked.

'Lots of them.'

'How can you be so sure?'

'Because all new reporters think they're original, witty and brilliant – and only their producers ever seem to realize that they sound just like the fellers they're replacing.'

'*I don't want to "carp" on about this,*' Jenkins said to the camera, '*but if you're hearing me – or perhaps I should say "herring" me – Mr Dumper, I really think you should examine your "sole" and ask yourself if this is the right "plaice" to leave your rubbish. This is Lynda Jenkins, for* Lunchtime News, *returning you to the aquarium – I mean, to the studio.*'

'That was awful,' the assistant groaned.

'Awful?' Hardcastle repeated. 'This isn't some highbrow current affairs programme, you know. It's *local lunchtime news*, watched by people who are too lazy or too stupid to be doing anything else with their time.'

'But surely we still have to have certain standards, don't we?' the assistant asked.

'We do have standards, lad – they're called viewing figures – and reports like that one are good for them.'

'Really?'

'You don't believe me? Then go into any pub you like tonight – and if you don't hear at least three fish jokes, you can have my job.'

Kate Meadows pulled up in front of the terraced house, then revved the engine of the Volkswagen convertible a couple of times before switching the engine off.

'Is she watching?' Meadows asked, from the corner of her mouth.

'I don't know for certain – but the lace curtain's certainly twitching,' Crane replied.

'Good enough.'

Meadows took a phone receiver out of her bag, and lifted it to her face.

'Hello, Jeremy, we've arrived,' she said.

'What are you doing?' Crane asked.

'I'm talking on the radio phone.'

'But this car doesn't have a radio phone.'

'True,' Meadows agreed. 'All I've actually got is this receiver, with a loose bit of cable hanging from it – but Mrs Lewis, squinting at us through the curtains, doesn't know that. To her, it'll look like the real thing.'

She smiled into the phone, said, 'God bless you, and all who sail in you,' and slipped the receiver back into her bag.

'You know what you have to do?' she asked Crane.

'I know what I have to do,' Crane agreed.

'Then let's get this show on the road,' Meadows suggested.

She got out of the car, walked up to the front door, and rang the bell.

The woman who answered the ring was in her mid-thirties, and had a pinched, dissatisfied face.

'Mrs Lewis?' Meadows asked brightly.

'Yes?'

'I'm Katie Quill, from the BBC.' She laughed, slightly awkwardly. 'Actually, that's not quite true. I work for Midnight Productions, which makes documentaries for the BBC. You've no doubt seen a few of them. *Sin in Soho*? *The Harrogate Wife Swappers Club*?'

'I don't think so,' Mrs Lewis said dubiously.

'Oh,' Meadows said, looking quite crestfallen. 'Well, never mind,' she continued, perking up. 'Our latest project – which we're all very excited about – is called, *Sexy Toys for the Sexy Suburbs*, and we're looking for experts in that particular field. In fact, that's exactly why we're here at your door.'

'I'm not following you,' Mrs Lewis told her.

Meadows giggled. 'I do get ahead of myself sometimes, don't I?' she asked. 'The fact is, you see, that one of my friends . . . well, she's into that sort of thing. And she said that she bought some of her best toys from your brother, and that he'd be just perfect for the programme. But the thing is, he's not at the address we have for him, and since one of his old neighbours said that you were his sister—'

'I don't know where he is,' Mrs Lewis interrupted.

'Well, that was a wasted journey,' Crane said, grumpily, turning back towards the car.

'Wait a minute, Daniel,' Meadows pleaded. 'You *really* don't know where he is, Mrs Lewis?'

'I *really* don't know.'

Crane had reached the Volkswagen and was already opening the passenger door.

'Come on, Katie,' he said. 'If we've hit a dead end here, I'm sure we won't have much trouble finding somebody else willing to work as an advisor for five hundred pounds a week.'

'Did you . . . did you say five hundred quid a week?' Mrs Lewis asked.

'Yes, that's the standard fee,' Meadows said, matter-of-factly. 'Of course, with overtime, it could work out to be considerably more than that.'

Mrs Lewis bit her lip. 'I'm sure our Brian would be more than willing to help you,' she said. 'But the thing is, you see, he's in a bit of trouble with the police.'

'Is he in jail?'

'No, no, nothing like that. But the bobbies are sort of looking for him.'

'I don't think that should be a problem. *Half* our advisors are wanted by the police for one thing or another, but that's really of no interest to us. *Our* only concern is to get our programme made.'

'There's a pub at the end of the street called the George and Dragon,' Mrs Lewis said. 'If you could be in there at nine o'clock tonight . . .'

'Nine o'clock?' Crane repeated. 'I was planning to be back in London by *nine o'clock*.'

'Six, then,' Mrs Lewis said, desperately. 'I'm sure I could have him there by six.'

Crane made a great show of thinking about it. 'Six o'clock on the dot,' he said finally. 'If he's a minute late, we'll be gone.'

'He won't be late,' Mrs Lewis promised.

'He'd better not be,' Crane said, unrelentingly.

'Would it be all right if I stood some of the team in the incident room down?' Beresford said, hating himself for having to ask.

'Why not?' Paniatowski replied dispiritedly. 'They can at least find something useful to do back at their own stations. Until we get some new leads – *if* we get some new leads – all they're doing here is sitting on their hands.'

'We'll get leads,' Beresford said loyally.

'I don't see how,' Paniatowski countered. She lit up a cigarette, though she didn't really want it. 'Tell me honestly, Colin, if it wasn't for the red shoes, would we be linking these two murders together at all?'

'We might,' Beresford said. 'After all, they were both whipped.'

'Yes, but the whippings were so different,' Paniatowski said. 'Just as everything else about the murders was different. If we assume the late Mr Taylor Brown was guilty . . .'

'He was. It was just a stroke of luck that we found some of Elaine Kershaw's nightdress in the remains of the fire at the bottom of his garden – I'll admit that – but we *did* find it.'

'. . . then we also assume that the reason he killed Elaine – or got his partner to kill her – was to get his revenge on Kershaw.'

'True.'

'But if that's the case, why did he have Grace killed as well? She can't have meant anything to him. And it wasn't a practice run, because, as we've already said, the two murders were so different.'

'Maybe Grace's murder was meant to be nothing but a distraction,' Beresford suggested. 'Maybe he thought that if we were looking for Grace's murderer, we'd have less resources to devote to finding Elaine.'

If that was the plan, it worked, Paniatowski thought. And it worked because I *let* it work – because I was so angry that Grace had no one else fighting for her that I focussed a lot of the investigation on her. But did I focus *too* much?

The phone rang. It was Shastri.

'I have finished the autopsy on Elaine Kershaw, Monika,' she said.

Not, 'How are you on this fine day, my dear Chief Detective Inspector?' Paniatowski noted.

Not, 'If you are planning to burden a poor Indian doctor with even more corpses, could you please tell me now, so I can cancel what little life I still have left outside work.'

No, just, 'I have finished the autopsy on Elaine Kershaw, Monika.'

Shastri not only cut up dead women, she knew when she was talking to one on the phone – and *that* was why she had put aside her customary levity.

'Did you discover anything interesting?' Paniatowski asked, though her heart wasn't really in it.

'I discovered several interesting things,' Shastri said, 'and when you have a little free time, Monika, I suggest you come down to the morgue, so that we can discuss them.'

'I've got some free time now,' Paniatowski said.

And that was no lie, because, without any new leads to follow, she had all the time in the world.

TWENTY-TWO

There was no doubt at all that Brian Waites would be able to pick out the two people he was supposed to be meeting, Crane thought. The rest of the customers in the George and Dragon were clearly ordinary working people – shop girls and foundry workers, painters and hairdressers – while he and Meadows, in all their finery, stood out like a beef supper at a vegetarian feast.

It was one minute past six when the man entered the pub. He was wearing a typical salesman's suit – the sort of suit which proclaims to the customer that while he might quite like to make the sale, he was certainly not desperate to. He was perhaps a couple of years younger than his sister, and though he could not have been called handsome, he had a certain buccaneering air about him which many women might find attractive and which also hinted that he knew a good, dirty sex toy when he saw one.

Waites walked over to their table, and looked down at them.

'So which one of you would be Miss Quill?' he asked, then

laughed – as if to suggest that even though he had made the joke himself, he hadn't heard it before and really found it quite witty.

'I'm Katie Quill,' Meadows said, 'and my friend is Detective Chief Superintendent Crane of the Vice Squad.'

'Ho, ho, very droll,' Waites said, though he obviously considered it well below his own contribution in the comedic stakes.

'Do take a seat, Mr Waites,' Meadows invited, and once he had sat down she reached into her pocket, held out her warrant card, and said, 'Surprise!'

Waites would have been back on his feet in a second, had it not been for the fact that Crane's heavy hand had already descended on his shoulder.

'Take it easy, Brian,' Crane said. 'You nearly knocked our drinks over.'

'This is entrapment,' Waites complained.

'In strictly legal terms, it's nothing of the kind,' Meadows said. 'What it actually is, is two smart bobbies running rings round a greedy little bleeder with itchy fingers.' She paused for a second. 'But that's neither here nor there,' she continued, 'because we haven't come to arrest you – we're here to make a deal.'

'A deal?' Waites said, licking his lips.

'That's right,' Meadows agreed, 'and here's how it works. You help us with our investigation and we'll pretend we've never seen you. On the other hand, you fail to help us and we'll have the cuffs on you before you can say "kinky boots". Because we like making arrests, don't we, Detective Chief Superintendent Crane?'

'We love it,' Crane said.

'What do you want me to do?' Waites asked.

'We want you to tell us about a couple of pairs of red, high-heeled shoes,' Meadows told him.

Shastri led Paniatowski into the morgue's staffroom.

'If you wish, I can get you a cup of coffee from the machine,' she said. 'We call it "death warmed up", but that is more a reflection on the macabre way we see things here than on the coffee itself, which is really quite nice.'

'I don't feel like a coffee,' Paniatowski said.

'Very well, then let us sit down,' Shastri suggested.

They sat facing each other.

'Am I right in assuming that this case is causing you more

difficulties than most?' Shastri asked. 'That it is, perhaps, putting your career in some jeopardy?'

'More or less,' Paniatowski agreed.

'You are not likely to be drummed out of the service though, are you?'

'No, not quite that.'

'So if the worst comes to the worst, you will probably be moved to some sort of administrative post?'

'That's right – chief inspector in charge of female officers' welfare and paper clip sorting,' Paniatowski said bitterly.

'I wonder if you have looked at the positive side of that,' Shastri said. 'You would certainly be healthier, because without the strains of your current position you would probably smoke and drink less.'

'Or more – because I'd be so bloody bored.'

'And you would have more time to spend with Louisa.'

'Yes, but would I be any bloody good for her?'

'I do not quite follow.'

'Louisa's the most important thing in the world to me – by far – but my job comes a very strong second. It's what I do. It's what I am. It defines me. Without this job, I wouldn't be the mother Louisa knows. I'd just be the shell of what I used to be.' Paniatowski paused. 'We've never had a conversation like this one before,' she continued, suspiciously. 'Why are we having it now?'

'Perhaps it is because, when you entered the morgue, I saw the light of hope in your eyes – as if you were expecting a miracle from me.'

'You've pulled off miracles before,' Paniatowski pointed out.

'Yes, I have,' Shastri agreed. 'But I am afraid that this time I have failed you. I can offer you no clues to your killer. In fact, I am not sure if, legally, he can be called a killer at all.'

'What!'

'Mrs Kershaw died of a heart attack. Her heart had a congenital weakness, though it's more than possible that she was not aware of it. She could have died walking down the street – or sitting at home watching television.'

'But surely what caused the heart attack was the wounds on her back,' Paniatowski protested. 'They were horrific. They almost cut her in half. Even a healthy person might have a heart attack under those conditions.'

'The whipping was indeed very vicious,' Shastri agreed. 'But it was inflicted post-mortem.'

'Are you sure?'

'I'm absolutely sure.'

'But why would anyone do that?'

'I have absolutely no idea.'

It was crazy, Paniatowski thought. It was completely insane. 'And that's it?' she demanded. 'That's all you've got for me?' She was suddenly drowning in guilt. 'I'm sorry,' she added hastily. 'I know you did you best, like you always do.'

'There is one more thing,' Shastri said, throwing Paniatowski a bone, even though she was sure it contained nothing nourishing.

'Yes?'

'The two women were dressed in identical made-to-measure shoes.'

'I know.'

'But Grace could never have walked in the pair she was wearing. She had surprisingly large feet for a woman her size, and taking even a few steps in them would have been agony.'

She didn't *have to* walk in them – Paniatowski thought. All she had to do was *stand* in them – with her arms chained above her head – while the killer lashed her with his whip.

'Elaine's shoes, on the other hand, were a perfect fit,' Shastri continued. 'Don't you English have a phrase for that? Something about fitting like a glove?'

'That's right.'

'Then Elaine's shoes fitted her like a glove. And so did Grace's shoes.'

'I thought you said that Grace's were much too small for her,' Paniatowski said.

'Ah, I have not made myself clear,' Shastri replied. 'When I put *Grace's* shoes on *Elaine's* feet, they too fitted her like a glove.'

'Tell us about the Lady Zelda shoes,' Meadows said.

'A lovely piece of merchandise, they were,' Brian Waites said. 'I'm not into that sort of kinkiness myself – I'm more the straight on top, wham, bam, thank you ma'am type of feller – but I have to admit that just holding them made me feel a wee bit horny.'

'How fascinating,' Meadows said. 'Remind me to look you up if I ever feel like being treated as a piece of meat.'

'There's no need to be like that,' Waites said, offended. 'I can be a real gentleman, too, when the situation calls for it.'

'You sold two pairs of the shoes to the same customer, didn't you?' Crane said.

'That's right, I did.'

'And also a Bride of Dracula corset?'

Waites chuckled. 'And much more besides. She was my best customer – she must have bought half the catalogue. And some of the stuff – like the red shoes – was such a turn-on for her that she bought a spare.'

'She!' Meadows exclaimed. 'Did you say *she*?'

'That's right.'

'You're sure you're not confusing things? You're certain it wasn't a man you dealt with?'

'Like I said, she was my best customer. I'm not likely to confuse *her*, now am I?'

Meadows remembered what she herself had told Crane in the Pride of Bolton: *the killer has a vision of how this whole grisly business should be carried out – and those red shoes are part of it. They're in his head. He's got to have them – whatever the consequences.*

And she still believed that, though now she was beginning to see that whilst he might have been compulsive, he had been far from reckless.

'Did she have a man with her, this customer of yours?' she asked Waites.

'No.'

He had been very clever, Meadows thought.

He chooses a woman to be his agent. She is probably someone he does not find attractive enough to kill for pleasure – because that kind of woman would only complicate his dealings with her. But he knows, right from the beginning, that she will have to die anyway – cold-bloodedly, calculatedly – because she is a link in the chain which will lead back to him.

'Actually, what I just told you isn't strictly accurate,' Waites said. 'Her husband *was* there on one occasion – but I don't think he meant to be.'

'What do you mean by that?'

'I'd made an arrangement to call round in the afternoon, but one of my other appointments had fallen through, so I dropped by late morning instead. The husband was upstairs. I think he must have been shaving or something, because he had the radio on. Anyway, possibly *because of* the radio, I don't think he even knew I was there until he'd started coming down the stairs.'

Meadows felt her pulse rate jump.

'What did he look like?' she asked.

'I couldn't really say.'

'You *saw* him, didn't you?'

'Yes, but only from behind, because I was talking to the customer, and by the time I turned, her husband was already heading for the kitchen.'

So he could leave by the *back* door, Meadows thought.

So he wouldn't have to walk past Waites, and let the salesman get a good look at him.

'You must have got *some* impression of the man,' she said.

'He was a tall man, with broad shoulders.'

Not Taylor Brown then, but his partner, Meadows thought.

'Can you tell me anything else about him?' she asked.

'I'd guess he was about fifteen or twenty years older than her.'

'What makes you think that?'

'Well, for a start, his hair was nearly white.'

'Lots of men go prematurely white.'

'And there was the way he walked – it wasn't a young man's walk.'

'How do you know he was her husband?'

'She said he was.'

'What happened next?'

'She stood up and followed him into the kitchen.'

'Did they speak?'

'Yes.'

'And are you going to tell me what they said – or do I have to guess?' Meadows demanded.

'Oh, sorry. She said something like, "Don't you want to come and see the exciting things that Brian has brought with him, darling?" And he said, "I've not got time now, sweetheart. But you know what I like, and I trust your judgement."'

They did *sound* like husband and wife, Meadows thought.

But she knew just how clever men like him were at role playing – because she was pretty good at it herself.

And the woman? Was *she* playing a role?

Possibly not. Possibly she had convinced herself that he *did* care for her – and that he *was* almost her husband.

She couldn't have known, poor deluded soul, what her ultimate fate would be – or that this chance encounter with Brian had probably shortened the time before she met it.

'Think about the next question very carefully,' Meadows said. 'Is it possible that the woman wasn't buying the clothes for herself, but for someone else? Is it possible that she was just acting as an agent?'

'Anything's possible, I suppose,' Waites admitted. 'But I don't think it's very likely, because most of the stuff she bought was made-to-measure.'

So she must have been approximately the same size as Elaine and Grace, Meadows thought.

The killer had certainly worked things out very carefully!

'I'll need this customer's name,' Meadows said.

What she was in fact asking for, she realized, was the name of a dead woman, who was probably in a shallow grave somewhere on the moors by now. It might not even be her *real* name that she had given him. But at least it was a start.

'I don't remember her name,' Waites told her.

'The name is part of the deal,' Meadows said coldly. 'If you *don't* give it to us, we'll arrest you.'

'Honestly, I really *can't* remember,' Waites said worriedly. 'It was in my order book, but I threw that away after I'd done my runner with the money from Ajax.'

'The address, then!' Meadows snapped.

'That was in the order book as well,' Waites said frantically.

'Get the cuffs out, Jack,' Meadows said to Crane.

'I remember what the house looked like, though,' Waites said in desperation. 'It was one of those big old-fashioned jobs. You know what I'm talking about – the kind of house that has a third floor where the servants used to sleep.'

'A Victorian house?'

'Yes, that's it.'

Meadows had a sinking feeling in the pit of her stomach.

'And where is this house?' she asked.

'It's in Whitebridge.'

Meadows and Crane exchanged glances.

'Describe the woman to me,' Meadows said.

'She's in her early thirties. Not my type, but rather attractive. She has a slim build – a bit like you – only much shorter,' Waites said. 'Hang on, I think the name's coming. The first name, at least. It was Ellen!'

'Ellen?'

'No, that's not quite right. It was Elaine. I'm sure of it now. And I've remembered something else.'

'Go on.'

'That time I called when her husband was there, and he went straight to the kitchen . . .'

'Yes?'

'She didn't say, "Don't you want to come and see the exciting things that Brian has brought with him, *darling*?" She said, "Don't you want to come and see the exciting things that Brian has brought with him, *Tom*?"'

TWENTY-THREE

Since Kate Meadows had begun the tale of her trip to Bolton, she had had the full attention of the others.

Now, as the tale drew to a close, Paniatowski said, 'You're sure that it's the right house?'

'It's the right house,' Meadows confirmed. 'We brought Waites back to Whitebridge with us. He didn't want to come, but we gave him no choice in the matter. We parked in a lay-by on the ring road, and told him to direct us to the house where he'd sold the red shoes. He took us straight there.'

'It's Kershaw!' Paniatowski said. 'It's been Kershaw all along!'

She should have worked that out long before now, she told herself angrily. Instead of trying to bury an unpleasant part of her past at the back of her mind, she should have been using it – holding it up as a lens through which to examine the present.

*   *   *

It is late at night, and almost everyone has left the station, but there is still a light burning in Kershaw's office. Paniatowski knows it will be a sign of weakness to appeal to him – yet again – to do something about the photographs which keep appearing, but she is desperate.

His door is partly open – just wide enough for her to see that he is sitting at his desk with a glossy magazine on his left and a pot of glue and a pair of scissors on his right.

She flings the door open.

'It was you!' *she screams.* 'You were the one who was doing it!'

For a moment he looks shocked, then the calm for which he is justly famous around police headquarters returns to him.

'We could have been very good together, Monika,' *he says.*

Yes, we could, she thinks. I could have loved you. I could have cherished you. We could have spent the rest of our lives together.

'But you refused to bend,' *he says.*

'What do you mean?' *she asks – confused, perhaps almost hysterical.*

'I don't want my women to have an inner strength,' *Kershaw says.* 'I want them to draw their strength from me.'

'So that was what it was all about,' *she says.* 'You wanted me to break down!'

'Yes,' *Kershaw says, almost tenderly.* 'But only so I could build you up again. Only so I could mould you. We could have been very happy together, Monika,' *and now the tenderness has been replaced by a harsh edge,* 'but you had to spoil it, didn't you? You wouldn't cry! You refused to cry!'

He blames me, she thinks incredulously. He thinks it's all my fault. If things have gone wrong, it's not because he has a warped view of life, it's because I refused to share it with him.

'I'm going to report this,' *she says.*

Kershaw chuckles. 'I wouldn't do that, if I was you.'

'Why not?'

'Because I'll deny it. And who will the top brass believe? An inspector with a solid record, who has earned the respect of everyone who's ever worked with him? Or a chit of a girl who's somehow – more by luck than judgement – managed to wangle the job of detective sergeant.'

He's right, she realizes. Not about the second part – he couldn't

*be more wrong about her – but when he says that no one will
take her word against his.*

'I can't possibly work with you any more,' she says.

*'Work for me, you mean,' he says, with a hint of anger. 'Work
under me. Well, fortunately, you won't have to. I'm being promoted
and moved into uniform. By next week, you'll have a new boss
– a Scotland Yard reject by the name of Charlie Woodend. And
if you want my advice, you'll treat him with more respect than
you've treated me.'*

*'Respect!' she repeats, astounded. 'Up until five minutes ago,
I had nothing but respect for you.'*

But he's no longer really listening to her.

*'Give Woodend what he wants,' Kershaw says. 'If he likes
giggling schoolgirls, be a giggling schoolgirl. If he wants to take
dirty pictures of you, tell him there's nothing you'd enjoy more.
Bend to his will.'*

No! Paniatowski thinks.

*She will never become a plaything for her new boss, she
promises herself. She will maintain a strictly professional relationship, and if that doesn't work, she will leave the force.*

*But the damage Kershaw has done to her has cut deeper than
merely her career, she realizes. She trusted him. She may even
have loved him. And now that he has betrayed her, she is not
sure she will ever be able to trust or love a man again.*

'I still can't believe that Mr Kershaw's the killer,' Beresford said.

'That's because you keep seeing him as the man he wants you
to see him as, rather than the man he actually is,' Paniatowski
countered. 'For Christ's sake, look at the evidence, Colin! It
wasn't some crazed killer with a grudge against Kershaw who
bought the red shoes – it was Elaine! And Kershaw knew she'd
bought them. He was even there once, when the salesman called.'

'All right, so they were into sadomasochism,' Beresford
conceded. 'I wouldn't have thought it of him, but that's not the
point. The fact that he indulged in perversion doesn't prove either
that he killed Grace or that he faked his wife's kidnapping and
then flogged her dead body.'

'So what do you think happened?' Paniatowski demanded.

'Someone broke into the house, kidnapped Elaine, and took
the shoes and the corset at the same time,' Beresford said.

'And how would this person know he'd *find* the shoes there?'

'Perhaps Mr Kershaw and his wife belonged to some kind of sadomasochistic club,' Beresford suggested.

'A sadomasochistic club,' Paniatowski repeated. 'Do such things exist, Kate?'

'Oh yes,' Meadows replied, matter-of-factly.

'And what goes on there?'

'It depends on the club. There are no hard-and-fast rules. Sometimes they swap partners. Sometimes, one partnership will put on a show for the rest. And in some clubs, you hardly even speak to the other members – it's enough for you to know that while you're doing your own thing, you're surrounded by like-minded people doing theirs.'

'Well, there you are, then,' Beresford said.

'*Where* am I?' Paniatowski asked.

'The man who kidnapped Elaine was a member of the same club.'

'Really!' Paniatowski said. 'Well, let me ask you this. You know Kershaw – or think you do. Can you really see him sharing his wife – even at a distance – with *anybody*?'

'No, I can't,' Beresford admitted. 'So maybe the kidnapper didn't even know the shoes would be there, but once he saw them, he decided to take them along.'

Paniatowski sighed, then she turned to Crane. 'Would you like to tell Inspector Beresford – who's older and much more experienced than you, so should know better – why this line he's taking is a load of crap?' she asked.

'I'd rather not, boss,' Crane said uncomfortably.

'It wasn't a request,' Paniatowski told him.

Crane cleared his throat. 'Mr Kershaw said he was desperate to get his wife safely back, but he did absolutely nothing to assist the investigation. He didn't tell us his wife liked to be whipped . . .'

'I don't see how that would have helped,' Beresford protested. 'That was a part of his private life which he wanted to *keep* private. He had no way of knowing then how things would develop.'

'Shut up and listen!' Paniatowski ordered. She turned to Crane. 'Start again, Jack.'

'He didn't tell us his wife liked to be whipped, even when

Grace's body was found,' Crane said. 'He denied ever having seen the red shoes before, though he must have known, when he saw that Grace had been wearing a pair of them, that that was another thing which tied her death to Elaine's disappearance. He didn't tell us that the corset Grace was wearing belonged to Elaine, nor did he—'

'Enough!' Beresford said. 'I've heard enough.'

What was it Jack Crane had said about the way the killer had positioned Grace's body, he asked himself.

'I think he did it because he hoped we'd waste our time searching for a meaning, instead of directing our energy at any other leads we might come up with. And it worked out perfectly for him, didn't it – because that's exactly what we have been doing.'

And what had he himself said in reply?

'But exactly what kind of man would think that way? It's almost as if . . .'

Almost as if he was a bobby!

But he'd never followed that thought through, had he?

And perhaps the *reason* he hadn't was because there was some part of his brain which was warning him that once he began suspecting a policeman, it would inevitably lead him to Tom Kershaw.

And he simply hadn't been ready to admit it could be Tom Kershaw – because Kershaw was one of his heroes!

'I've been an idiot,' he told Paniatowski. 'Of course it's Kershaw. It *has* to be Kershaw. He decided to kill his wife . . .' He paused for a moment. 'That has to be our starting point, doesn't it?'

'Yes, it does,' Paniatowski agreed. 'He decided to kill her, but he didn't have to – because nature beat him to it.'

'But he wouldn't necessarily have known that,' Crane said. 'He probably thought that it was what he was doing to her at the time which killed her.'

'We're getting ahead of ourselves,' Beresford said. 'He decided to kill her – for reasons we don't know, and may never know – but he was well aware, as a policeman, that the husband is automatically a suspect. So he had to do something to distract attention away from him – and what better way than to create the impression that it was the work of some psychopath. But for

that to fly, there had to be a minimum of two deaths – and that
was why he had to kill Grace.'

'But why did he fake his own wife's kidnapping?' Meadows
asked. 'Wasn't that an unnecessary risk? Wouldn't it just have
been easier to pretend to Elaine that everything was normal, and
keep her at home until the time came to kill her?'

'Unless she *already* suspected that he wanted to get rid of
her,' Crane said. 'If she did, then he had to lock her away somewhere safe before he killed Grace – because, given her suspicions,
Grace's death would have really put the wind up her.'

'Especially if she found out that Grace was wearing a pair of
her shoes,' Paniatowski said. 'And Grace *had to* be wearing those
shoes, in order to tie the two murders together.'

'Where did he take Elaine, once he'd faked the kidnapping?'
Meadows wondered.

'Could have been anywhere,' Beresford said. 'A lock-up
garage. An abandoned house on the moors. He'd have had
hundreds of choices. And it doesn't really matter, anyway,
because now she's no longer there, we have no proof that she
ever was.' He lit up a cigarette. 'When you think about it, we
don't have proof of *anything* – at least, anything that will stand
up in court.'

'Maybe you'll find some kind of evidence in his punishment
room,' Meadows suggested.

'In his *what*?' Paniatowski asked.

'His punishment room. His torture chamber. His pleasure
palace. Whatever it was he decided to call it.'

'Will he have one?' Paniatowski asked.

'Oh yes.'

'And do you have any idea where it might be?'

'It'll be in his house.'

'But we searched the house from top to bottom when Elaine
supposedly went missing,' Beresford pointed out. 'There was no
sign of anything like that.'

'It'll be there,' Meadows said confidently.

There were lights on in every room of George Baxter's house,
and as she walked up the path to the front door, Paniatowski
could hear the sounds of a party going on inside.

She could have married George, she thought, and if she had,

this house and this party would have been hers. And even though she hadn't wanted to marry him – and knew she wouldn't have been happy if she had – she couldn't help feeling a little jealous, and a little resentful, of the woman who had taken her place in his life.

She rang the door bell, and it was Baxter himself who answered.

'Oh, for God's sake, Monika, can't you see I'm entertaining?' he said exasperatedly.

'Sorry, sir, I'll arrange my next murder investigation at a time which is more convenient for you,' Paniatowski said.

Baxter bowed his head slightly. 'I suppose I asked for that,' he admitted. He looked back over his shoulder into the hallway. 'I wanted to call the damn party off when they found Elaine's body, you know, but my wife pointed out – quite rightly – that none of the guests have any connections with either the police or the Kershaws, so it wouldn't have been fair to them.'

'Can I come in?' Paniatowski asked.

'Yes,' Baxter said. 'I mean, no,' he quickly amended. 'It would just annoy Jo. She thinks I spend far too much of my time on police business as it is.'

Besides which, she doesn't like me, Paniatowski thought. And I certainly can't blame her for that.

Baxter stepped back into the hallway, and picked up a set of keys from the hall table.

'We'll go out to the garage,' he said. 'That way, we won't disturb anybody else.'

He led her around the front of the house, and glancing through the window, Paniatowski saw that the party was in full swing.

Well, jolly good – and jolly nice! she thought sarcastically.

It was a big garage, and Baxter's and his wife's cars only occupied the front half of it. The rest of the space had become a combination workshop and storeroom. There was a carpenter's bench in one corner – saws and chisels hanging neatly above – and a large chest freezer in the other. Between the two were shelves, some containing canned vegetables, and others pots of paint and brushes. Three of the shelves in the centre were devoted exclusively to Baxter's fishing gear.

'It's a bit nippy at the moment, but once the heating kicks in, it'll soon warm up,' the chief constable said, clicking a switch on the wall. 'Now what can I do for you, DCI Paniatowski?'

'I'd like your permission to apply for a search warrant for Chief Superintendent Kershaw's house, sir,' Paniatowski said.

Baxter looked as if he'd just been hit with a shovel.

'Dear God, is there no end to your vindictiveness?' he asked. 'And hasn't Tom Kershaw already suffered enough?'

'Nowhere near as much as Grace Meade,' Paniatowski countered.

She told him about the shoes, and the corset, and how Kershaw had denied any knowledge of either.

'So why did he want to kill Elaine?' Baxter asked, with a chilling calm.

She would have preferred anger, she thought. Anger would have been easier to deal with. But this calm – as sharp as a surgeon's knife – was something else. With this calm, he would shred all her arguments and leave them in pieces at her feet.

'Well?' Baxter repeated. 'Why did he want to kill Elaine?'

'We don't know,' she admitted. 'We can only speculate.'

'So speculate.'

'He didn't want anyone to know about his fetish. It would have destroyed the image that everyone has of him. And that image – his reputation – is very important to him. That's why he was never at the house when the salesman called. That's why he shredded the skin on her back when she was dead – because he wanted to remove all traces of the minor scars she'd acquired from her beatings over the years.'

'I still haven't heard a motive,' Baxter said.

'Perhaps Elaine was tired of keeping it a secret. Perhaps she was ashamed and wanted to confess. Or perhaps she felt no shame at all, and wanted everyone to know *that*.'

'Interesting,' Baxter said, in a tone that really meant 'fanciful'. 'Let's move on to the fact that he kidnapped his own wife.'

'All right,' she agreed, knowing this was the weakest point of her whole argument.

'You don't know where he kept her, do you?'

'No, we don't.'

'But wherever she was, she must have been alone for much of time, because Tom Kershaw was very much in evidence around police headquarters.'

'That's true.'

'So, given that some considerable time elapsed between the

kidnapping and her death, will you admit that there was at least a slight possibility of someone else finding her?'

'I suppose so.'

'And what would have done more damage to Tom's reputation – to be known as someone who likes to give his wife a gentle whipping, or to be known as a man who kidnapped his wife with the intention of killing her?'

'It was a risk, but he's always been a risk taker,' Paniatowski said stubbornly.

'You see, if Elaine had died before the prostitute—'

'Grace!' Paniatowski said fiercely. 'Her name was Grace.'

'All right,' Baxter agreed. 'If Elaine had died before Grace, you might have been able to argue the case that Tom killed the second woman in order to make it look as if he had no connection with the death of the first. But as it is, you're claiming that first he kidnapped Elaine, then abducted and killed Grace, *then* killed Elaine and . . .'

'I've explained why he had to kidnap her when he did,' Paniatowski protested.

'No, you haven't,' Baxter contradicted her. 'You've raised some improbable theories and put forward some unsubstantiated speculations. And that's all. I admit that what you've told me about the shoes and the corset raises questions – but that's all it does. You simply don't have a case.'

'So you won't allow me to search Kershaw's house again?'

'I most certainly will not.'

Did her case make sense, or was it really no more than fancy? Paniatowski asked herself.

Was Baxter acting in the measured, statesmanlike way a chief constable should, or was he merely out to protect his friend?

She no longer knew what was reasonable and what was not.

But she *did know* that, as tired and frustrated as she was, she felt an overwhelming urge to lash out at something – and since Baxter was there, he would do just fine.

'Well, you have to give Tom Kershaw one thing,' she said. 'He may be a murderer, but at least he has spirit enough to organize his life for his own comfort and convenience.'

'What do you mean by that?' Baxter asked – taking the bait, just as she'd hoped he would.

'You could have a snooker table and a dartboard in here, just like Tom's got in his basement,' she said. 'But you're so henpecked that all you've got is cans of vegetables and your wife's deep freeze!'

'It's *my* deep freeze,' Baxter said, stung.

'What?'

'I said it's my deep freeze. It's where I keep what I catch on my fishing trips with Tom.'

'If Elaine had died before Grace, you might have been able to argue the case that Tom killed the second woman to make it look as if he had no connection with the death of the first,' Baxter had said.

'I know how he did it!' Paniatowski shouted. 'I know how he bloody did it!'

TWENTY-FOUR

C hief Superintendent Kershaw met them at his front door. 'You've got a nerve coming here!' he said angrily.

'No, sir, we've got a search warrant,' Paniatowski said, holding the document up for him to see.

'Does the chief constable know about this?' Kershaw demanded.

'The chief constable? Your fishing pal and fellow communicant at St Mary's Church? Yes, he knows.'

Knew, but was not happy about it.

'If you're wrong about this, Monika,' he'd said at the end of their long discussion in his garage, *'you'll have ruined my relationship with one of the best policemen I've ever worked with. And when he sets out to destroy you – and he will – I won't lift a finger to help you.'*

'I'm surprised to see *you* here, Colin,' Kershaw said to Beresford. 'You used to work for me. I'm the one who guided you on to the right path. Without me, you wouldn't be where you are today.'

'That's true,' Beresford agreed

'And you've been a guest in this house. I've invited you here when other – higher ranking – officers would have given their eye-teeth to be in your place.'

'I know.'

'And don't you have *any* sense of loyalty?'

'I have a very strong sense of loyalty,' Beresford said.

And he was thinking, that's why I'm here, putting my career on the line – yet again – for Monika.

'It's strange you haven't asked *why* we got a search warrant sworn out,' Paniatowski said.

'I *know* why you got it,' Kershaw said. 'You want to try and prove that I killed my wife.'

'*And* Grace Meade,' Paniatowski said. 'But, of course, Grace doesn't matter. She never did. Shall we go inside?'

Kershaw stepped aside to let them enter the hallway.

'The law requires that you do not impede our search in any way—' Beresford began.

'Don't try to tell me what the law says,' Kershaw interrupted angrily.

'. . . but should you wish to accompany us on that search, we have no objections.'

'Oh, I'll accompany you, all right,' Kershaw said. 'Have no doubts about that.'

They started in Kershaw's study. They did not expect to find anything there, but it was all part of the softening up process.

'You handled the whole thing very cleverly,' Paniatowski said, as she opened a drawer. 'I'm especially impressed by the way that – right from the start – you did everything you could to draw suspicion away from yourself.'

'Is this the point at which I'm so impressed by your superior intelligence that I break down and confess?' Kershaw asked.

'Reporting your wife missing at the same time as Grace Meade disappeared was a master stroke,' Paniatowski said. 'We didn't see how *one* man would have the time to kidnap *two* women, so we were forced to the conclusion that the kidnapper must have a partner. It took us quite a while to work out that there only ever *had been* one kidnapping.'

'So now you're saying that this Grace girl wasn't kidnapped after all?'

'No, I'm saying that *your wife* was never kidnapped.'

'You found the heel of her shoe at the bottom of the garden,' Kershaw pointed out.

'Ah, so now you admit it was *her* shoe,' Paniatowski said.

'You found the heel of *a* shoe at the bottom of the garden,' Kershaw amended.

'Crashing your car into that oak tree was the second master stroke,' Paniatowski continued. 'Who would ever have suspected a man who was so panicked by his wife's disappearance that he almost killed himself?'

'I *could have* killed myself,' Kershaw said.

'No, you couldn't. You're a good driver, and you weren't panicked at all. You were in complete control of yourself, and you timed it just perfectly.'

She moved on to the filing cabinet.

'And then there was your insistence on being part of the investigation. What could be more natural than a distressed husband who *wanted* to be part of the investigation? But you're too good a policeman not to know that would never be allowed.'

'Oh, so I'm a good policeman now, am I?' Kershaw asked, sarcastically.

'You've *always* been a good policeman,' Paniatowski replied. 'I've never denied it.' She flicked through a file and replaced it in the cabinet. 'What else did you do? Oh yes, you forced your way into the morgue, demanding to see the body, because you thought it might be your wife's. But you knew it wasn't – because you knew *exactly* where she was.'

'And where *was* she?'

'We'll come to that later. And, of course, Sergeant Lee caught you going through your old case files. He thought you were looking for the man who might have kidnapped Elaine, but what, in fact, you were looking for, was a man you could convincingly *fit up* for the kidnapping. You didn't find one, but then you remembered Taylor Brown, who hadn't been one of your cases at all, but would do just perfectly.'

'It's not a question of remembering anything. He and his scumbag partner – who you still haven't caught – kidnapped my wife,' Kershaw said.

'And so that's why you went to see him in the cells – to find out what he'd done with her?'

'Yes.'

'You went to see him in the cells to make it *appear* as if you wanted to know what he'd done with your wife. And then you hit him. You expected to be disciplined for that, but given your circumstances, it was never going to be more than a slap on the wrist – and it all added to your credibility.'

'You planted Elaine's nightdress in Taylor Brown's garden,' Beresford said, 'but whereas a lesser man would just have left it there, you made it look as if he'd tried to destroy it.'

'You'll live to regret turning on me, Colin,' Kershaw said.

'Well, that's enough foreplay,' Paniatowski said. 'Let's get on with the main event.'

'Your flippancy is not appreciated,' Kershaw said sternly.

'Oh, I'm sorry, sir,' Paniatowski said. 'I'll phrase it another way, shall I? We'd like to go down to the basement now.'

The basement looked exactly as it had done the last time they were there. There was the dartboard in one corner, with the bar next to it, the poker table with its straight-backed chairs, the large television with its easy chairs, and the bookcase on the far wall crammed with books on sport.

And there was still a large empty space at the foot of the stairs, too.

'This is where you're going to put the cabinet which will hold your sporting trophies, isn't it?' Paniatowski asked.

'It's where I *was* going to put it,' Kershaw said. 'Such things seem of no interest now.'

'So when it arrives, you'll just send it back?' Paniatowski asked.

'I expect so. I haven't really thought about it.'

'He must have ordered it,' Paniatowski said to Beresford.

'What do you mean, boss?'

'If he expects he'll send it back, he must already have ordered it.'

'That makes sense,' Beresford agreed. 'Who did you order it *from*, sir?'

'I don't remember.'

'But you must have the invoice around here somewhere.'

'I expect so.'

'Then we'd like to see it,' Paniatowski said.

For the first time since they'd entered the house, Kershaw was looking rattled.

'Perhaps I got confused,' he said. 'God knows, after all that's happened, I'm entitled to be.'

'Confused about what?' Paniatowski asked.

'Confused about the trophy case. Maybe I only *meant* to order it.'

'Or maybe you never thought of ordering it at all,' Paniatowski suggested. 'Maybe you simply didn't have the space for it until the night Elaine died.'

'What are you talking about?' Kershaw demanded.

'How wide would you say that bookcase is, Colin?' Paniatowski asked, ignoring him.

'Must be at least three feet,' Beresford said.

'Do you think you could move it on your own?'

'No problem, boss. Especially if I took all the books off it first.'

'There are some very rare and valuable books in that bookcase,' Kershaw said. 'You leave them alone.'

'Funny, isn't it?' Paniatowski mused. 'His trophies mean nothing to him now that his wife's dead, but he still cares about his books. Shift it, Colin!'

Beresford walked over to the bookcase, took hold of one end, and gave it a tentative tug.

'I don't think I'll have to take the books off it,' he said. 'It appears to be on some kind of a hinge.'

It would have to have been, Paniatowski thought. Logic determined that it would have to have been. But she still felt a huge wave of relief when Beresford confirmed it.

'Open it,' she said.

'Before you do that, there's something I want to say,' Kershaw told her. 'I loved my wife, and she loved me.'

'I don't doubt it,' Paniatowski said.

And she didn't. It had been obvious, when talking to her sister and mother, that Elaine had loved Kershaw. And though she had once thought that Kershaw had planned to murder Elaine, she now realized that the anonymous note he had dropped through Crane's letterbox told quite a different story.

'I never did anything to Elaine that she didn't want me to do,' Kershaw said. 'She liked to be hurt – and she liked having power over me.'

'Power over you?' Paniatowski repeated incredulously. 'You were the one with the whip.'

'I told you once that the only reason I wanted to break you

down was so I could build you up again – mould you,' Kershaw said. 'Do you remember that?'

Paniatowski glanced across at Beresford, but her inspector seemed to have been struck temporarily deaf.

'Yes, I remember that,' she said.

'Elaine showed me that was not the way to true happiness. I didn't have to break her. I didn't want to break her. Yes, I was the one with the whip, but she was the one who decided when I could use it.'

She was a very different kind of woman to me, Paniatowski thought. And perhaps – despite the meek little mouse she was when he married her – she was a much stronger one.

'Go on,' she said aloud.

'She knew how much I desired her,' Kershaw continued, 'and that showed in everything she did – the way she looked, the way she spoke, the way she walked. She had a confidence – a certainty about herself – that few men could resist. Wherever she went, men's eyes followed her.'

Paniatowski looked at Beresford, and Beresford – who had been to her barbecue, and now seemed to have got his hearing back – just nodded.

'Do you want to tell me how it happened?' Paniatowski asked.

Kershaw shrugged. 'Why not? Once you open up the bookcase, it won't matter anyway.'

Elaine has been in bed with the flu, but she is over it now. She feels so much like her old self that she rings Tom in the middle of the day.

'Any chance of you slipping home for a while,' she purrs seductively into the telephone.

'I'd like to,' Kershaw admits, 'but there's a firm rule in my team that unless there's a real emergency . . .'

'Who made that rule?' Elaine asks.

'I did.'

'Then if you made it, you can break it.'

'You're wrong about that, my love. It's precisely because I made it that I can be the last one to be seen to break it.'

'Then don't be seen to break it,' Elaine says. 'Slip away quietly.'

'I don't think I—'

'But it's been such a long time since we did it,' Elaine says huskily.

'I'll see what I can do,' Kershaw says, weakening.

He arrives home half an hour later, and she is waiting for him.

'I'll be very gentle,' he promises.

'There's no need,' she tells him. 'I'm fine. It's been over a week since you've had any fun – let yourself go!'

When he chains her to the wall, he already has an erection so hard that it seems to belong to a much younger man. He lifts his whip, and lashes it across her back.

'That's lovely,' she gasps.

When they have finished with the whipping, he will carry her up to their bed, and it will be wonderful, he tells himself.

He whips her again – harder than before.

And this time she doesn't groan.

This time she makes a roaring-gurgling noise, as if all the air is being expelled from her lungs.

And then she goes limp.

He unchains her, and lays her on the ground. He has no doubt she is dead, and no doubt he has killed her.

For five minutes, he weeps uncontrollably. And then, as his brain begins to override his emotions, he stops.

Elaine is dead, his brain tells him. There is nothing he can do about that. But if he is to survive – if he is to continue being the man he always has been – he must take action now.

'I had to do something,' Kershaw told Paniatowski. 'I couldn't see everything that I'd worked for all my life go to waste.'

'And what you did was to come up with the idea of a serial killer,' Paniatowski said. 'Your initial thought was to make Elaine his first victim, and someone else his second. But if you did that, the police would already have been investigating you by the time the second body turned up – and who knows what they might *already* have found. So how much better it would be if the idea of the serial killer was established *before* Elaine's body was discovered.'

'What do you expect me to say?' Kershaw asked.

'Nothing,' Paniatowski told him. 'Nothing at all. Open the bookcase, Colin.'

Beresford swung the bookcase open, to reveal the room which lay beyond it.

It was not a big room – possibly only a little larger than the kitchen range and fireplace which had once stood there – but it contained much of interest. There were manacles on the wall, with whips hanging next to them. There was a clothes rail, from which were suspended many of the articles Elaine had bought from Brian Waites. And there was a large chest freezer.

'That used to be next to the stairs, didn't it?' Paniatowski asked, pointing at the freezer.

'Yes.'

'It's where you stored the fish you caught on your expeditions with good old Georgie Baxter.'

'Yes.'

'You moved it into your little torture chamber . . .'

'Don't call it that!'

'. . . took out all the fish – which you later dumped – and set it to super-freeze. And when you thought it was cold enough, you put Elaine inside. And that's where she stayed, all the time that twenty or thirty policemen were tramping all over the house, looking for clues to where she might have gone.'

'But before you did your stunt of crashing into the roundabout, you went out and picked up a prostitute who was roughly Elaine's size,' Beresford said. 'You brought her back here, gave her a quick – but extremely cruel and violent – whipping, smothered her, and put her in the freezer with Elaine.'

'It was a question of measuring one life against another,' Kershaw said.

'Was it?' Beresford asked – and any trace of the admiration he might once have had for Kershaw was now quite absent.

'Of course it was,' Kershaw replied. 'The girl I killed was achieving nothing with her life, and would probably have been dead in a couple of years anyway. I thought her death would enable me to continue being a powerful force for good in the community.'

'You flayed Elaine's back to cover up the scars of her previous beatings,' Paniatowski said.

'That wasn't Elaine!' Kershaw told her. 'It was a cadaver. Elaine was long gone from me by then.'

'You can't have entirely believed that, or you'd simply have just dumped her somewhere, just like you dumped poor Grace,' Paniatowski said. 'But you didn't do that. You laid her out on a table in the mill, and you covered her with a white sheet. And then you sent me an anonymous note, to make sure that we'd find her before the rats did!'

'You're right,' Kershaw agreed. 'I couldn't bear the thought of the rats getting at her.'

'By the way, how long was it before you decided the freezer was cold enough to put Elaine into it?' Paniatowski asked.

Kershaw shrugged. 'I don't know. An hour? An hour and a half?'

'Had rigor set in?'

'No,' Kershaw said, puzzled. 'But it often doesn't in that time. Why do you ask?'

'Forensic science has come a long way since the last time you investigated a murder,' Paniatowski said. 'If Elaine had been dead for an hour and a half before she was frozen, I think Dr Shastri would have been able to tell.'

Kershaw's face collapsed. 'What are you . . . what do you mean?'

'She might well have been dying when you put her in that freezer – but I don't think she was quite dead,' Paniatowski said.

TWENTY-FIVE

The man standing on the platform at Whitebridge Station had curly hair which flopped over the collar of his old royal air force greatcoat. The coat was open, despite the cold weather, and under it he was wearing a pair of shabby cord trousers, a flowery shirt and a suede waistcoat.

It was almost impossible to work out whether he was an old hippy, a tramp or an eccentric millionaire, Paniatowski thought, but she didn't really care which it was, because she was much more intrigued by the question of why Lucy had asked to meet her here.

The man in the greatcoat noticed her standing there, and made a beeline for her.

'Are you Monika?' he asked.

'That's right.'

He held out his hand.

'I'm Jasper – Lucy's pimp.' He noted her refusal to take his hand, and laughed. 'I'm not really her pimp. That's just our little joke.'

'Then what are you?' Paniatowski asked, stony-faced.

'I'm her supervisor.'

'And what about her do you supervise?'

Jasper looked puzzled for a moment, then he laughed again, and said, 'Of course, you don't know. I'm supervising her doctorate.'

A nun, carrying a suitcase, emerged from the waiting room.

'Ah, here she is now,' Jasper said.

Lucy walked up to them. 'I'm sorry, Monika, I know I should have warned you,' she said. 'But really, I couldn't resist seeing the look on your face when you saw me.'

'So you're a nun,' Paniatowski said. 'And a virgin?'

'And a virgin,' the other woman confirmed. 'I'm Sister Lucia – though you can still call me Lucy.'

'And you've been doing research on the prostitutes of Whitebridge?'

'If we don't understand them, how are we ever going to be able to help them?'

'And now you're leaving?'

Lucy sighed. 'I have a very liberal mother superior, and an extremely liberal bishop, but even they baulked at the idea of continuing my research when one of my subjects was murdered.' She put down her case and took Paniatowski's hands in hers. 'That's why I asked you to meet me, Monika. I wanted to thank you for what you did for Grace. There were only four of us who cared anything about her.'

'I was one, and you were the second, and Marie was the third,' Paniatowski said. 'Who was the fourth?'

'God, of course,' Lucy said. 'He cared – He cared more deeply than we ever could.'

'You must be very angry about having to abandon your research,' Paniatowski said, changing the subject, as she usually did when God came up.

'Angry?' Lucy repeated. 'With whom?'

'With your bishop and your mother superior.'

'Of course I'm not angry with them. It is not my place to question their decisions – it is my place to obey.'

The train rattled into the station, and they walked to the edge of the platform.

'Perhaps one day you will return to your faith,' Lucy said.

'Perhaps I will,' Paniatowski agreed. 'But, if I was you, I wouldn't hold my breath while I was waiting.'

Jasper opened the door, and he and Lucy climbed aboard. Then Lucy turned, and pulled down the window.

'With God's help, I will become a good nun,' she said, 'but even without His help – and I dare say this only because I know He is all-merciful and all-forgiving – I think I could have been a very successful prostitute.'

Paniatowski grinned. 'You'd have had them queuing up at the door,' she said. Then the guard blew his whistle and the train pulled away.